IRREPARABLE HARM

BY USA TODAY BESTSELLING AUTHOR

MELISSA F. MILLER

BROWN STREET BOOKS

Contact the author at melissa@melissafmiller.com

Published by Brown Street Books.

For my parents.

It took me almost forty years, but here it is.

and

For my husband David, who, in a very real sense,

made this book possible.

1

Somewhere in the air over Blacksburg, Virginia

The old man checked his new gold watch, given in appreciation for his fifty years of service to the City of Pittsburgh. He lifted the window screen and pressed his head against the oval window in the side of the plane. The glass was cold against his papery skin. Somewhere, out in the darkness, the Blue Ridge Mountains of Virginia rose up from the land. He looked hard but couldn't see them.

He pulled the screen back down, more sharply than he'd intended, and glanced over at his seatmates. They didn't react to the noise. Next to him, sat a thin, college-aged girl who had squeezed herself into the middle seat, jammed her earbuds into her ears, and closed her eyes, lost in her music; beside her, a businessman, mid-level management, no higher, judging by the wrinkled suit and battered briefcase. Like a good business traveler, he used the flight to catch up on his sleep. His head lolled back on the headrest and his leg dangled into the aisle.

The man coughed into his fist and remembered the last time he had flown. It had been almost ten years. His youngest daughter and her husband, the struggling actor, had flown him and his wife out to Los Angeles to be there for the birth of their first child—his fourth grandchild, but the first girl. Maya had entered the world squealing, and, at least based on the weekly phone calls he had with her mother, it seemed she hadn't ever stopped. He chuckled to himself at the thought and immediately felt his eyes well up. He blinked and twisted the thin gold band on his ring finger. His mind turned to his Rosa. Fifty-two years together.

He hacked again and dug a handkerchief out of his pocket to wipe his mouth. After folding the white cloth back into a careful square, he checked his watch again, fumbled with the smartphone on his lap, squinted at it to confirm the coordinates were correct, and hit SEND. Then Angelo Calvaruso sat back, closed his eyes, and relaxed—completely relaxed—for the first time in weeks.

Two minutes later, Hemisphere Air Flight No. 1667, a Boeing 737 en route from Washington National to Dallas-Fort Worth International, slammed into the side of a mountain at full speed and exploded in a fiery wave of metal and burning flesh.

~

The offices of Prescott & Talbott
Pittsburgh, Pennsylvania

SASHA MCCANDLESS BLEW the eyeshadow residue off the tiny mirror of the makeup palette she kept in the top left drawer of her desk and checked her reflection. The drawer was her home away from home. It held a travel toothbrush and toothpaste, a tin of mints, an unopened box of condoms, makeup, a spare pair of contact lenses, a pair of glasses, and a brush. She smiled at herself and opened the drawer again, tore open the box, and popped a condom into her beaded handbag.

She shrugged out of the gray cashmere cardigan she'd worn over her black sheath dress all day and kicked off her pumps. She dug around in the credenza behind her desk until she found her fun shoes under a pile of discarded draft briefs, destined for the shredder. She pushed the papers aside and pulled out her shoes. She was wrestling with the tiny red strap on her left stiletto when she heard the ping of an e-mail hitting her in-box.

"No, no, no," she moaned, as she slowly straightened. She had not had a proper date in weeks. She hoped against hope that the e-mail would reveal no emergency motions, no ranting clients, no last-minute calls to substitute for a deposition in Omaha, or Detroit, or New Orleans.

She needed a steak, a bottle of overpriced red wine, and candlelight. She did not need another night of lukewarm Chinese takeout at her desk.

Almost afraid to look, she clicked on the envelope icon and breathed out, smiling. It was just a Google news alert about a client. She had set up news alerts for all the clients she worked for. It always impressed the partners when she knew what was going on with their clients before they did. Scared them a little, too.

Hemisphere Air was Peterson's biggest client. She opened the e-mail to see why it was in the news. Maybe a merger? It was one of the healthier airlines and had been looking to pick off a smaller competitor, especially after Sasha and Peterson had gotten it out of that little antitrust mess.

Sasha's green eyes widened and then fell as she scanned the e-mail. Flight 1667, three-quarters full, en route from D.C. to Dallas, had just crashed in Virginia, killing all 156 people onboard.

She wriggled out of the party shoes and picked up the phone to ruin her date's night. Then she dialed Peterson's mobile number to ruin his.

Noah Peterson's home phone rang at almost the same moment his cell phone began to blare out some unrecognizable piece of classical music in the public domain. Both sat on his bedside table. Noah didn't lift his head from his magazine.

Laura waited a minute to see if he would move. He didn't, so she sighed deeply, placed a bookmark in her novel, and reached over to shake his arm. Noah had developed a habit of dozing off while reading in bed. Laura had no idea how he found that position comfortable enough for sleeping, and she didn't understand why he was so tired all the time lately. He'd always kept long hours at the office, but the pace seemed to be getting to him more these days.

"Noah, phone. Phones, actually." She shook his forearm harder.

Noah started and pushed his reading glasses, which had slid down his nose, back up to the bridge. He grabbed his cell phone and passed the house phone to Laura to deal with. Squinting at the display, he recognized Sasha McCandless' office number.

"Mac, slow down," he said over the torrent of words pouring out of his senior associate. Then he sat, silent, listening, his shoulders sagging under the weight of what Sasha was saying.

Laura tugged on his sleeve, covering the mouthpiece with her hand, and stage whispered, "It's Bob Metz."

Noah nodded. Metz was the general counsel of Hemisphere Air.

"Mac, Metz is on my home line. Stay put. Make some coffee. I'll see you soon." He flipped the phone shut.

Laura handed him the house phone and he headed into his closet to dress while he placated the troubled man on the other end of the line.

Soft warm light puddled down from the brass-armed sconces that bracketed each side of the headboard, bathing Laura in a romantic glow. She'd paid a princely sum for that attractive lighting, but it was rarely used for its intended purpose. In hindsight, reading light would have been more useful. She scooted over to claim the center of the king bed with its high-thread count sheets and cashmere blankets; it sounded like she would have the luxury all to herself tonight. Again. She opened her book to the marked spot to resume her reading.

2

Bethesda, Maryland

Jerry Irwin sat in his dark office, the only light the glow of his computer monitor. He tapped out a quick message: *Demo completed successfully, as we are sure you've heard. Second display to occur on Friday. Interested parties to submit confidential bids by midnight Friday.*

Irwin read it over twice to make sure it struck the right tone: succinct and confident, but not brash or boastful. Satisfied, he ran the concealment program and sent it out to a select list.

He powered off the computer and rose from

his ergonomic desk chair, whistling tunelessly. It wouldn't be appropriate to celebrate until the bids were in and the winner had paid, but he thought a glass of good scotch was in order.

3

The offices of Prescott & Talbott
11:50 p.m.

By the time Peterson had driven in from his center hall Colonial in Sewickley, Sasha had brewed a pot of strong coffee; assembled a crew of exhausted junior associates, pulled from various late-night document reviews; and passed out copies of the barebones media reports on the crash and a one-pager about Hemisphere Air's corporate culture and litigation philosophy.

The gathered associates were tired but excited. The promise of action energized them. They had spent long weeks, if not months, of twelve- to fifteen-hour days reviewing thousands upon thousands of electronic documents for privilege and responsiveness for use in cases they would never come any closer to. Each sat at the gleaming conference room table praying this horrible plane crash would be his or her ticket out of document review hell.

Peterson swept into the room. Despite—or maybe because of—the fact that it was almost midnight and his biggest client was in crisis, Peterson looked fresh and unperturbed. He wore creaseless khakis and a pink golf shirt.

Sasha handed him a mug of coffee and a set of the handouts.

He leaned in and said, “These are real Prescott folks, right?”

She nodded. Prescott & Talbott had dealt with the trying economic times by creating a caste system of lawyers. Contract attorneys—deemed unfit for true employment on the basis of academic achievement or social standing—were brought in to staff the largest of the document reviews and paid an insulting hourly rate for their efforts. Not only would they miss out on the prestige of partnership, but the salaries they earned wouldn’t make a dent in the tens (or, more likely, hundreds) of thousands of dollars of law school loans they’d accumulated.

The contract workers were supervised by staff

attorneys—deemed fit to receive a pay check and benefits directly from Prescott & Talbott, but still not good enough to be real Prescott attorneys. The staff attorneys did scut work and were forbidden from signing documents bearing the firm letterhead; they were branded as "staff attorneys" on the firm's website and business cards and were under no illusions about the dead end nature of their position.

The staff attorneys, in turn, were supervised by junior associates—the bright-eyed men and women who watched Peterson from their seats around the table. They had been at the tops of their law school classes; editors of journals; the spawn of the old money families who golfed, swam, or prayed with the Prescott & Talbott partners; or some combination of the three.

Assuming they didn't get chewed up and spit out by the firm, these junior associates would one day reach Sasha's level. As an eighth-year associate she worked directly with clients, stood up in court and argued, and had primary responsibility for writing briefs and running small cases. On a big case, like the crash would be, she'd handle the day-to-day supervision of the case team and work with Peterson on strategy.

And, provided Sasha didn't burn out, she would soon reach the level of income partner. In the spring, Prescott & Talbott's equity partners would hold a vote and almost certainly would offer her income partnership. Which would mean she had reached the top of a very tall greased pole. Only a handful of the dozens of eager young attorneys who began work each September at Prescott would make it that far. That was the good news. The bad news was all her achievement would land her right at the bottom of a taller, greasier pole: the one standing between her and equity partnership.

Peterson gave her a nod, letting her know he appreciated her judgment. Sasha felt a small thrill of satisfaction at having pleased him and then an equally small pang of disgust at caring about pleasing him. She shrugged off both emotions and poured herself another cup of coffee.

Peterson pulled out the chair that had been left empty at the head of the table and looked around the table. He met each set of eyes and held his gaze for a moment to let the seriousness of the evening's events sink in.

"For those of you who don't know me, I'm Noah Peterson, the managing partner of the complex litigation department here. For those of you who don't know Hemisphere Air, it is one of Prescott's oldest clients and, each year, one of our biggest clients in terms of hours billed and revenues collected. Hemisphere Air is a proud

Pittsburgh institution and will be looking to us to help it weather this terrible tragedy."

Sasha glanced up from her notepad to make sure everyone was nodding in all the right places. They were.

She turned back to drawing up a master task list and making tentative assignments. The immediate issue was to find the best available legal assistant and get him or her put on the case. An excellent legal assistant was more valuable than all the expensive, untested talent sitting around the table.

She looked up again when she heard her name.

"Sasha McCandless will run the team. Sasha is well acquainted with this client and its needs. If you have questions or concerns, you will direct them to Sasha." *And not to me, you peons,* was left unsaid but not unclear.

Eight sets of eyes shifted from Peterson to Sasha. She put down her pen.

"We'll meet right at 8:30 every morning for a quick status update and to hand out the day's priority assignments. Beginning now, you work exclusively for Hemisphere Air. If you need me to run interference with anyone to get you off other matters, tell me now; otherwise, I expect you'll clear your plates entirely of other work by the end of the day tomorrow."

Sasha waited a beat to see if anyone had a problem with that. No one did. At this point in their careers, they would chew their arms off to get out of the document review trap.

They could hardly have imagined that, as shiny new lawyers, they would spend their days, nights, and weekends staring at computer screens, reading one inane e-mail after another —sifting through the forwarded jokes, spam advertisements for Viagra, and mundane details of a client's new transportation benefit in an effort to find evidence of insider trading, an antitrust conspiracy, or legal advice regarding some action of the company. Sasha felt sorry for them. At least when she was cutting her teeth on document reviews, she got to travel to exotic locations like Duluth and paw through boxes of yellowing paper in unheated warehouses instead of being subjected to some stranger's collection of Internet porn.

She continued, "We're going to have to hit the ground running. Our working assumption is the first group of plaintiffs will file tomorrow. Whoever files first has a good shot at being named class counsel and, if this ends up with a bunch of consolidated cases, MDL coordinating counsel."

She met with a few blank stares.

"MDL—multidistrict litigation?" she prompted them.

It was criminal, the way firms like Prescott demanded the brightest legal minds and then prevented them from actually practicing law for the first several years of their careers.

Once they started nodding again, she went on, "We'll need someone to do a conflict of laws analysis, on the off chance the first case is filed in Virginia—the site of the accident—but it's safe to assume we'll be in federal court here, in the Western District of Pennsylvania."

Joe Donaldson had a question. "How can you be so sure? Just because Hemisphere Air is headquartered here? Why would plaintiffs take on Hemisphere Air where it has home court advantage?"

"That's a valid point, Joe. Look out that window behind you."

Joe and the four other attorneys on his side of the table swiveled their chairs to look where she pointed. The three people seated across the table from them half-rose from their chairs and craned their necks, so they could see, too. Only Peterson didn't move. He just smiled.

"See the Frick Building?" It was a squat stone building, lost in a sea of glass high-rises. "The entire building is dark, right? Except for a row of five windows, four floors up."

The junior attorneys' heads were bobbing in agreement. They turned back to face her.

"Those are Mickey Collins' offices. Mickey's one of the most successful plaintiff's attorneys in town. The Aston Martin parked right under the security light in the lot next door is his. I've been working here eight years and I can count the number of times I've seen it in the lot after six p.m. He's in there, working the phones, trying to find the widow of someone on that flight so he can head into court first thing in the morning and file with a named class representative. You can count on it."

Joe looked down, sheepish.

"Hey, it was a good question, Joe." Sasha valued someone who would speak up in a group. "Why don't you work on putting together background information on whichever Western District judges are the most likely candidates to be assigned the next MDL case filed here?"

"Will do." Joe sat up straighter.

"Good. Anyone want to volunteer for the conflict of laws analysis?"

Kaitlyn Hart raised her pen. "I'll do it."

"Great." Sasha turned to Peterson. "Are you meeting with Metz tomorrow, Noah?"

"Yes. He's coming here for a lunch meeting. We'll do it in the office. The press will be all over their offices tomorrow."

"Okay. That means I'll need both memos by mid-morning, so I can review them before Noah and I meet with in-house counsel."

Joe and Kaitlyn both nodded, as they scribbled notes on their legal pads.

"The rest of you will get your assignments at the morning meeting."

Sasha felt a smidgeon of guilt that the others had been pulled off their late-night document review tasks only to hurry up and wait, but that was just a fact of big firm life. It could be maddeningly inefficient.

"Any other questions?"

No one spoke. A few people shook their heads.

It was nearly one in the morning. Time to cut people loose.

"Then we're done. See you in the morning."

4

Outside Blacksburg, Virginia

As a weak autumn sun rose over the mountains, the recovery team combed through what was left of Flight 1667. It was only October, but a hard frost blanketed the ground.

The men and women who had started out as a rescue team late the night before were chilled through and exhausted. Once they had wheeled out the bright work lights and seen the crash site, they'd known there'd be no rescuing, and the adrenaline that had propelled them out of their warm beds had drained away.

Now—under the supervision of a cluster of

glum and mostly silent TSA and NTSB officials —the volunteer firefighters, EMTs, and local police officers worked shoulder to shoulder, bagging and cataloguing charred body parts, twisted curls of metal, shards of cell phones and laptops, and scraps of rollerboard bags.

Marty Kowalski spotted a piece of polka dotted fabric and bent, knees cracking, to inspect it. It was roughly the size of a sheet of loose-leaf paper and had once been a cream color, dotted gaily with light pink, mocha brown, and soft blue circles. It looked somehow familiar, but Marty couldn't put his finger on why.

Where had he seen fabric like this before? His tired brain searched his memory but came up empty. He turned the fabric over and it stuck; the backing was some kind of plastic that had partially melted into the ground. As Marty pulled it free, the plastic liner jarred something in his memory, and he realized he was looking at what remained of a diaper bag: a cheerful pastel pattern, lined with a protective plastic covering.

A mother had carefully counted out the diapers she'd need for the flight, adding a few extras just in case. Then, she'd folded in a case of wipes and a travel-size tube of soothing diaper cream, tossed in a soft toy or board book to keep the baby entertained on the plane, and probably shoved a well-worn blanket or stuffed animal on top.

Now, all that was left was this torn scrap of the bag, and mother and baby were scattered among the ashes blowing across the smoky field. Marty's stomach seized. He hurried over to the tree line in case he was going to be sick.

Marty leaned over, bracing his stiff hands on his thighs, right above his knees. He heaved, but nothing came up, so he spat a few times and then wiped his mouth with the back of his hand. As he straightened up, he spotted bright metal glinting in the brush. He kicked the growth aside with a steel-toed boot and stared. A badly dented, stainless steel box roughly the size of his toolbox at home lay on its side. It had been painted bright orange. The words "FLIGHT DATA RECORDER DO NOT OPEN" were stenciled on in large black letters.

"Hey!" he shouted, "I found it—I found the black box."

People started running toward his voice from all directions.

5

Pittsburgh, Pennsylvania

Not quite four hours after she'd gone to bed, Sasha's eyes flipped open exactly five minutes before her alarm was set to go off, as they did every morning. She stretched to her full length, pointing her toes and spreading her arms above her head, fingertips hitting the headboard. She sat, arched her back, rolled her neck, and switched off the still-silent alarm.

The genius of her loft-style condo was that her bedroom was just three steps up from the kitchen with its oil-rubbed bronze appliances (the new stainless, according to her realtor). She made the short walk to the kitchen and had an oversized mug of very hot, very strong black coffee in her hand before she'd fully awakened.

Sasha had learned quickly that grinding the beans, setting up the water, and putting the coffee maker on the timer the night before made for much easier mornings. She even set out the mug the night before, putting it right beside the machine on the recycled glass countertop (deemed the new granite by the same realtor).

She had briefly dated Joel Somebody or Other, a coffee purist who'd been appalled when he witnessed this routine. He had lectured her about the oils in the beans and the temperature of the water. At their next—and last—date, he'd presented her with a small French press and suggested she learn the art of crafting her coffee one perfect cup at a time.

She'd tossed the French press in a drawer, where it remained, still in its box. She'd tossed Joe back into Pittsburgh's shallow dating waters, unwilling to indulge his coffee-related snobbery.

What she sacrificed in flavor by setting up the coffee at night was more than offset by the immediate delivery of caffeine that greeted her each morning.

She carried the coffee back into the bedroom, where she pulled on her running shoes. She'd also learned that sleeping in her workout clothes instead of proper pajamas made for easier mornings.

Then it was into the bathroom to wash her face, brush her teeth, and pull her hair back into a low ponytail. She headed out to the small foyer, where she pulled on the fleece jacket that hung by the door, jammed a baseball cap on her head, and shrugged into her backpack. She checked to make sure the door locked behind her and jogged down the stairs to the lobby.

Eight minutes after getting out of bed, Sasha burst out the door to the street and filled her lungs with the cold air. As she ran through Shadyside, up to Fifth Avenue, she felt her legs loosen and her stride lengthen.

Mondays through Saturdays she ran from her condo to her Krav Maga class. She'd taken the hand-to-hand combat classes since law school. Krav Maga kept her mentally sharp. Not to mention, she was almost 5'3" tall—as long as she was wearing three-inch heels—and a whopping ninety-seven pounds. That put her at a distinct size disadvantage against anyone other than third graders. Knowing how to shatter a kneecap gave her some comfort when she was walking to her car late at night or brushing off the advances of some drunk on the rooftop deck at Doc's bar.

After the class, depending on where she'd left her car the night before, she either ran back home to get ready for work or ran straight to Prescott & Talbott's offices and showered at the firm gym, where she kept a supply of business clothes.

Sundays she neither worked out nor worked. She slept until noon and then spent the afternoon at her parents' house, staying for dinner with her brothers, their wives, and her assorted nieces and nephews.

By the time she showered, dressed, and stepped off the elevator into Prescott's offices six days a week at eight a.m. sharp, takeout cup from the coffee shop in the lobby in her hand, Sasha was alert, loose, and ready for her day. No one asked if she'd spent her morning learning how to crush a windpipe with the blade of her forearm, disarm someone wielding a knife, or subdue an attacker using an arm triangle chokehold, and she never mentioned it.

6

Bethesda, Maryland

Tim Warner had the bad luck to be the first one in the office on Tuesday morning, as he was most mornings. He'd never really been a morning person, but when he started working at Patriotech, he learned he got most of his work done before his colleagues arrived for the day and started peppering him with questions about how many vacation days they had left and when their worthless stock options would vest.

Even though his job was mundane, Tim felt lucky to have landed a position shortly after graduation, especially in a recession. His salary sucked, that was for sure, but he did have an impressive-sounding title—Director of Human Resources—which was made somewhat less impressive only if one happened to know he directed a staff of zero.

Tim told himself he was making an investment in his future. Patriotech, as a technology startup in the defense sector, was well-positioned to go public within a few years. At least that was what the CEO, Jerry Irwin, had said when he'd interviewed Tim for the position of human resources specialist. After the interview, Tim had been inspired by Irwin and his vision for the company, so he'd leapt at Irwin's offer to come aboard with a fancier title and stock options, despite the paltry pay.

In the two months he'd been at Patriotech, Tim had remained impressed by Irwin's vision, even as he'd grown to hate and fear the man. Tim lacked the technical background to understand the product Patriotech had developed, but he assumed Irwin's violent outbursts and rapid mood swings were a sign of his genius. Or more accurately, he hoped they were a sign of his genius, because Irwin was making his life miserable.

Tim stooped and picked up *The Washington Post* before swiping his access card in the reader by the lobby doors. Once inside, he flipped on the lights and took the newspaper from its biodegradable green bag, scanning the headlines before he deposited the paper on Lilliana's desk in the reception area. What he saw below the fold ruined his day: "Hemisphere Flight from National Airport Crashes into Mountain in Virginia; No Survivors."

Tim skimmed the article to confirm what he already suspected—the downed flight was bound for Dallas—then hurried into his cubicle in the back corner of the office, pulled out a personnel file, and dialed Angelo Calvaruso's home number.

After he hung up with Calvaruso's newly minted widow, he sat perfectly still, cradling his head in his hands, for a long while. He stayed immobile when Irwin came into the office and breezed past him on his way to his glass-walled corner office.

After another minute, he steeled himself and walked over to Irwin's office. His legs felt like they were encased in rock. At just twenty-three, Tim had never had to deliver news like this before; he wasn't sure how to go about it.

He rapped softly on the open frosted glass door. Irwin looked up from his *Wall Street Journal.*

"Tim," he said. Then he waited.

For a moment, Tim had an overpowering feeling Irwin already knew, but he dismissed it as wishful thinking. Irwin read nothing but *The Wall Street Journal* and technical journals, claimed not to own a television, and listened only to classical music on satellite radio in his BMW. There was no way he would have heard about the crash.

Tim swallowed, his mouth suddenly dry. "Uh. Jerry, I don't know if you heard but . . um ... there was a plane crash late last night . . ." He trailed off.

"Oh?" Irwin said.

"Yeah, um ... well . . .," Tim took a breath, and the words tumbled out of their own volition, "there were no survivors, Jerry. Angelo was on the plane. I'm so sorry."

Irwin just looked at him.

"Angelo? Calvaruso? The consultant?" Tim prompted him, thinking Irwin might be blanking on the name. Or maybe he was in shock, Tim thought.

"Oh," Irwin said again, finally. "Tell Lilliana to send his family flowers when she gets in." He turned back to his paper. Tim was dismissed.

Tim walked back to his cubicle, wrinkling his brow in confusion.

Just one month earlier, Irwin had insisted Patriotech hire Calvaruso as a technical consultant under a one-year, $150,000 contract. Tim had gone to see Irwin when the order crossed his desk, and Irwin had blown up at him. In fact, he reflected, it was after their confrontation that Irwin had really started to make life unbearable.

Tim couldn't understand what Irwin had been thinking. Not because the contract payment was four times his own salary—well, not only because of that. Angelo Calvaruso was a seventy-two-year-old retired snowplow driver for the City of Pittsburgh. Tim found it unimaginable Calvaruso had technical expertise worth what Irwin wanted to pay him.

Irwin had exploded when Tim questioned his decision. His face had darkened, and an ugly raised vein had begun to pulse at his temple. He'd screamed so close to Tim's face that Tim had been able to count the fillings in Irwin's teeth and feel the heat from his breath. He'd told Tim to draw up the contract and keep his worthless opinions to himself.

Tim had rushed to prepare a contract then snuck into Irwin's office and left it on his desk when he was out at lunch. He got it back signed, along with a note to get keyman and travel insurance on Calvaruso in the amount of one million dollars each.

Tim had scoffed at the idea that the old man's technical skills or knowledge—whatever they were—could possibly be so critical to Patriotech's business that they needed keyman insurance on him, but he didn't dare raise it with Irwin. He simply called the company's broker and got the coverage.

Now, after all that, Irwin seemed completely unfazed that the old man had died after having worked for the company for just four weeks.

Then, a very ugly thought occurred to Tim: Patriotech had paid Angelo Calvaruso exactly $12,500. Rosa Calvaruso was about to collect a million bucks under the travel policy, and Patriotech was going to collect the same amount under the keyman policy.

7

The offices of Prescott & Talbott

Sasha crossed Prescott's gleaming lobby, her heels clicking against the polished marble floor. Her mind still on the knife attack she'd successfully warded off in class, she smiled hello at Anne, the silk-voiced receptionist who'd been greeting visitors to the firm since Sasha was in diapers. Anne nodded back, her headset bobbing; she was already busy fielding calls.

Sasha ignored the bank of internal elevators across from the reception desk and headed up the curved staircase, taking the four flights as quickly as her heels would permit. On four, instead of going straight to her office, Sasha detoured down a long corridor and poked her head into one of the interior offices. All attorneys, except for the contract attorneys, had offices along the exterior walls of the building; each office had at least one window. The legal assistants and document clerks had windowless offices along the interior wall. The contract attorneys were relegated to crowded, charmless, communal work rooms lined with computers and devoid of privacy.

"Hey," Sasha said, startling the slight African-American woman whose back was to the door. Naya Andrews' head swiveled at the sound of Sasha's voice.

"Mac," the older woman said, smiling. "Where've you been hiding?"

Naya and Sasha had spent most of the summer working on a trade secrets case that had settled on the morning the trial was scheduled to start. During the trial preparation, Sasha had been nicknamed Mac, and, at least as far as Naya and Peterson were concerned, it had stuck.

"I've been locked away working on an appellate brief. How's your mom doing?"

Naya's smile faded. "About the same. Some days she knows who I am, some days she doesn't."

Naya's mother had Alzheimer's, and Naya was

doing her damnedest to keep her in her home. She'd declined to the point where she needed round-the-clock care, though. Naya's brothers and sister either couldn't or wouldn't help with the costs of full-time in-home care, so she was shouldering the expense herself. For now, at least. Naya had pared her own expenses to the bare minimum and was pouring almost everything she earned into paying for her mother's care. Sasha wondered how much longer she could afford it.

"I'm really sorry, Naya."

Naya pasted her smile back on, all business. "So, what brings you down this hallway?"

Sasha nodded, indicating the *Post-Gazette*'s website open on Naya's desktop. Not surprisingly, news of the crash was front and center on the local paper's website, as well as in the print edition. Sasha had scanned the headlines in the lobby coffee shop; the crash took up the entire front page. Naya followed Sasha's gaze to the monitor and looked back at her.

"Metz called Peterson last night," Sasha told her. "The team's already in place, except for a legal assistant. You want in?"

"Hell yeah!"

Naya's eagerness was partly professional and partly pragmatic. The case would involve high stakes and interesting work, as well as lots of overtime. Unlike the attorneys, legal assistants at Prescott were eligible for overtime pay. A senior legal assistant who worked a lot of overtime would bring home more than the contract attorneys and most of the junior staff attorneys. Naya had never shied away from long hours, but now with her mother's condition worsening, she was more willing than ever to volunteer for extra work.

Sasha knew Naya would jump at the chance to get on the team, but she also knew she didn't have the juice to get Naya pulled off her other matters. Legal assistants also differed from most junior lawyers at Prescott in that the partners didn't view them as fungible. The smart partners realized good legal assistants were irreplaceable assets and protected them accordingly.

Whether the associates Sasha had tapped for her team realized it or not, there would be little to no pushback about her pulling them from their document review assignments. As an honest, if tactless, partner had once noted, junior associates were like goldfish: if you lost one, you flushed it and replaced it with another one just like it.

Sasha asked, "Are you sure you can swing it?"

Naya inventoried her brutal workload in her head. "Yes," she said simply.

Sasha smiled. "Team meeting at eight thirty. Mellon Conference Room."

Naya called after her, "Thanks for thinking of me, Mac."

Sasha drained her coffee as she rounded the corner by the kitchenette. Each of Prescott's eight floors had its own coffee and tea station. Prescott provided free drinks for its employees. Whether out of generosity or the belief that caffeine-wired lawyers billed longer hours, Sasha neither knew nor cared. She tossed the takeout cup into the recycling bin and poured a fresh cup into a navy blue and cream mug emblazoned with the firm logo.

A hostess was assigned to staff each kitchenette during business hours, charged with brewing fresh coffee; restocking milk, sugar, and cream; cutting lemons for the tea drinkers; running the Prescott & Talbott mugs through the dishwasher; and keeping the area spotless. Most of the hostesses were older women—widows whose pension and social security payments weren't quite enough to get by on—and a few were young women, very young, Asian immigrants.

Sasha's personal ranking system put the coffee hostesses somewhere below a good legal assistant but well above the first-year associates. She smiled at Mai, the hostess—who had retreated to the supply closet when Sasha had approached—and raised her mug in a salute on her way out.

Sasha was well aware that she, too, had once been a hapless first-year associate, and she knew that, just as she had, some of the current crop would blossom into real attorneys. Her cynicism stemmed from the knowledge that most of them would be long gone before she could tell whether they had what it took to be lawyers.

The reality of being handed a six-figure position with no real-world experience and no meaningful guidance tended to cause one of two reactions: One, the new lawyer was paralyzed with fear and refused to make any judgment calls or take any proactive steps. Or, two, he or she swung to the complete opposite end of the spectrum and became a self-important twit, abusing secretaries and barking out bizarre and wrongheaded orders to anyone in earshot. Both styles were a recipe for failure. The deer-in-the-headlights types generally faded away after a few years, and the Napoleons usually flamed out in spectacular, scandalous fashion.

Every crop of associates had just a handful of survivors. Some were those who had gone to law school as nontraditional students. They were older and had been in the workforce—many even kept working while in law school. Maybe they even had kids already. To them, the stakes were higher, the prize of the high-paying job sweeter.

Others were the golden children. They were the offspring of lawyers and judges and had grown up knowing they were destined for the corner office. Whether it was nature or nurture, they were programmed to succeed, whether they wanted to or not.

Sasha had gone to law school straight from college, but she sometimes thought of herself as part of the nontraditional student group. She was nontraditional for Prescott & Talbott, at least, because she'd grown up poor. Not *poor* poor, to be sure, but working class poor.

Sasha approached the rarified world of Prescott & Talbott and everything it signified differently than her colleagues who'd grown up with maids, vacation homes, and country club memberships. She worked as hard as she could, saved as much of her salary as she could, and took care to dress and speak like one of *them*, but she never pretended to be anything other than what she was: a half-Russian, half-Irish working-class kid with no pedigree to speak of.

8

At eight twenty-five, Sasha walked into the Mellon conference room. Instead of numbering the conference rooms, the decision makers at Prescott had chosen to name them after prominent old Pittsburgh families and luminaries. Sasha assumed all the industrialists and robber-barons whose names graced the conference rooms had once been clients of the firm; some still were.

She knew for a fact the naming system was confusing to everyone from new employees to clients to visiting attorneys. There were seven floors of offices, each home to four conference rooms, and a second floor conference center, which held another eight. That made for a total of thirty-six conference rooms, none of them numbered or identified by location.

As she entered the conference room, Sasha smiled to see Lettie, her secretary, fussing around with the catering tray and restacking napkins and coffee stirrers that had been stacked perfectly neatly in the first place, as far as Sasha could tell.

"Hi, Lettie."

Lettie looked up from the pastries. "Good morning, Sasha."

Sasha waited for the barrage of information that was coming. Lettie Conrad had gone to secretarial school right after graduating from Sacred Heart High and took her career seriously. She was pleasant, meticulous, always helpful, talkative, and probably one of about four people who knew exactly where every conference room was by name.

Lettie took a breath and launched in. "After I saw your e-mail, I reserved this conference room for one hour a day for the next month. That's as far out as the scheduling software will let me block out, but I'll talk to Myron about extending it. I ordered breakfast for twelve and coffee for eighteen."

She paused and pursed her lips to remind her boss how she felt about her coffee consumption and then continued, "I arranged for Flora, from the secretarial pool, to be assigned to the work station right outside. She can make copies, set up conference calls, or whatever you need. If you need me, though, just buzz me and I'll be down as soon as I can."

Sasha nodded, peering through the door at Flora, who smiled widely and waggled five very long, dark purple fingertips at her. Sasha glanced down at Lettie's short, neatly trimmed nails and made a mental note not to ask Flora to do any word processing.

"Sounds good, Lettie. Thanks."

"Oh, I almost forgot." Lettie's hand snaked behind a coffee carafe and reappeared holding a clear plastic cup of yogurt parfait and a spoon.

"Here. I know you won't eat that stuff," she nodded toward the danishes and softball-sized chocolate muffins on the catering tray, "so I ordered this for you. Yogurt and granola. Please eat it."

She placed the cup in front of Sasha and patted it gently.

"Thanks."

Lettie turned to leave, then remembered something and turned back. "How was your date?"

Sasha looked at her blankly.

"Your date? With the architect?"

"Oh. I had to cancel because of the plane crash."

Lettie fixed her with a long, disapproving look but said nothing.

She crossed paths with Peterson on her way out and greeted the senior partner formally, "Good morning, Mr. Peterson."

"Good morning, Mrs. Conrad."

Noah might not have been able to pick any of the junior associates out of a lineup, but he knew all the veteran staff members by name and, in most cases, knew their spouses' and kids' names, too.

He crossed the room and plucked a frosted cinnamon bun roughly the size of a salad plate off the tray. As he raised it to his lips, he tilted his head toward the door. "Is your secretary angry with you?"

Sasha shook her head. "More like disappointed in me," she said, prying the domed lid off the parfait. "I canceled another date last night."

Peterson laughed softly. "She'll never get you married off at this rate, Mac."

He sat down at the head of the table and turned his attention to his cinnamon bun, as its frosting began to ooze down the side, coming perilously close to his muted, silk tie.

Despite Prescott's move to a business casual dress code during the tech boom in the late 1990s, Peterson, like many of the older partners, still wore suits most days. Sasha, who joined the firm after the switch, did too. She figured the senior attorneys were more comfortable in business suits because they'd worn them for decades. She wore suits for the practical reason that most casual clothes in her size involved glitter, ruffles, and lace and made ample use of the colors pink and lavender.

She could, however, find petite suits and have them altered to fit. Pants were problematic—too much tailoring involved—so she had settled on a uniform of sorts. She wore sheath dresses with matching jackets. Occasionally, she swapped out the jacket for a cardigan.

Today, because she would be sitting in on the meeting with Metz, she was wearing one of her most conservative suits. A navy sheath with white piping and a long matching jacket. She'd added pearl earrings and a choker and had pulled her hair back into a low, loose chignon. She watched Peterson appraise her. She knew she'd pass muster. Not like the legendary flameout of an associate who'd shown up for a client meeting with a new neck tattoo peeking out from above his collar. She couldn't even remember his name, but he lived on as a cautionary tale to new hires.

"Did you line up a paralegal?"

Legal assistant, Sasha thought, but didn't bother to correct him. "Naya Andrews."

"Excellent." Peterson dabbed the icing from his lips with a napkin. There was something dainty about the gesture. He scowled at his watch. "It's 8:32. Where is everyone?"

"Probably wandering the halls trying to figure out which room is Mellon."

Peterson half-smiled, conceding the point. He brushed a stray piece of lint off his jacket lapel. "We're in Frick for the lunch with Metz."

Sasha poured herself a cup of coffee and looked out the window toward Point State Park and the three rivers that met there. The sun was struggling out from behind the clouds but the water looked gray and cold.

Sasha had been disappointed to learn as a child that, despite Pittsburgh mythology, the rivers didn't really form a triangle. Her disappointment had been tempered some when her father told her there were actually four rivers. A secret river flowed underground, beneath the city. In fact, it was this fourth, unnamed river that provided the water for the enormous fountain at the Point.

She turned away from the window and took the seat to Peterson's right as a small group started to filter into the room. She smiled a little at the symbolism. She was widely perceived as Peterson's right-hand woman; she figured she might as well make it official.

She watched with mild interest while, as a mass, the lawyers claimed the seats furthest from her and Peterson—as though they were going to avoid being called on by sitting in the back of a law school lecture hall. After depositing their legal pads, pens, and Blackberries at their seats, most of them headed for the drinks and pastries. Kaitlyn stood over the tray, her hand hovering above a cruller for a long minute, before she pulled it away and chose a muffin instead. Apparently, she'd convinced herself the muffin was a healthier choice despite it being nothing more than a slab of chocolate cake in a paper liner. She'd learn. New associates were always enthusiastic about the ample free food at Prescott & Talbott—until the freshman fifteen appeared out of nowhere.

Naya came in, ignored the food, and took the seat next to Sasha. She handed Sasha a folder. "Articles on the crash. Check out the flagged one."

Sasha flipped through the printouts until she came to one marked with a red sticky flag. It was from the *Pittsburgh Tribune-Review*, the more conservative of the city's two daily papers. In the grand tradition of local papers, its coverage of the event was focused on the regional angle. There was a sidebar describing Hemisphere Air as a Pittsburgh company, headquartered in the South

Hills, and a longer piece listing the known crash victims who had ties, however tenuous, to Western Pennsylvania.

Naya had highlighted one victim whose connection wasn't at all tenuous: a retired city laborer named Angelo Calvaruso, who lived in the Pittsburgh neighborhood of Morningside, had been on the doomed flight. The brief biographical information said he had recently been hired as a consultant by Patriotech, a Bethesda, Maryland company, and was survived by his wife, Rosa, four children, and four grandchildren.

Sasha scanned the other names on the list. Some victims had relatives in Pittsburgh. One had graduated from Carnegie Mellon University in the late 1990s. One was a former local weatherman who had moved up to a station in Virginia. But Mr. Calvaruso appeared to be the only resident of Pittsburgh who had been on the flight.

She looked at Naya and said, "We found the class representative."

Naya nodded, her braids bouncing, "It's gotta be him."

Peterson must have caught a snippet of the conversation. His head swiveled their way, his eyes interested. Sasha handed him the printout, and he skimmed it, stroking his left eyebrow with his index finger as he read. "Looks like he'll be the guy."

Sasha turned back to Naya. "Do you know anyone in the clerk's office?"

Noah, Sasha, and Naya knew Mickey Collins had either stumbled upon the existence of the late Angelo Calvaruso the night before or, at the latest, when he read this morning's paper. They had no doubt he'd already paid Rosa Calvaruso a visit, consoled her in her time of grief, and promptly signed the widow up as his class representative. If he hadn't, the lion of the plaintiffs' bar was slipping.

With a named representative onboard, Mickey would have slapped together a complaint to get on file first thing in the morning. Hell, he'd probably been waiting outside the federal courthouse when it had opened. The complaint itself would likely be laughable—heavy on emotion, thin on allegations—but that wouldn't matter; he could amend it later. What did matter was getting their hands on a copy of the complaint before Mickey started calling his reporter buddies, so they could help to prepare Metz for the inevitable press inquiries.

The joke underlying all this urgency was, under the federal rules, Mickey had sixty days after filing before he had to serve Hemisphere Air with a copy of the complaint. Sixty days in a mass accident case was a lifetime. Even if Mickey waited two months to officially serve their client, the assembled lawyers would spend every one of those sixty days gathering information and performing research to aid in the company's defense.

Naya was still murmuring into the phone on the credenza, her back to the room, but Peterson was tapping his ring finger against the mahogany table. *Clink. Clink. Clink. Clink.* His wedding band beat out a rhythm. Not slow, not fast. Steady. Unrelenting.

Sasha willed herself not to slam her own hand down on top of his to quiet it. "Noah, do you want to go ahead and get started?" she said instead.

"Let's."

Sasha raised her voice a notch to be heard over the Tuesday morning quarterbacking of the previous night's Steelers game. Most of the group had probably set their DVRs to record it while they worked. "Okay, let's get started." She stole a glance at the time on her Blackberry display. "It's twenty to nine. When I said eight thirty, I meant eight thirty. For today and today only, I'll give you the benefit of the doubt that you were looking for the conference room. Going forward, be here on time. A few minutes early if you want to get your grubby hands on the breakfast treats."

Eight heads bobbed their understanding. Kaitlyn opened her mouth, probably to apologize, but Sasha didn't give her the chance. "Naya Andrews will be the legal assistant on this case."

Naya, still on the telephone, turned slightly and shot the group a peace sign. Or the devil's horns. From this angle, Sasha wasn't entirely sure which, and, knowing Naya, she figured they were equally probable.

"Naya is a tremendous resource and we're lucky to have her on our team. We need to use her time wisely. Any assignments for Naya are to run through me. If I approve it, then you can ask Naya to do it. On the flip side, if Naya asks you to do something, you should assume she's already talked to me about it and get right on it."

Sasha hoped they all caught the subtext. They weren't to give the legal assistant any bullshit assignments or busy work—or worse, personal errands to run—and they weren't to give her any lip if she asked them to do something. Despite the warning, Sasha fully expected at least one, probably two, of the lawyers sitting at the table to violate the simple instructions. And heaven help the one who did; Naya would waste no time setting the offender straight and would throw in a few choice cracks about his or her looks, breath, or fashion choices.

Naya placed the receiver back in the cradle and returned to her seat.

"So?" Peterson asked.

"Well, Mickey did file this morning, but get this: Calvaruso's *not* the named rep."

"What?" Peterson and Sasha said together.

"I know, weird, right? The deputy clerk said the putative class representatives are listed as Martin and Tonya Grant."

"Grant?" Sasha retrieved the article from in front of Peterson and started flipping through it. "Here we go. Celeste Grant, getting her masters in social work at the University of Maryland, is survived by her parents, Tonya and Martin Grant of Regent Square. She was on her way to a training session for some humanitarian group she had signed on to work with in South America next summer."

Peterson groaned. Sasha knew what he was thinking: the parents of a graduate student devoted to helping people made for pretty sympathetic plaintiffs. True, but she would have gone with Rosa Calvaruso. A widow, particularly one who wasn't well off,—which this one almost assuredly was not, given her address and her late husband's job—would resonate more with a Pittsburgh jury. Not that this case would ever see a jury. Hemisphere Air would settle if Prescott couldn't get the case dismissed or the class claims kicked on legal grounds. But still, Sasha wondered, what was Mickey Collins thinking?

"What was he thinking?" she said aloud.

Peterson raised his shoulders in a dismissive shrug. "Perhaps the widow told him she wasn't interested."

Several pairs of eyebrows shot up around the room. Even these inexperienced attorneys found the idea that a would-be plaintiff would turn down a potential jackpot a bit hard to swallow.

"Maybe she was in shock," Kaitlyn offered.

"Maybe." Sasha turned back to Naya. "Who caught the case?"

Naya grinned. "Judge Dolans."

The Honorable Amanda Dolans, the last of the Clinton appointees still sitting on the Western District bench, was notoriously pro-plaintiff.

Joe Donaldson cleared his throat. "Uh, Sasha, I e-mailed my memo to you just before the meeting, so you probably didn't get a chance to see it yet." He spoke with effort, like the words were lodged in his throat, fighting not to come out.

"No, Joe, I didn't."

His eyes, already bleary from the late night spent researching and drafting the memo, clouded over as he broke the news. "Um, well, of the three sitting judges who have MDL experience and who don't currently have an active

MDL case on their dockets, Judge Dolans is the worst for us."

Sasha smiled. "Of the other two, who would have been the best?"

"Either one would have been much better. Mattheis is a pro-business Bush appointee. Westman is an Obama appointee, but his decisions have been very well-reasoned. They both have good track records with MDLs. Mattheis just settled an enormous antitrust MDL, so he probably won't be assigned another one for a while. But, man, it's bad luck we got Dolans and not Westman. Based on the opinions I looked at last night, she finds a way to rule for the plaintiff every time."

He finished and dropped his gaze to his half-eaten doughnut, ashamed, as though he were somehow responsible for the case being assigned to an unfavorable judge.

"Rewrite the memo to focus on Westman, summarize his significant opinions, and attach copies of them."

Joe looked up.

"Mandy Dolans is Mickey Collins' ex-wife. She'll recuse herself as soon as the complaint gets to her chambers. She always does when one of his cases is assigned to her. From what I hear, the divorce was ugly."

Joe smiled, equal parts relieved Dolans

wouldn't be hearing the case and chagrined he didn't think to research the judges' personal lives.

"It's difficult being married to a lawyer," Peterson announced to no one in particular.

Naya shot Sasha a look.

Is he okay?

Sasha shrugged and moved on, "Each of you will be responsible for putting together a dossier on one of the victims. Look for criminal records, unpaid parking tickets, compromising Facebook pictures, internet forum posts, anything you can find that they wouldn't want us to know about. Naya will e-mail around an assignment list. I'll take Calvaruso. Kaitlyn, once you finish the conflicts analysis, you take Celeste Grant."

Ordinarily, Sasha would have taken Grant herself, but something about Calvaruso was bothering her. She wanted to check it out.

Parker, a blonde who looked like she should be riding a horse in a Ralph Lauren ad, raised her hand. "Why are we digging up dirt on the crash victims?"

Sasha glanced at Peterson to see if he wanted to field this one. It was the type of question he was an expert at turning around, obfuscating the moral issue so completely that you ended up wondering how lawyers could claim to represent their clients' interest if they *weren't* trashing the plaintiffs. Peterson didn't look up from his mug.

"Don't think of it as digging up dirt on the victims," Sasha said. "To properly defend Hemisphere Air, we need to understand our opponents—their motivations, their strengths, and their weaknesses."

Parker twirled a long strand of hair around her finger and just looked at her.

"You'll be surprised at how much damaging information is out there about people. Last year, Noah and I were defending UPMC against an employee who claimed he couldn't work because he had a debilitating fear that the building was toxic even though the results of environmental studies showed it wasn't. But he said he experienced all the symptoms of sick building syndrome whenever he came to work."

She waited a minute to let her colleagues scoff and laugh derisively. It was absurd now, but at the time the medical center had been staring down the barrel at a high seven-figure demand and there was nothing funny about the case.

She went on, "Plaintiff's counsel retained a doctor from New Mexico who touted himself as the leading expert in this area. A three-minute Google search revealed a state medical board decision revoking his medical license, a Justice Department investigation into possible Medicare fraud for bogus billing of nonexistent treatments, and a federal court decision barring him from testifying because it viewed his opinion as junk science. After a very entertaining deposition of the good doctor, the plaintiff voluntarily dismissed with prejudice in exchange for our not filing a motion for sanctions and fees. Could we have really served UPMC's interests in that case if we hadn't thoroughly researched our opponent? Of course not."

The assembled attorneys bobbed their heads, sold on the idea. Caught up in the moment, they failed to appreciate the difference between discrediting a for-hire whore selling his opinions to the highest bidder and destroying the shell-shocked family members' memories of their loved ones—men and women who were just trying to get from Point A to Point B.

If averages held, two of the associates sitting around the table would stumble onto that distinction at some point. And one of them would care. That one would become a former Prescott attorney. The other would someday pick out the furniture for a corner office.

The meeting broke up and people drifted out, talking about how awesome it must have been to shove that expert down plaintiff counsel's throat.

Sasha stayed behind to cadge the remaining pastries for Lettie and her friends. On her way out, she stopped to offer one to Flora, who deliberated before settling on a muffin.

"Thanks," she said, peeling back the paper with her purple talons.

Naya came out of the conference room and caught up with Sasha at Flora's work station. She put a hand on Sasha's arm to keep her there.

"What's going on with Peterson?" Naya asked.

Sasha shrugged. "I honestly don't know."

"Well, you'd better be ready to take the lead during the meeting with Metz. Look at him." Naya pulled Sasha back into the doorway.

Noah Peterson sat in the now-darkened, otherwise empty conference room, his eyes still on the mug on the table in front of him.

9

Bethesda, Maryland

Jerry sat at his immaculate desk, running through the details of Friday's upcoming exercise in his head. It was critical that second display of his technology go off with the same precision as had the first. Everything depended on another flawless performance.

One positive result could be considered a fluke or chalked up to luck, but two consecutive positives would be viewed as proof Irwin could consistently deliver what he promised: the ability to take down a commercial airliner without unbuckling your seatbelt. And that capability would fetch a fantastic sum on the not-exactly-open market. More than enough for him to disappear forever.

Jerry rehearsed the plan again. He found no vulnerabilities, but he would keep running through it, probing for weaknesses until he identified them. Then he would fix them. Because he was Jerry Irwin. He wondered if he could be considered a bona fide evil genius.

The chirping telephone broke into his thoughts. He glared at it, waiting for Lilliana to pick it up. Then he realized his desk phone wasn't ringing. He reached into his top desk drawer and grabbed the prepaid cell phone. Only one person had the number, and it was only to be used to convey key information.

"Hello?" Jerry waited to hear what his partner had to say.

The voice on the other end was urgent but measured. "Hemisphere is meeting with the law firm today. And the NTSB found the black box already. That's sooner than we'd hoped. It means the lawyers will start digging around, probably before Friday. We just need to stay focused."

Jerry took in the news. He thought hard. Then he said, "Okay."

Damage control wasn't his responsibility. All he had to do was crash one more plane.

He hung up and ran through the plan again.

10

Pittsburgh, Pennsylvania

It stood to reason they were meeting with Metz in the Frick Conference Room.

Frick had a postcard-worthy view of the city. From its wall of windows, downtown's skyline was on display. On a clear day, the working barges that crossed the city's rivers zipped by like dragonflies in the distance, and, at night, the high-rises glittered with lights. Each Fourth of July, the firm opened its doors to employees and their families to watch the fire-works display from the room.

In addition to the view, Frick was one of the largest conference rooms (wholly unnecessary for a three-person meeting) and the most opulent (wholly necessary for a meeting with a very important client like Hemisphere Air). An original painting by Mary Cassatt, a native of Pittsburgh, hung on one wall and competed with the view.

Sasha turned her attention from the Cassatt hanging on the wall to the distressed man sitting at the table.

Bob Metz looked like a man who hadn't slept in a week. He was usually disheveled; his hair unruly, his custom-made suits rumpled. But his normal disarray had an air of too rich and not vain enough to care—like Angelina Jolie caught in sweatpants and a baseball cap picking up a quart of rice milk.

Today he looked more like a professional athlete who'd spent the night in a holding cell after shooting up a strip club. Actually, he reminded Sasha of that Nick Nolte mugshot that had been all over the Internet back in 2002. Not that Metz would be caught wearing a Hawaiian shirt, no matter how dire the situation.

He had a day's growth on his chin and cheeks, his reddish blond hair was uncombed, and his striped necktie was tied in a sloppy four-in-hand knot that would have earned him detention in his boarding school days.

Sasha wasn't sure who was in worse shape—

her client or her boss. Peterson at least looked presentable. But he was still lost in thought and saying random things. Sasha doubted he was up to the task of providing the thoughtful advice for which Hemisphere Air shelled out eight hundred dollars an hour.

In his panic, Metz didn't seem to notice his trusted counselor's near-catatonic state. So, Sasha took charge of the meeting and set for herself the same goal she had every time she babysat her nieces and nephews: no blood; no property damage in excess of a hundred dollars; and everybody eats something.

She turned to Metz, "Bob, I know this is a stressful situation, but you should eat."

She pointed at his untouched plate of Virginia spots, which Peterson had brought in from the Duquesne Club because they were Metz's favorite dish.

Peterson was busy ignoring his own plate of spots. Sasha wasn't a fan herself, although admitting as much about the breaded, white fish of indeterminate origin would be tantamount to heresy around Prescott & Talbott's offices.

Metz shoved the spots around on his plate with his fork, dragging them through the beurre blanc sauce but not eating them. Peterson carefully buttered a hunk of warm bread. Neither man spoke.

She tried again. "Bob, why don't I fill you in on what we've learned thus far."

She winced when she heard herself say "thus" but pressed on. "Mickey Collins filed, as you know. We're making a copy of the complaint for you, but it's nothing impressive. The real news is the case was assigned to Judge Dolans, who will recuse, given her personal history with Collins. Judge Westman is the most likely. . . "

Metz interrupted her, "They found the black box."

The black box, often the sole survivor of a plane crash, isn't really black. It's bright orange.

Sasha supposed it might be charred black after a fire. She'd never seen one; she'd just worked with the data they'd preserved. The box contained two separate recorders; one recorded cockpit conversation and background noise, which often became unintelligible screaming at the end, and the other recorded literally hundreds of data points about the flight—things like speed, altitude, and fuel flow. Of the two, the voice recording was the more dramatic, but the flight data usually proved more helpful in piecing together exactly what had happened.

"That was quick. Were both recorders intact?"

Sasha looked sidelong at Peterson to see if he was even feigning an interest. He wasn't.

Metz nodded. "The NTSB called about seven

this morning. Vivian flew to D.C. to act as Hemisphere Air's representative in the lab while they cracked it open. The cockpit voice recorder and the flight data recorder are both in pristine shape. They won't have to do any reconstruction." Metz glanced at Peterson then fell silent.

Bob Metz was a good guy. He was polite, considerate, and political without being oily. He was not a legal scholar. He'd earned gentleman's Cs through college and law school and had relied on his family connections and charm to get where he was in his career.

Metz would do—always did—whatever Noah Peterson told him he should do. Although everyone in the room knew it, they all pretended not to. Instead, Peterson would couch his instruction as a suggestion, so that when Metz invariably followed it, he could act as though he'd independently evaluated and agreed with the advice of his legal counsel.

This arrangement usually suited both client and attorney just fine, but at the moment, Metz's trusted counselor seemed to be counting the fibers in his cloth napkin. Or maybe he wasn't even seeing the napkin.

"Did Vivian hear the playback from the voice recorder?"

Metz sighed, ran his hand down his tie, smoothed out some wrinkles, and said, "She said that first the pilot says something like the onboard system reset itself and was now locked in with new coordinates. Co-pilot checks them, agrees. They try to reset them, you know, override the autopilot, but nothing happens. They got out a mayday transmission, but barely. After that, she said it was just, uh, screaming. I think some praying." Metz closed his eyes.

"And the data recorder information bears that out? The onboard computer changed the coordinates all by itself and couldn't be overridden?"

"Yes. Oh, and the plane accelerated right before impact. No one else knows any of this yet—not even anyone inside the company. The TSA and NTSB asked Vivian to keep it to herself until they complete their initial analysis of the data, but, of course, she told me. And this conversation is privileged, so, I figured it's okay to tell you."

Sasha tried to imagine how the crew must have felt, watching the mountain loom closer and being unable to do anything to stop the plane from plowing into it. Powerless.

But the facts, horrible as they were, seemed to be helpful to Hemisphere Air's defense. Either Metz was in complete shock or she was missing something.

She tried to pull Peterson into the conversation. "Noah, based on what Vivian's learned from the NTSB, don't you think it sounds like Hemisphere Air has a good indemnification claim against the manufacturer? Who was it—Boeing?"

Peterson nodded absently.

Metz shook his head. "We don't."

Sasha spoke slowly, almost as if he were a child. "Bob, if a plane suddenly changes its coordinates and locks them in, that's not pilot error or a maintenance problem. In my view, that would result from a manufacturing defect. You can turn to Boeing for that."

Metz shook his head again, miserably. "Not this time. You know how if you make aftermarket modifications to your car, you void the warranty?"

"Sure."

"We modified that plane. Over Boeing's express objection, we installed the RAGS link."

"The what?"

Sasha thought she knew everything there was to know about Hemisphere Air's business, and she had never heard of RAGS.

Peterson shook his head. He didn't know about it either, assuming he had even heard what Metz had said and wasn't just randomly moving his head.

"RAGS," Metz said. "The Remote Aircraft Guidance System."

Peterson, finally brought to life by the

prospect of a legal malpractice claim, asked one question.

"Did Prescott & Talbott opine on the advisability of installing this RAGS link?"

Metz pushed his plate away.

"You did. Well, not you, of course, someone in your contracts review group. You told us not to do it. But Vivian insisted."

Not good for Hemisphere Air. Good for Prescott & Talbott, though. Peterson's shoulders relaxed and he went back to staring off into space.

"What exactly is a RAGS link, and why did Vivian want it so badly?" Sasha asked.

"RAGS was conceived after 9/11. The TSA put out a call for technology companies to develop systems to safeguard the skies. Most of the responses were ideas to reinforce cockpit doors or onboard scanners to detect metal that made it through airport screening. You know, responding to the attack that already happened, not protecting against the next thing. But an outfit called Patriotech developed a program that could tap into the autopilot system in the event of a hijacking. Basically, it would allow an air marshal to control the plane remotely, from the cabin. He could thwart the hijackers without being detected, avoiding a dangerous mid-air confrontation that could risk the lives of passengers."

Sasha shrugged, "Sounds like that's not a bad idea."

"Oh, it's not. And, early on there was a lot of excitement about it. The Air Marshals were considering it. They approached Vivian about participating in a pilot program, and you know Viv." Metz looked meaningfully at Peterson and then at Sasha.

Sasha actually didn't know Viv, but she knew of her.

Vivian Coulter was a legend around the office. She'd been one of the first women in the firm to make partner, which was quite an achievement during a time when female attorneys were routinely asked how many words per minute they could type. But, Viv's achievement was sullied by the fact that she'd made partner by backstabbing, undercutting, and sabotaging her peers and sleeping with her superiors.

After her elevation to partner, her already-unpleasant demeanor took a turn toward vile. She became a screamer; she was a terror to work for and impossible to please. She tore through associates at nearly the same rate she ran through husbands. "Viv" became a verb at Prescott & Talbott. As in, "I got vived hard yesterday" or "If you turn that memo in without proofreading it, the partner is going to viv your ass."

Finally, after her secretary had a full-blown nervous breakdown, complete with hospital stay, Prescott & Talbott managed to foist Viv off on its long-time client, carefully praising her work product while never mentioning her personality. And so, Viv Coulter became the Senior Vice President of Legal Affairs for Hemisphere Air. She was Metz's boss on the organizational chart, but she rarely involved herself in the day-to-day operations of the legal department.

Sasha, who joined the firm after Viv's long-awaited and heavily celebrated departure, had heard the in-house gig had mellowed Viv. Judging from Metz's expression, not by enough.

Peterson nodded. "I see."

"So, Vivian wanted to sign on for the RAGS pilot?" Sasha asked.

"Oh yeah. She thought it would be great publicity—Hemisphere Air doing its part to fight terrorism."

"But we advised you not to install RAGS?"

"Right. When we told Boeing about it, so we could get the exact specs for the autopilot program, their people said absolutely not to do it. RAGS hadn't even been tested in flight simulators at that point. They said there was no guarantee it might not malfunction and, well, cause a crash."

"But, Vivian wanted to do it anyway?"

Metz picked his story back up. "Right. So, we asked Patriotech to draft an agreement indemnifying us if RAGS did cause a problem with our systems. They didn't have any in-house lawyers and didn't want to spend the money on an outside firm, so I think their CEO drafted it. It was worthless. I sent it over to your contracts review folks to take a look, and they confirmed it offered us no real protection."

"Viv couldn't be reasoned with, so you signed it anyway," Peterson said.

"Worse. She said not to even bother with the indemnification agreement. She went ahead and had the RAGS link installed with no protection for Hemisphere of any kind."

Sasha and Peterson were quiet for a minute, thinking about that.

"On how many planes?" Sasha asked.

"I don't know."

"How many other airlines signed up for the pilot program?"

"I don't know. Everything was trade secret confidential. Patriotech didn't tell us much."

"Are you sure the system was installed on the plane that went down?"

"Yes, Viv told me. You can't tell her I told you.

She didn't even tell the TSA and NTSB. They didn't mention it to her, so we assume they don't know about it."

"How can that be? Weren't the Air Marshals part of the pilot program?"

Metz laughed sourly. "Yeah, funny thing. Right before the links were installed, Homeland Security backed out. They pulled the plug on the program. The official statement was they had concerns about the application falling into the wrong hands. Privately, they told us they didn't really trust their own people with it."

Sasha nodded. "I remember hearing about problems in the Air Marshal Service. After 9/11, they hired a ton of new air marshals, but they pushed through applicants with criminal records, psychiatric disorders, financial problems, that sort of thing. There was a lot of fallout."

"Right," Metz said. "Viv went ahead and had the links installed anyway. She figured she could lobby some senator she used to date or something to revive the program."

Metz cradled his head in his hands. He pulled his fingers through his hair and looked up. "So, you see where this leaves us? We modified the plane to install a completely worthless communications link. Now Boeing will claim the RAGS link caused the equipment failure."

Sasha caught Peterson's eye. He gave her a slight nod, as he said, "Actually, Bob have you considered the other possibility?"

Even off his game, Peterson could finesse this discussion so as not to drive the defeated man beside him even further into despair.

"What other possibility?"

Peterson spoke softly. "That the Air Marshals' scenario happened. Someone got a hold of this RAGS application and used it to bring down the plane deliberately."

Sasha and Peterson waited for it to sink in. When it did, they watched every bit of color drain from Metz's tired face. Then his hands started to shake.

SASHA AND PETERSON sent Metz home to try to rest. Then, by unspoken agreement, they got their jackets and headed to the bar at the Renaissance Hotel. It was close enough to walk to, but far enough from the office that they weren't likely to run into anyone. Not that many of Prescott & Talbott's lawyers would be found at a bar in the middle of a Tuesday afternoon.

They walked the four blocks in silence. The only sound was the clacking of Sasha's heels against the pavement as they hurried through the brisk air. When they entered Braddock's, they were met by a blast of warm air and a smile from Marcus, who was tending an empty bar.

"Counselors," he greeted them from behind the gleaming bar, already reaching for the bottle of McCallan 18 to pour Peterson his usual.

"Marcus," Peterson said in return as he took a seat away from the door and the television set to CNN. As he situated himself on the stool, he reached into his pants pocket and fished out his key ring, then tossed his keys on the bar so they wouldn't rip his suit pants when he sat. He'd learned the hard way that keys and Hickey Freeman suit pants did not mix well.

The sparkling ruby plane on his key chain charm caught Sasha's eye as it did every time. Hemisphere Air had given Noah a custom-made crystal globe of the earth, encrusted with the small ruby plane, in appreciation of a defense verdict he'd won while Sasha was still in law school. It had been a true bet-the-company case, with several billion dollars at stake. Noah treated the expensive trinket like it had come from a gumball machine, but he never missed the chance to tell the story of his victory.

The bartender muted the television's sound and put a dish of peanuts and the glass of neat scotch in front of Peterson.

Sasha perched on the stool next to Peterson,

her feet dangling several inches above the brass footrest that ran the length of the bar.

"Sapphire & tonic for you, Sasha?" Marcus asked, placing two bowls—one with cashews and one with blue-cheese stuffed olives—on the bar in front of her.

"Please." She smiled at the bartender and plucked an olive from the dish.

He returned quickly with a generous pour and leaned over the bar. "Are we celebrating a court victory this afternoon?" he asked, calculating his potential tip in his head.

"I'm afraid not today, Marcus," Peterson said. "In fact, we need to discuss some strategy."

"Got it," the bartender said, unoffended, and retreated to the far end of the bar, where he resumed drying glasses. He'd tended bar long enough to know when to make himself scarce. He wouldn't interrupt them again unless they called him over.

Sasha stirred the ice cubes around in her gin and tonic, thinking. After they'd gotten Metz to understand the possibility that the crash had not been an accident, they'd probed him gently to see if he knew anything else about Patriotech or RAGS, but they got nothing else out of him.

He had asked if he should tell the NTSB about the RAGS link. Peterson told him they needed to analyze the situation and determine the best way to self-report if it turned out to be the right thing to do.

Sasha figured both men knew they'd have to tell the government. They were just trying to buy time to see if the TSA or NTSB would find out on their own, so they wouldn't have to incur Viv's wrath. It would be a hell of a battle to convince Viv to disclose what would look like a mistake on her part. Sasha was glad that would be Peterson's job, not hers.

She took another olive from the dish on the bar.

"Noah, we have to find out if any other planes have the RAGS link installed."

Peterson nodded and took a long drink of scotch. "I agree. And tomorrow, once Bob has calmed down, we'll ask him to poke around discreetly and see if he can find out."

Sasha opened her mouth but Peterson cut her off. "Mac, I know what you're thinking, but we can't take this to Vivian until we know more. You don't know her like I do." He took another swallow.

Sasha bit back a response. It was true, she didn't know the woman, but surely Metz or Peterson could make her see the urgency. The trouble was Metz was terrified of her, and Peterson would only go to her when he was good and ready.

She sipped her drink and tried to think of another approach. It was hard to think because she had this cloudy feeling she was overlooking something. It had started during the morning's meeting and had grown stronger all day.

She closed her eyes to concentrate. What was she missing? She tried to remember when the feeling hit. Calvaruso. It was when Naya announced Calvaruso wasn't the class representative. How did the retired city laborer play into this?

She opened her eyes in time to see Peterson drain his glass and signal for another. Unable to decode what her brain was trying to tell her, she let it go for the moment.

"Um, Noah? Is everything okay? I mean, aside from the crash. You seem sort of distracted." Sasha chose her words carefully. Peterson was her mentor and she considered him a friend, but they rarely discussed their personal lives.

He looked at her, his cool blue eyes as sad as she'd ever seen them. "It's Laura, Mac. I think she's going to leave me." His gaze dropped to the bar and his shoulders fell.

"Leave you? Why would Laura leave you?"

Sasha had been to dinner at the Petersons' home several times and had spoken to Laura Peterson at dozens of Prescott & Talbott events. She seemed to dote on her husband. She spent her days decorating her house, gardening, and swimming. She was always talking about her book club and the charitable organizations she belonged to. Laura was the model Prescott & Talbott wife.

"I don't know. She just doesn't seem to care anymore if I'm around or not. Take last night. I had to come in to the office and she didn't say a word. Just went back to reading her book. Then, when I got home, she was sound asleep in the middle of the bed, as if she didn't expect me to return."

Sasha looked at him, at the pain etched on his face. "Noah, maybe she was just tired."

He raised his eyes to hers. "You don't get it, Mac. Or maybe you do and that's why you're single. The firm comes first, has always come first. When we were newlyweds, I was just starting out. I told Laura work had to come first for a couple years, until I'd proved myself. Then, it was until I made partner. Then, until I had a solid book of business. Then, until I was on the Management Committee. And every time I promised the balance would switch after I'd cleared the next hurdle, I meant it. But look at me. I'm sixty. I work constantly. I have no children, no grandkids, and a smart, gorgeous wife who has wasted her life sitting in an empty house waiting for me to be her partner."

Sasha saw tears in his eyes and forced herself not to look away. "Noah, if that's really how you feel, why don't you retire? You have more money than God."

"What about my clients? Do you think Metz could navigate this morass without me?"

"What about your wife?"

Noah shook his head. "Retirement? What would I do? Legal consulting?"

The cloudy feeling was growing stronger again. Sasha ignored it and said, "Then what about the P&T Sabbatical Program?"

The Sabbatical Program was another of the Prescott & Talbott Work-Balance Committee's misguided attempts to improve attorney morale. Any equity partner could apply for either a six-month or twelve-month paid sabbatical to recharge, pursue a passion project, travel, teach a class, volunteer, whatever. When the program was announced, it had an effect on attorney morale all right, just not the intended one.

Most of the morale issues had been raised by junior attorneys who felt they were being overworked and not given professional development opportunities and by young income partners who felt they were being overworked and undercompensated. A program for the guys at the top of the pyramid to take a one-year paid vacation while their underlings picked up their slack hadn't been wildly popular. It sounded like Peterson could use it, though.

"The sabbatical program, hmm. We could rent a villa in Spain. Maybe Italy. No, France. Laura likes France." Peterson sat up straighter. "I'm going to call Laura right now and suggest it. Thanks, Mac."

Sasha finally broke through her cloud as he was going on about his big plans. "Wait, please. Something you said about retiring. Legal consulting. That would be a logical second career for you, right?"

"Yes, Mac. What of it?" Peterson was impatient to plan his year in Provence.

"Just hear me out, Noah. Angelo Calvaruso was a city laborer. You know, the guys who drive the snow plows in the winter and cut the grass and trim the trees at the city parks in the summer. So, he retires and starts a job as a consultant for some Bethesda company? What sense does that make?"

Peterson just looked at her.

"None, right? It's been bothering me all morning. And I can't believe it didn't hit me when we were talking to Metz. The name of the Bethesda company that hired Mr. Calvaruso as a consultant was . . ."

Peterson beat her to it. "Patriotech."

Sasha picked up her bag and slid off the barstool. "I'm going to visit Mrs. Calvaruso."

Peterson nodded. "Take someone with you. And, Mac, be discreet. I guess I'll need to talk to Metz and Vivian about reporting this today after all." He signaled for Marcus to bring him a third scotch to fortify him for the conversation ahead.

"Good luck," Sasha said as she turned to leave.

11

Sasha walked back to the office. Her stomach was sour. It wasn't from the gin. She realized she couldn't intrude on Mrs. Calvaruso. Not today. She'd be no different from Mickey Collins and his band of ambulance chasers if she showed up unannounced at the widow's house.

She needed to get information about Calvaruso's job. She didn't have to get it from his wife. She took her Blackberry from her bag and pulled up Peterson's cell number. The call rolled straight to voicemail.

"Noah, I'm not going to see Mrs. Calvaruso today. I don't think it's the right course. I'll call Patriotech and talk to someone in human resources. I'll probably get more out of them than a grieving old lady, anyway. Don't worry, I won't mention RAGS. Will you call me after you talk to Metz and Vivian so we can regroup?"

She tossed the phone back in her bag, already feeling better. One thing Krav Maga had taught her was to follow her instincts. Always.

Back in her office, she ignored the lopsided pile of mail threatening to spill off her desk and her blinking voicemail light. She Googled Patriotech, and the first hit was the company's website. It was bare bones. There were no details about Patriotech's products; no press releases; no investor information; no management bios—nothing but a photo of the outside of an anonymous-looking building in a business park, with a main contact number and a street address below it. She memorized the number and closed her browser before dialing it. She didn't like to be distracted when she was on a call.

A pleasant, accented woman's voice answered on the second ring. "Good afternoon. Thank you for calling Patriotech."

"My name is Sasha McCandless. I'm an attorney with Prescott & Talbott in Pittsburgh. I'd like to speak to someone in your HR department."

After a pause, the voice said, "Uh, you'll want to talk to Tim ... I guess."

The woman didn't sound convinced, so Sasha asked, "What is Tim's title?"

"Oh, he's our Human Resources Director."

"That'd be great."

Sasha listened to an instrumental version of an old Journey song while the receptionist transferred the call.

"Um, this is Tim Warner. I'm the HR Director here."

Warner sounded very young and no more certain that he was the right person to handle the call than the receptionist had been.

Sasha repeated her name and explained that she was an attorney calling from Pittsburgh, then she quickly launched into the reason for her call. "I represent Hemisphere Air, which operates the flight that crashed last night. I understand one of your employees was on the plane. I'm very sorry." Sasha hoped she sounded sincere. She *was* very sorry.

Warner mumbled something about it being a tragedy. Sasha didn't think it seemed particularly heartfelt.

She plowed ahead, "It would be very helpful if you would send me a copy of Mr. Calvaruso's personnel file. Of course, if you prefer, I could get a subpoena *duces tecum* from the court ordering you to turn it over. Obviously, if you agree to send it voluntarily it would save everyone involved a lot of time and expense."

She was banking on Warner being intimidated by the Latin and too green to know it wouldn't be quite that easy to serve a subpoena to produce documents on Patriotech.

First, she'd have to get an attorney licensed to practice in Maryland involved, because she'd need the Maryland federal district court to issue a subpoena on Patriotech.

Then, if Patriotech got counsel involved (unlikely, she thought, given that the company drafted its own indemnification agreement with Hemisphere), there'd be objections, request for extensions, negotiations over the scope of the subpoena, and probably a demand for a confidentiality agreement that would also have to be negotiated.

And, she'd have to serve Collins, who would undoubtedly try to gum up the works, claiming the information she was looking for was irrelevant or, at a minimum, premature; and, frankly, he'd be right about that. In the context of the suit Collins had filed, she had no current need for Angelo Calvaruso's personnel file.

In short, she needed to convince Warner she was doing him a favor and get those files out of him informally.

"A subpoena?" Warner repeated, "Would there be a public record of that?"

"Certainly." She waited in silence while Warner weighed that information. After a long minute, she heard the clack of keys on Warner's keyboard and smiled.

Warner said, "Patriotech would be happy to cooperate, Ms. McCandless. There's no need to involve the court. What exactly do you need from us?"

"I appreciate that and, please, call me Sasha. I'm looking for whatever documentation you have regarding Mr. Calvaruso's job duties, benefits and salary, any performance reviews, an employment agreement, that sort of thing."

"Hmm . . ." Warner scanned the file names on his computer's directory. "Mr. Calvaruso only joined us about a month ago and he was technically a consultant, not an employee, so his file is going to be pretty thin. Can I just copy all the files I can access on our server that relate to his position or contain his name? I mean, if electronic files are acceptable? We try to operate as paperlessly as we can."

"Electronic copies are fine," Sasha assured him. "Actually, they're preferable. But, when you say all the files you can access, does that mean there are files you don't have access to?"

Warner paused before answering. His voice was sheepish as he explained, "Well, given the, uh, nature of our business, the R&D, and, um, proprietary confidential information, Patriotech takes measures to ensure the secrecy of our research." He hurried to add, "But, I think I can access all the files related to Mr. Calvaruso."

Sasha heard a desk drawer roll open, then Warner said, "Okay if I copy these to a thumb drive and pop them in the mail?"

"That's fine. If you wouldn't mind, please overnight it. It's really rather urgent."

"No problem. I have your firm website up right now. Should I just send it to your attention at that address?"

"That would be great." Sasha thanked him warmly and hung up. She felt just the tiniest bit bad about how easy it had been to bluff Patriotech's human resources director, but she knew Noah would be thrilled to have the files.

12

Bethesda, Maryland

Tim slid the thumb drive into a UPS envelope. He strained to think of a clever note to include, finally settling for "It was a pleasure to speak to you today. Please let me know if you need anything further." After addressing the envelope, he took one more look at the attorney's picture on her firm website. Sasha McCandless was a hottie. Dark wavy hair, bright green eyes, and a tight little body that her suit jacket couldn't hide. Tim thought he saw a hint of a smile playing on her lips.

Maybe he should ask Irwin if he could go to Angelo Calvaruso's funeral as a representative of

Patriotech, he thought. He *was* the Director of Human Resources, after all. It seemed appropriate for him to attend as a gesture of ... something. And he could call Sasha and ask her to get a cup of coffee or maybe a cocktail.

Tim checked his watch. It was close enough to five. He decided to call it a day and drop the package into the UPS box in the parking lot on his way out. He'd tell Irwin about the call tomorrow; presumably, he'd be pleased that Tim had shown the initiative to keep Patriotech from getting dragged into court. Irwin *hated* publicity. In fact, Tim thought, as he pushed in his desk chair and turned out his lights, Irwin might actually reward him for this one. That'd be a change.

JERRY IRWIN WATCHED from his floor-to-ceiling window as his worthless human resources director scurried to his dirty Honda. It wasn't even five o'clock and there was Warner sneaking out of work. Not that it mattered, Irwin thought, Warner was essentially useless and had been hired mainly because Irwin knew he'd be too stupid and inexperienced to ask any questions or to follow-up when he was fed a line of bullshit. Besides, by this time next week, Patriotech would be shuttered, he'd be long gone, and his hapless employees would be someone else's problem.

He swiveled his chair back to his desk and returned to the long-hand calculations he'd been working out on a legal pad. He knew he was counting unhatched chicks, but he couldn't resist running endless variations on how much he would profit from the sale of the RAGS technology. Even with the 40% split with his partner and even assuming a very conservative winning bid, Irwin knew he'd be hard pressed to spend his share of the take in his lifetime.

Behind him, on the return of his immaculate L-shaped desk, his computer screen displayed a pop-up alert notifying him that Warner had accessed flagged files. But Irwin was lost in thought, trying to settle on which of the islands on his short list would become his new home.

By the time he turned his attention back to his monitor and saw the notification, Warner was long gone with copies of files related to Calvaruso and his replacement.

First, Irwin pounded his fist on his desk until his knuckles bled. Next, he retrieved the prepaid phone from his desk drawer to tell his partner about the breach and his plan to remedy it. After explaining the situation, he hung up and returned the phone to the drawer.

Then, he took out a second prepaid phone—

even his partner didn't have the number to this one—and called the private security firm he'd placed on retainer when the project had gotten underway.

At the time he'd hired them, he wasn't sure what purpose the suit-wearing gang of thugs might serve. Now, he knew.

13

The offices of Prescott & Talbott
6:30 p.m.

Sasha tore through her e-mail inbox, trying to respond to as many of the messages as she could by seven o'clock. At seven, she would take a break to go pick up some dinner. Naya had stopped by to let her know she was ordering pizza for the hard-at-work Hemisphere Air team, but Sasha planned to pick up sushi.

She would need the fresh air. It was going to be a long night.

After a break for dinner, she would turn to

Joe and Kaitlyn's memos. They would likely require heavy comments and she wanted to give them back early enough that the junior attorneys could work through the night and have them rewritten and waiting on Noah's desk when he arrived in the morning.

Only then, would she think about tackling the stack of mail that Lettie had sorted and left on the corner of her desk.

Sasha knew she wasn't working at peak efficiency. She was distracted.

There had been no word from Peterson. No news couldn't possibly be good news in this case, she thought. Either he was still meeting with Viv and Metz, trying to convince them to go to the NTSB or the meeting was over and he hadn't been able to persuade them. In which case, he was no doubt washing away the taste of failure with more scotch.

Her desk phone rang. Hoping to see Metz's number, she glanced at the display before answering it. It was just the evening receptionist.

"Hi, Marie."

"Sasha, I have a gentleman who says he's been trying to reach Mr. Peterson all day. He's left several urgent messages but Noah hasn't responded. Now, he's asking to talk to the second in command on the Hemisphere Air team. May I transfer him?"

Second in command sounded military. But, odds were, it was a reporter. If so, Sasha had no comment. Whoever it was, if the guy were important, Peterson would have returned his call.

"Do me a favor, Marie. Put him into my voicemail."

"Sure thing, honey. Did you eat yet?" Lettie had deputized Marie as her stand-in mother hen after hours.

"I'm going to run out and pick something up," Sasha said and then hung up before Marie could lecture her.

She turned back to her e-mails until the voicemail light blinked red on her phone. The caller who was so interested in talking to Peterson was not a reporter.

"Ms. McCandless, this is Special Agent Leo Connelly calling from the Federal Air Marshal's Pittsburgh Field Office. I urgently need to speak to you or Mr. Peterson regarding the Hemisphere Air matter. When you get this message, please call me at 412-555-1600."

Agent Connelly's tone was measured and serious.

Sasha stared at the notes she'd scrawled while listening to the message, hoping they'd give her a clue as to what to do next. Where the hell was Peterson?

She was just about to call his home number,

when Parker appeared in her doorway, swaying slightly.

"Do you have a minute?"

She tucked a strand of expensive honey-streaked hair behind her ear, revealing a diamond earring the size of Sasha's thumb.

Sasha glanced at the time. She'd called in her sushi order nearly twenty minutes earlier. "Just one."

She gestured toward the guest chair, but Parker leaned against the door frame.

"Okay, so, I was having drinks . . ."

"You went to happy hour? You're on a trial team."

"Uh, it was a preexisting commitment?" Parker's cheeks flushed as she realized maybe she should have cancelled her plans.

Sasha scribbled a note to lay out her expectations more fully at the next day's meeting.

She looked up from her notepad and watched Parker's blush deepen. Finally, she said, "So, do you want to tell me about your date or not?"

Parker forced out a small laugh and twisted the ring on her right ring finger. It sported a stone that made the earrings look like chips in comparison. "It wasn't really a date. I've hung out with this guy off and on since law school, and now he works for Mickey Collins. So, he had to get back to the office, too. It was just a couple quick drinks, Sasha."

This was going from bad to worse. Aside from the surprise that Parker was slumming with a mere plaintiff's attorney—which Sasha chalked up to rich girl rebellion—she was skirting a very thin line ethically.

"You do know that you cannot discuss the case with this guy, right? Tell me you didn't discuss the case."

If they had to remove Parker from the team, Peterson would be livid.

"Of course not!" Parker had the good sense to sound scandalized. "We only talked about the newspaper reports, and, I guess the complaint, but that's public record."

Sasha narrowed her eyes. Not believable. Lawyers were notorious for honoring client confidentiality in the breach. If strictly observed, the confidentiality rules would put a real crimp in the age-old sport of trading war stories. Most attorneys do discuss their cases with outsiders, they just never identify the client involved by name. That compromise position clearly wouldn't work for Parker and her friend. Everyone at Mickey's shop was working on the crash. Had to be.

"So, I mentioned that I was surprised by their choice of class rep. Oh . . ." Parker trailed off and chewed on her bottom lip. "That's okay, right? I mean, the complaint is public, and that article named that Caruso guy."

"Calvaruso." Sasha corrected her and ignored the question.

"Sorry, Calvaruso. My friend, Chase, said Collins called everyone into the office last night after the crash and offered a $5,000 bonus to whoever found him a class rep. Chase has a cousin who works for a corporate travel service, so he called her to see if she could find any reservations for the flight. She found Mr. Calvaruso's reservation, booked through Patriotech by a Mr. Irwin, and told Chase that Calvaruso had flown from Pittsburgh to D.C., had a layover, and then was booked from D.C. to Dallas."

She paused.

Sasha got the sense the younger woman was waiting for praise, so she said nothing.

Parker went on, a bit deflated, "So, anyway, Chase found Collins right away and told him about Mr. Calvaruso. He said Collins was really excited until he mentioned Mr. Irwin's name. Then, Collins immediately said no way, Calvaruso wouldn't work. But he didn't say why, and Chase said he got sort of angry when Chase tried to press him about it. A couple minutes later, another associate came up with the Grants, and Collins went with them."

Sasha stood and gathered up her office id badge, wallet, and cell phone. Parker's story was interesting, but it was time to pick up her take-out. "Thanks for bringing this to me, Parker."

They walked down the hall together. Sasha stopped in front of Parker's office.

"If you want to stay on this trial team, work on your assignment. Act like a grownup making six figures, not a princess. No more happy hours. If you can't do that, you go back to document review. Is that clear?"

Parker flushed. Anger flashed in her eyes, followed by shame. She said, "Crystal."

"Good," Sasha said and left to go get her dinner.

Back in the office, Sasha checked in with the team. She noted Parker had joined them in the work room.

Finally, she sat at her desk and wolfed down her sushi. She quieted her mind and drank a glass of water, then she closed her office blinds against the dark. The view from her window, although not as stunning as that from the Frick, was pretty—especially at night, when the lights on the surrounding office buildings glittered in the Monongahela River below. She closed the blinds even though she enjoyed the view, because she did not like the way she felt sitting in her brightly lit office at night: like she was on display in an illuminated box.

Before turning to the memos, she tried Peterson's cell phone again. Once again, the call went straight to voicemail. She was just about to call his home number when she noticed the message light on her phone was blinking.

Hoping it was Peterson and not the air marshal, Sasha tapped in her voicemail code and waited. The call had come in at 7:22 p.m., while she'd been walking over to Sushi & Rolls. She didn't recognize the number, but the 202 area code was D.C.

Um, hi, Ms. McCandless. I wanted to let you know ... oh, uh, this is Tim. Tim Warner from Patriotech. I wanted to let you know that I put that package in the mail this evening and, also, I plan to be in Pittsburgh to attend Mr. Calvaruso's funeral, whenever that is. I was thinking maybe it would be helpful to meet ... You know, in case you have any questions about the files or just to have a cup of . . .

Sasha could hear faint knocking in the background.

Okay, there's someone at my door. Anyway, this

is my cell phone number, 202-555-0808. Call any time. Coming!

The knocking grew louder, then Warner was opening the door, but he hadn't ended the call.

Yes? Can I help . . .. Hey! What do you think ... You guys can't just barge in here!

Another voice, rough and deep, broke in. Sasha could make out muffled words.

You Warner? You stole something of Mr. Irwin's and he wants it back.

Then Warner again.

Irwin? I **work** *for Mr. Irwin. You must be confused.*

You can give us those files or we can take them. Your choice.

Files? What, wait ... I'm,. . . I'm the Human Resources Director.

A sound like a door slamming shut filled Sasha's office through her phone's speaker box. Then, Warner's quavering voice gave way to shouting that she could not decipher. She strained to listen, but what followed was a cacophony: grunts, moaning, and a whimper. The cell phone clattered like it had hit the floor and picked up some banging noises. The noise continued until the message reached the voice-mail system's time limit.

Sasha's mouth was dry. She picked up the

handset and replayed the message, hoping to hear something different this time. She did not.

She pressed 9 to save the message and tried to slow her heartbeat before dialing Warner's cell phone number. It rang and rang. Warner didn't pick up. Neither did his voicemail.

She called Peterson's home number. No answer. She left a message, apologizing for bothering him at home and saying it was urgent that she speak to him.

Sasha put the receiver back in its cradle. She stood and started pacing in front of her window. She opened the blinds to look out at the night skyline, but did not see it.

She closed her office door and thought hard.

She could fairly assume that something bad was happening or had happened to Warner because he copied Calvaruso's files for her. The situation he was in was her responsibility.

Her current marching orders from Hemisphere Air were not to divulge the existence of the RAGS program. Because she hadn't heard from Peterson, she had to assume that position has not changed.

She couldn't call the police or the feds. There was no way to involve the authorities without breaching her obligation to maintain the attorney-client privilege and protect Hemisphere Air's confidential information.

Ethically, she could do nothing that would lead to the discovery of the RAGS program. Morally, she had to do something to help Warner.

That left only one course of action.

14

Washington, D.C.

"Welcome to our nation's capital," the pilot said through his tired, plastered-on smile.

Sasha smiled back and slung her backpack over her shoulders as she stepped off the plane into the tunnel leading to the gate. D.C.'s Reagan National was quiet at this hour. Although it was just past nine thirty, the smoothie stands and pizza places were all closed and the sports bar was almost empty. She walked along the hushed terminal, head down, checking her phone for e-mails, voicemails, and texts.

She'd managed to catch the last flight out of

Pittsburgh and had spent the drive from the office to Pittsburgh International working her cell phone, making flight and hotel arrangements, leaving messages for Naya, Peterson, and the team, and repeatedly trying Warner's cell phone with no success. While she was out of reach during the short flight, she knew Naya would be busy getting Sasha the information she needed.

As Sasha boarded the escalator down to the ground transportation area, she found what she was searching for: a text from Naya with Warner's home address. Because she was Naya, she had the foresight to also include the neighborhood and a suggested route.

Sasha shivered against the chill in the air in line at the cab stand. As much as she wanted to stop by the hotel and change into warm, comfortable clothes, she didn't want to waste any more time. She'd go straight to Warner's apartment. Another hour or so in heels and a suit wouldn't kill her.

"Virginia, Maryland, or D.C.?" the airport worker asked, handing her an information sheet about D.C. taxi fares.

"D.C."

He motioned to the cab second in line and the driver popped the trunk. Sasha shook her head and clicked it closed, before sliding into the back seat with her backpack in hand.

"How are you, tonight?" she asked the cab driver, whose license hanging from the passenger side sun visor identified him as Hakim.

"Very good. Nice weather, no?" Hakim smiled at her in the rearview mirror.

"Yes. I'm going to 3426 16th Street N.W. in Mt. Pleasant. Between Newton and Monroe."

"You wanna take Rock Creek Parkway, yes?"

Sasha checked the text from Naya. "No, let's take 15th to 16th, please."

Hakim nodded his approval and pulled out. D.C. cab drivers, in Sasha's experience, were always asking you what route you wanted them to take. But, politely suggest a route to a New York cabbie and you were likely to find yourself on the receiving end of a tirade, if you were lucky, or deposited on the side of the road, if you were not.

As Hakim cruised up the mostly empty streets, she tried Warner once more and, again, got no answer and no voicemail. So, she settled back and listened to Hakim's cell phone conversation with a woman, presumably his wife. He was speaking Amharic. There was a large Ethiopian population in D.C., and Sasha had heard plenty of Amharic during her college years at Georgetown.

She knew enough phrases to order dinner at an Ethiopian restaurant, but not enough to understand the cab driver's end of the conversation. But, she could hear the unmistakable, universal wailing of a colicky baby coming through his handset, even in the backseat. Hakim spoke rapidly in a soothing tone, but it didn't seem to be helping either mother or child.

He hung up abruptly and pulled into a courtyard that fronted two massive, white brick Wardman buildings dotted with stone balconies. An old-fashioned street lamp sat in front of the entrance to 3426, the larger of the two, and cast a glow on Hakim's cab.

"Do you need a receipt, miss?"

"Yes, please." It remained to be seen if this trip would qualify as a business expense or a personal frolic and detour.

Sasha handed him a twenty and took the receipt. He waited for her to tell him how much change to give back.

"Keep it."

"Thank you, miss. I can wait for you?"

Sasha looked out the window and saw a steady stream of headlights headed southbound, toward the Madison and downtown. Most of those cars would be cabs.

"No need. Please, buy your wife some flowers, though. And tell her to hang in there."

He smiled at her in the rearview mirror. She grabbed her backpack and got out of the cab.

As Hakim pulled away, she checked the apartment number that Naya had texted. 840. At the entryway, a metal box listed resident names and codes. She punched in the number for Warner's apartment and waited. No response. As she was reaching for her phone to try to raise him on his cell phone again, the lobby door swung open. A sweater-wearing beagle and an enormous muzzled dog, a Belgian shepherd maybe, came bounding out the door, followed by a small, dark-haired woman, not much taller than Sasha.

"Oh, hold that, please!"

The woman stopped the door with her foot and Sasha slipped in, shouting her thanks over her shoulder, as the dogs and their owner headed out for their walk.

The lobby was faded with time. Its gray-veined white marble, ornate gold-framed paintings, and vases of fresh flowers were leftovers from a more glamorous past.

Sasha boarded the ancient elevator and pressed the button for the eighth floor. The only sound was its groaning.

She stepped out into a narrow hallway. Her approach to Warner's door was silent, thanks to the thick, wine-colored carpet. She could feel her heart thumping as she approached the apartment.

She raised her fist to rap on the door. As soon as she touched it, it swung inward slightly. Not locked. She pushed it halfway open and tilted her head to see around it. The entryway was dark. Streetlights shining through the French doors that led to the balcony cast some light, but all she saw was the outlines of furniture.

"Tim? Mr. Warner? It's Sasha McCandless. Hello?"

No response.

She hadn't come all this way to stand in the hallway. She walked in and reached down to turn on a small lamp sitting on an antique, or at least old, telephone stand.

As she straightened to standing, she turned and found herself staring at the barrel of a gun. She estimated it was eight inches from her face. Maybe closer.

"Don't move," said its owner in a soft voice. He looked to be about six feet tall, solidly built, but not bulky. He had a lean, fit runner's frame. Part Asian, maybe? Definitely big for an Asian guy. He wore neat, close-cropped dark hair, a clean shave, and a decent suit. He assessed her with a calm and serious look.

Her brain clicked off and her training kicked in.

She stood completely still, her hands at her side, and waited for the man to tell her to put her hands up.

"Put your hands up."

As instructed, Sasha raised her hands up and also moved them forward, pushing the gun to the side and away from her face. *Redirect.*

At the same time, she wrapped her left hand around the barrel and pointed it down toward the man's hip. *Control.*

She drove the blade of her sharp, bony right elbow into his sternum and used that momentum to hammer his nose with her right fist. As his head bobbled back from the blow, she brought her right hand down to the base of the gun's grip. With both hands now tight around the gun, she twisted them sharply, rotating the gun 180 degrees. *Attack.*

His bone made a sickening crack as his trigger finger broke, and she turned her hands back, and pulled the gun from him. *Take.*

She held the gun with both hands. With a deliberate motion she pointed it at the center of his chest and hoped he couldn't tell she'd never handled a gun before.

The entire sequence had taken less than a second.

He stared at her, blood pouring from his

nose, his right hand dangling awkwardly by his side. Then he started to laugh.

"You could have just returned my call, Ms. McCandless."

She didn't speak.

He started to extend his hand, as though to offer her a handshake with his mangled, swollen finger.

"Don't." She raised the gun and aimed it at his head.

He stopped mid-gesture. "I'm Agent Leo Connelly, Department of Homeland, with the Federal Air Marshal Service. I wish I could say it's nice to meet you."

She kept the gun trained on him. "ID. Slowly."

He reached into his jacket pocket with his good hand and retrieved a worn, brown leather wallet. One handed, he fumbled with it until it flipped open to display his credentials.

She leaned in to look at his identification, keeping one eye on him and the gun raised.

"May I have my gun back now?"

"Not yet. Why didn't you identify yourself when I came in?"

"No time, Ms. McCandless. You were too quick for me."

"I said my name. Why did you draw your gun?"

"I may know who you are, Ms. McCandless. That doesn't mean you aren't a threat."

"You can call me Sasha. What are you doing here?"

"I could ask you the same thing. Do we really need to have this conversation at gunpoint?"

Sasha lowered the gun to her side. "No signs of Warner?"

"No. The place is empty." Connelly was speaking through a continuous stream of blood from his nose.

"Sit down. I'll get you a towel." She headed for the kitchen, following the glow from the stovetop light.

"And some ice." Connelly yelled, "I think you broke my finger."

Sasha returned with two striped dishtowels. One for his nose, the other wrapped around a cold pack she found in the freezer.

"I'm sure I broke your finger," she told him. "That was the goal, at least."

He shook his head, spraying blood on his shirt.

"Either Warner is a total slob or someone trashed this place pretty thoroughly," Sasha said, finally looking around.

The couch had been overturned, its cushions sliced open with foam spilling out of them. The desk chair was upside down. Its leather seat had also been slashed. Warner's unopened mail and piles of magazines cascaded across the floor. The drawers had been pulled out from the desk, their contents scattered. Two cheap art prints were leaning against a wall, their glass cracked.

"Someone was looking for something," Connelly agreed. "Any idea what?"

"How should I know?" She wasn't about to tell a federal air marshal they were looking for files Warner had removed from Patriotech at her request.

"What are you doing here?"

She answered truthfully, if incompletely. "Warner left me a voicemail message tonight. Not long after you did, actually. It was interrupted when his doorbell rang. And I heard some kind of altercation, it sounded bad."

"So you just hopped on a plane and flew down here to see if he was okay?"

She shrugged. "That's the kind of girl I am."

"Huh." Connelly examined the bloodied dish towel, then leaned forward and pinched his nose. "I think you might have broken my nose, too."'

Sasha wasn't sure how to respond, so she didn't. She walked through the dining room into a short hallway that led to Warner's bedroom. She flipped the light switch and stuck her head in.

The bedroom had been torn to pieces, too.

Dresser drawers emptied. Boxes, bags, and entire shelves pulled from the closet. Another framed print—this one of waves breaking against a lighthouse—was propped against one wall, its glass splintered. The king bed had no pillows or linens, just a bare mattress.

She turned out the light and returned to the living room. Connelly was perched on the edge of an armchair that had been cut open. Stuffing and springs stuck out all around him.

"Did you notice his bed has been stripped?"

"Yes."

"That's not good," Connelly told her.

Sasha had already surmised as much.

She didn't want to talk about it. Instead, she asked him, "Did you find a cell phone? Or hear one ringing?"

"No." He stood up. "Gun, please." He held out his left hand, palm up. Sasha placed the gun in it, glad to be rid of it.

He engaged the safety and slipped the weapon into his jacket pocket. "Let's go."

"Where?"

"The alley." He inclined his head toward the French doors.

Warner's balcony overlooked a long alley. It was dark except for a single light, which was positioned over a dumpster.

"Wipe your prints off the freezer and the lamp," Connelly said.

She rubbed the surfaces with the sleeve of her jacket.

He balled up both dish towels. "Put these in your backpack. We were never here."

She took the towels and stuffed them in the bag, and they walked out of Apartment 840, leaving the door ajar.

THEY STOOD in the narrow alley. The back of Warner's building ran the entire length of the right side. The left was a row of backyards for a block of townhouses. Each townhouse boasted a tiny, maybe ten foot by twenty foot, yard.

Most of the owners seemed to have given up the dream of green space. In the shadows, Sasha could make out multilevel decks, a gravel dog run, some concrete patios, and one sad-looking sandbox and slide sitting on a patch of cracked cement. A row of chain link fences, some more crooked than others, framed the yards, abutting crumbling retaining walls. The alley was a good six feet lower than the row of retaining walls. And, except for the lone light shining down on the dumpster, it was perfectly dark. A plump rat darted out from under the dumpster and headed into the weeds.

"Give me those towels, would you?" Connelly said over his shoulder, as he walked over to the dumpster. She handed him the dish towels, and he wrapped them around his hands as makeshift gloves before prying open the lid.

"Can you hold this open?" he called from within the bin.

Sasha held the lid, her head turned away from the smell, as Connelly dug through the bin, tossing bags of trash out and on to the ground. It didn't take long to find a plaid blanket, rolled up lengthwise, like a rug.

Connelly unwrapped it to reveal a blood-stained tan sheet. He carefully pulled the sheet aside. The body was that of a young man, probably in his early twenties. Sandy brown hair, matted with blood. His face had been bashed in. The entire left side was collapsed and misshapen.

"Well, that's Warner," Connelly said. "I ran his name through the database earlier. What's left of him matches his driver's license photo."

Sasha looked down into the dumpster at Warner's ruined face. The bile rose in her throat, acidic and sharp. Someone had killed this man—kid, really—because of her.

15

After a heated discussion about whether they could really just leave Warner's body in a dumpster, Sasha and Connelly ducked out of the alley and walked a block south on Sixteenth Street to catch a cab.

Connelly had been adamant that they couldn't wait for the authorities, which struck Sasha as bizarre—wasn't *he* the authorities? And Sasha had been equally insistent that they couldn't fail to report a murder.

So, they'd compromised. Connelly had called a friend in the District of Columbia's U.S. Marshal's Office and told him to forward the location of the body to the District of Columbia police as an anonymous tip picked up in the course of the NTSB's crash investigation. Sasha figured that was more or less true and that she probably wouldn't get disbarred if the unvarnished truth ever came to light. Probably.

Sasha scanned the street for a cab, trying to keep her mind blank to crowd out Warner's sightless eyes and bloodied face.

"Do you have a hotel room?" Connelly asked.

"Sure, at the Madison. "

"Cancel it. You're staying at the Hotel Monaco. I'll have my office get another room."

"No thanks. I'll be fine at the Madison."

"I'm not asking."

"Excuse me?"

"Here's what I know about you, Ms. McCandless. You're interested in the fatal crash of a commercial airliner, you showed up at the apartment of a dead man, who you claim is a stranger, and you committed assault and battery against a federal agent. Your choices are the Hotel Monaco or a cell."

Sasha stared at him.

A white and green taxi cab came to a stop beside them. Connelly slid into the back seat and waited for her to make a decision. She climbed in after him and slammed the door. They rode in awkward silence for several blocks.

Sasha spoke first. "So, Connelly? Irish?"

It seemed disrespectful to Warner to make small talk, but they could hardly discuss a murder in the backseat of a cab.

"Vietnamese-American. But, yeah, my mother's ancestors came from Ireland. My mom was a military nurse in Vietnam. My father was a Vietnamese farm boy. Just like the GIs who fathered and left behind kids during the war. Only, I obviously came to America. When she started showing, she was discharged. She didn't know my father's last name and never told him she was pregnant." Connelly recited his background in a deliberate, bored tone that did not invite questions.

"Oh. My dad's Irish and my mom's Russian. All my brothers got good Irish names—Sean, Ryan, Patrick—but mom had visions of a little Russian ballerina and overruled Mary Patricia."

"You're no ballerina," Connelly said, rubbing the bridge of his nose.

From the bruising and swelling, it looked like he'd been right. She probably had broken it. Sasha couldn't feel too sorry about it, though. He had been pointing a gun at her.

The driver cruised into a spot at the entrance to the hotel. The building itself was a grand, white-columned presence. It fit right in with the federal buildings in the surrounding blocks.

Inside, the lobby had been remodeled and updated to show travelers just how hip and whimsical they were to be staying here. A fireplace, a water feature, and a beaded room divider competed for attention.

Connelly drew several sidelong glances from the two women behind the front desk but neither mentioned his blackening eyes or blood-stained shirt. The older of the two was telling him about the complimentary happy hour held in the library each evening.

"Would you like a pet goldfish during your stay?" The younger woman smiled at Sasha.

"No, thanks. I would like an in-room coffee maker, though."

She'd stayed at enough chic hotels to realize that amenities like goldfish and happy hours didn't always go hand-in-hand with necessities like a coffee pot or horizontal work space in the room.

"Certainly, we can arrange that for you."

Sasha took her key and waited by the elevators for Connelly, who joined her carrying a fish bowl. A small orange goldfish swam around in rapid circles.

"Seriously?"

He ignored her. "Trinka at the front desk says the bar next door will be pretty quiet on a Tuesday night, if there's nothing going on at the MCI Center. Why don't we change and get a drink? We need to talk about some things."

"Are my options a drink with you or a cell?"

"Pretty much."

AFTER CHANGING INTO CASUAL—AND in Connelly's case, blood-free, clothes—they walked through a courtyard to the Poste Brasserie, the restaurant on the ground floor of the building adjacent to the hotel. The bar was a little too light and airy for Sasha's liking. Lots of blonde wood and modern light fixtures, with sufficient wattage to let the equally blonde crowd see and be seen. The music was loud and frenetic, and the conversations ran together in a buzz.

She led Connelly to a booth on the far end of the bar, near the windows and away from the mingling crowd. A boyish waiter in a white shirt and black vest hustled over and took their drink orders. A Yuengling for Sasha and a mineral water for Connelly. They waved off the small plates menu.

"You don't drink?"

"I drink. But, first I need to satisfy myself that you're not a problem."

"A problem?"

"Problem, suspect, choose your word." Connelly planted his forearms on the highly polished table and leaned in toward her. "Sasha, tell me what's going on." He watched her face.

"It's not that easy, Agent Connelly. I have a duty to my client . . ."

"Hemisphere Air? Who you represent in connection with the crash?"

"Right."

"So Warner's death is related to the crash."

"I didn't say that," Sasha protested.

She couldn't tell Connelly about the RAGS link. If she could confirm he already knew about it, she could discuss it with him.

Metz had said the feds didn't know the system had been installed on the downed plane. But why else would Connelly be interested in Patriotech?

"Look," she continued, "I don't mean to be unhelpful. I really don't. But I am boxed in by my ethical obligations. Why don't you help me out here?"

"Help you out how?"

"If you could answer some questions for me, I would have a better sense of what I can and cannot share with you."

Connelly's lips tightened into a slash, but he kept his tone neutral. "This isn't a game."

"I know it's not a game. I just helped you unearth a corpse from a dumpster. I want to cooperate with you and your agency. But I'm constrained by the rules of professional responsibility. I can't divulge any confidences that my client shared and I can't tell you anything that would be detrimental to my client. It's not that I won't or don't want to, I *can't*."

Sasha stopped talking as the waiter came back with their drinks and two glasses. He poured Connelly's water into one and looked at Sasha. "Would the lady care for a glass for her beer?"

"No thanks, the lady's not that classy."

She took a long pull on the beer. It was perfect. Cold and bitter.

She waited until the server had moved on with the unused glass to continue. "I do want to help you, and I might be able to, if we can figure out the parameters together."

Connelly made a show of placing his big hands on the table, palms up, like he was saying here are all my cards. "Ask your questions."

"What were you doing at Warner's place?"

Connelly shook his head. "That's classified."

"Why are you interested in Patriotech?"

"Classified."

Sasha stared at him. Connelly shrugged.

She switched tacks. "It was awfully easy to disarm you. Don't you guys get any kind of training? I mean, they let you carry a weapon on a plane even though a girl my size can take it away? Doesn't make me feel very confident as a member of the flying masses." She raised her bottle to hide her smile.

His face showed no reaction, not even a flicker. But his hands involuntarily, slightly, began to curl into fists. Then he caught himself and stopped them, wincing because he'd tried to bend his busted finger.

"One," he told her, "I am not a field agent anymore. I am a special investigator with the OIA, temporarily assigned to the Pittsburgh office. So, no need to worry about my abilities to protect you in the air. Two, you seem quite capable of protecting yourself. What was that, Krav Maga?"

Sasha nodded.

He continued, "Thought so. I admit when I saw you, I made a series of assumptions based on your gender, size, and status as a law-abiding citizen and officer of the court. I obviously miscalculated the danger you posed. But, three, as a federal air marshal, I have qualified with the highest degree of marksmanship and am also proficient in hand-to-hand combat. You got very lucky today."

"If you say so. OIA, that's Office of Internal Affairs?"

"Correct."

"Internal Affairs is investigating a commercial airline crash?"

Connelly looked at her. She watched him deciding whether he could tell her. He was trying to assess if she could help him.

She waited.

He made up his mind. "I had been in Pittsburgh investigating anonymous comments someone out of that office has been making on the internet. Someone is divulging SSI."

"SSI?"

"Sensitive security information. Unclassified, but not for public dissemination."

"And this SSI leak is related to the crash?"

He drained his water glass before answering. "No. I don't think so, but there was an air marshal on that flight, so I have to be sure. Because if there is a link, the leaker just went from facing a reprimand to being screwed. Life in prison screwed, if he's lucky. Death penalty screwed, if he's not."

"So what were you doing at Warner's? And how'd you get in?"

"I imagine I got in the same way as you. Some kind resident held the door for me." Connelly paused, then he said, "Okay. I'll show you mine. Warner's name popped through the SAR initiative."

She looked at him blankly.

"Suspicious Activity Reporting. You know, 'if you see something, say something.'"

"The thing at Wal-Mart, where they tell you to report anything unusual?"

"No way do you shop at Wal-Mart."

It was true. She was a Target woman.

"Whatever. That spy on your neighbors program?"

"It's not a spying program, Sasha. It's a program designed to harness the eyes and ears of the citizenry to aid the government in responding to threats. The program crosses multiple agencies, and, in addition to asking everyday Americans to be alert, it contains a specific financial crimes component that asks bankers and others to report suspicious activities. Mostly money laundering, tax evasion, that sort of thing."

It sounded exactly like spying on your neighbors to Sasha, but she just nodded.

"Once the victim list started coming in on the crash, we ran it through the SAR. The system flagged Angelo Calvaruso's name."

She interrupted. "The system? I thought there is no system—just a mishmash of different agencies' databases that don't talk to each other."

Connelly nodded. "That used to be true. Since 9/11, we've made a lot of headway in cross-referencing information, particularly with the nationwide Guardian database. That's how Mr. Calvaruso's name came up. An insurance broker had submitted a tip to the Maryland database when Patriotech purchased keyman insurance on him."

"Why? *I* think it's insane for a tech company to buy keyman insurance on a retired snowplow driver, but if an insurer was willing to write the policy, how could they turn around and say it's suspect?"

"Who knows why? The notes just say the broker thought it was odd Patriotech bought keyman and life insurance, but no health insurance. Apparently the three usually come as a package. And, also, the broker noted that Mr. Calvaruso had an Italian-sounding name."

She arched an eyebrow. "What? The Mafia?"

"The tips aren't always of the highest quality, I'll grant you, but information is always good to have."

The bar was emptying out. The noise level had dropped, so she lowered her voice. "Whatever. How'd you get from Calvaruso to Warner?"

"He was listed as the contact at Patriotech. When the name popped, I called him. He had already left for the day. I hadn't heard back from Peterson—or you, I might add. The first twenty-four hours of an investigation are make it, break it time, so I figured I'd pay Mr. Warner a personal visit at home. We were probably on the same flight, because I hadn't been there more than a few minutes when you walked in and attacked me. Your turn. What were you really doing at Warner's apartment?"

He moved his water glass two inches to the left so it lined up exactly with her bottle.

"Attacked you. Nice revisionist history, Agent Connelly." Sasha took her time phrasing her story. She wanted to come across as forthright and open without actually revealing too much.

"Okay. Something about Calvaruso didn't sit right with me. The news reports said he was a retired city laborer who had been working as a consultant for a defense tech company. I mean, that's strange right there. Then, plaintiff's counsel didn't name him as the class rep. For a lot of boring legal strategy reasons, he was the obvious choice. It just seemed weird. So, I had a choice. Call and bother his widow or try to get more info about him some other way. I figured I would try his employer first. I spoke to Warner, who agreed to send me a copy of Mr. Calvaruso's personnel file."

She stopped to finish her beer. Put the bottle back on the table two inches off center of Connelly's glass and watched his face. His right eye twitched but he resisted the urge to move it.

"He just offered to send you the file?"

"I have my ways." She smiled.

"What? You reach through the phone and punch him in the nose?"

She rolled her eyes but continued, "I suggested it would be better to give it to me informally than to make me get a subpoena."

Now he arched an eyebrow. "You think you could get a subpoena for that?"

She shrugged. "Maybe. Doesn't matter. *He* thought I could."

"So, you decided to pick up the file in person?"

She took a minute. Replayed the voicemail in her head. "No. Not long after I got your message, I got one from Warner, calling from his cell phone. He wanted to ... actually, I think he was asking me out. Said he was coming to Pittsburgh for Calvaruso's funeral and maybe we could get together. Then, there was a knock on his door and I heard, I guess, an altercation."

"What kind of altercation?"

Sasha looked at him. "I think I heard him getting beaten to death."

She took her phone out, called her voicemail system, skipped over the eight new messages that had piled up in her box, and retrieved Warner's message. Then, she hit the button to turn on the speakerphone and laid the phone on the table. She kept the volume low, so they both leaned in and hunched over the phone to hear. They sat there in silence and listened to Warner's recorded screams.

Just like a black box, she thought, pressing 7 to save the message. She turned off the phone and looked back at Connelly.

He was still leaning forward, tense. Ready to spring into action. "Irwin had his own employee killed?"

Sasha shook her head. "I have no idea. Sounds that way."

The cell phone rang. They both jumped.

She glanced at the display. It was Naya. She answered, and Naya started to talk immediately. Sasha listened for a long time. She didn't interrupt. She glanced once at Connelly, then said, "Okay. I'm leaving now."

She hung up and looked across the table at the federal agent. "Noah Peterson is dead."

16

Jerry Irwin's house, Potomac, Maryland

The two giants in Irwin's study stared at the geometric pattern on the rug. They didn't want to meet his eye. He glared at them from behind the glass and steel desk. He'd been asleep when they'd called to tell him they'd killed Warner by mistake and had failed to retrieve his files.

Now, he was wide awake and irritated. His mind was a wonderful machine, but it needed to be babied, like a classic car or an orchid or some shit. He needed ten hours of sleep to perform at peak efficiency. He could not afford a sleep deficit. Not this week.

"I hired you to take care of problems, not cause them," he said.

The older one nodded his agreement. Neither spoke. The dead kid had a skull like an overripe melon. They hadn't even hit him that hard, but they'd learned in their line of work not to make excuses with their clients. Very bad men had little patience for explanations. This angry nerd was not their usual client, but they figured the safest course was to treat him like any other criminal and stay quiet.

Irwin sighed and dialed his partner's number, still glaring at the men in front of him, who continued to focus on the rug.

"It's me," he said. "My goons got overzealous and killed the guy without getting the files out of him. A woman lawyer called the main number today and spoke to him. She was from some firm in Pittsburgh, but my useless receptionist can't remember her name or the name of the firm."

"It's probably the associate, McCandless. Don't worry," his partner reassured him, "the company's lead outside lawyer died in a tragic accident tonight. They'll be scrambling to deal with that for the rest of the week."

Irwin didn't want the power balance to shift, and it would if he didn't clean up his own mess. "Tragic. Even so, I am going to send these morons to Pittsburgh to tie up loose ends. McCandless? What's her first name?"

"Sasha. See if they can get something out of her before they kill her, why don't you?"

Irwin gritted his teeth. "Right."

He clicked off the phone.

"Okay, assholes" he said. "Redemption time. You're going to Pittsburgh. Find a chick lawyer named Sasha McCandless. Listen carefully now. Find out what she knows. If she has files, get them from her. Got it? Don't kill her and then tell me you're sorry you didn't get the files. Do you think you can handle that, you mental midgets?"

The younger guy glanced sidelong at his partner, looking for a signal that he could start pummeling Irwin.

But the older guy straightened up and said, "Yes. We've got it. You know there's an extra fee for travel, right?"

Irwin cocked his head, started to object, and then decided it wasn't worth it. "Whatever. Fine. Just don't screw it up this time. Now get out. I have to get some sleep."

SIXTY MILES AWAY, Sasha and Connelly were traveling north on Interstate 70. They'd just passed the exit for the Antietam Battlefield. In a few minutes they'd be through Hagerstown and would be crossing over the Mason-Dixon Line from Maryland into Pennsylvania.

"Did you know the Mason-Dixon had nothing to do with slavery?" Connelly said. "It was laid to settle a property dispute between the Calvert family of Maryland and the Penn family of Pennsylvania."

Sasha glanced at him in the rental car's rearview mirror. It was the first time he'd spoken since the car had been delivered to the hotel. He'd tried to convince her that Peterson wouldn't be any less dead if they waited and took the first flight out in the morning, but she finally got him to understand she was driving back with or without him. He'd blustered and threatened to arrest her, but, in the end, he'd yanked open the rear passenger door and flung himself and his bag across the seat.

She hadn't much cared whether he'd been sleeping back there or just sulking. The silence had been welcome.

Now, she met Connelly's eye in the mirror and said, "Is that so?"

"Mmm-hmm. American history major."

Several minutes later, the road changed from smooth blacktop to bumpy and cracked. Pennsylvania's Department of Transportation crews had taken over road maintenance several hundred feet before the official sign welcoming hapless travelers to the Commonwealth and it showed.

"Welcome to Pennsylvania," she told him as they were jostled along.

Connelly forced a laugh. They drove in silence for a spell. Then he said, "You don't think it was an accident, do you?"

He meant Peterson. After she'd hung up, Sasha had told him what Naya had told her. Peterson's car was found wrapped around a tree a few blocks from his home. He'd apparently hit it at a high rate of speed and was declared dead on the scene. Everyone was assuming he'd been driving under the influence. Naya had added that the Prescott power brokers were hard at work trying to convince the coroner's office not to run a blood alcohol test. Sasha hadn't seen a reason to share that piece of information with the air marshal.

Now, in answer to his question she said, "No. I don't."

He waited.

She kept her eyes on the bands of luminescent paint stretching out ahead of her. "Noah was a heavy drinker. But he'd been drinking hard since before either of us was born. He was an *accomplished* drunk. I've seen him have a four-martini lunch and then cross-examine an expert witness and just shred the guy. He Irished up his coffee every morning for his commute to the office. But, he never, ever slurred his speech, let alone wrecked his car. He used to brag about threading the needle."

"What's that?"

"When he lived in the South Hills, he had to drive through the Fort Pitt tunnel every night. You know it?"

The tunnel was the handiwork of a city planner who'd been born to design carnival rides. Southbound, it was a bi-level bridge, with two lanes of traffic shooting into the two levels, while ramps from major highways fed into it from east and west. It was nerve wracking to navigate while sober, let alone after having had a few.

"Sure."

"Peterson could speed through that approach and the tunnel after shutting down a bar. No problem."

Connelly seemed to accept this navigational feat as evidence of the dead lawyer's drunk-driving prowess.

"You think Irwin had your alcoholic boss killed?"

"I don't know. The timing's pretty convenient."

"Did he know you talked to Warner?"

"Not sure. Like I told you, I was supposed to

go see Mrs. Calvaruso. It felt too, I don't know, sleazy to pump a widow for information the same day she learns her husband's died. So, I left Noah a message saying I was going to call Patriotech instead. I don't know whether he got it."

"Let's assume he was murdered. It's hard to believe Irwin would have the reach to find him and have him killed from D.C. So, odds are he has a local partner. Any candidates spring to mind?"

Connelly sounded uninterested, almost bored, like he knew the answer would be no, but he was asking anyway because that's what a good investigator did.

"Mickey Collins." The name clicked into place like the last tumbler of a combination lock. "It's gotta be."

"The plaintiff's attorney?"

"Right," she said, shot through with excitement now. She wasn't sure which was racing faster—her heart or her mind. "It explains everything. Why he didn't name Calvaruso as his class rep, why he flipped out when his associate mentioned Irwin's name. He's in on it."

"In on what exactly?"

In on the RAGS link application. But, she couldn't tell Connelly about that. Sasha caught herself before she pounded her fist on the steering wheel.

"It's a long story."

The Starbucks mermaid flashed by on a sign advertising their approach to Breezewood, the self-proclaimed "Town of Motels." It was an ugly, neon commercial stretch of fast food joints, gas stations, and, as promised, ample cheap hotels offering free cable and clean rooms on their magnetic-lettered signs.

The stretch was an anomaly that resulted when I-70 was built in the 1960s. Apparently, the then-prevailing rules made it prohibitively expensive to connect I-70 directly to I-76, the Pennsylvania Turnpike. So, the little strip, less than a mile long, served to feed traffic from one interstate to the other.

As Sasha had learned at a mind-numbing transportation law continuing legal education seminar, the rules had long since been loosened. But the commercial enterprises that relied on the travelers forced to drive through the junction had lobbied hard and successfully to prevent re-routing. That left Breezewood as one of only two numbered interstate roads in the United States to have a traffic light. She forgot where the other one was located.

Sasha wondered if she should share the town's tale with the American history major in the backseat. If she did, it would be the first time she had put her transportation law knowledge to use. For some reason, her continuing education requirement snuck up on her every year and she ended up at seminars like transportation law or elder rights—things that had no relevance to her practice.

She opted to skip the history of Breezewood and said, "I need a coffee."

She didn't give him a chance to respond. Just jerked the car into the left lane and sped toward the green and white coffee shack. She could buy some time. And caffeine.

He waited in the car while she used the restroom and bought a Venti vanilla latte. She preferred black coffee, but Starbucks' brew always tasted burnt to her. The sugar would give her an energy boost, anyway.

She tossed an overpriced, square bottle of water into the back seat for Connelly and slid the coffee into the center console cup holder before she burned the skin off her hand. That was going to need to cool down before she attempted to drink it at 70 miles an hour.

As she eased out into the meager traffic and entered the tollbooth plaza, she returned to his question.

"Here's what I can tell you ethically. I have reason to believe the crash wasn't an accident and that Mr. Calvaruso may have been involved in causing it. If I'm right, I think Mickey Collins and Irwin are behind it together."

"How good is your information?" He sat up straight, wide awake now.

That was the question she'd asked herself while the half-asleep barista stumbled through the milk-steaming process at the coffee stand. If she *knew* for a fact that Calvaruso had used the RAGS link to crash the plane, she could arguably tell Connelly everything. The potential to stop another crash could trump her duty to keep the information confidential. Maybe.

The problem was that she didn't know. She suspected. Her suspicions were growing stronger as dead bodies were piling up, but she couldn't violate her ethical obligations to Hemisphere Air because she had a hunch.

She stretched her arm as far as she could out the window in an effort to reach the ticket hanging from the automatic machine. Almost got it. She put the car in park, popped off the shoulder harness, opened the car door halfway, and snagged the ticket. Then she reversed the sequence and pulled out.

"It's pretty good. I hope I can confirm it when I get Calvaruso's file. I think that's why Warner was killed. Irwin knows there's info in that file that ties him to the crash."

She brought the car back up to speed and

they bumped along the toll road, which somehow managed to be in even worse repair than Interstate 70.

Connelly worked his jaw in the backseat. She watched in the rearview mirror as he tried to decide whether to ream her out for meddling in his investigation or to pump her for what she knew. She figured his curiosity would win out.

She picked up the still-steaming coffee cup and blew across the opening of the lid. As she juggled the hot cup and the steering wheel, Connelly's feet and then his legs appeared in her peripheral vision. He was scissoring himself over the center console. She swept the cup out of his path. His torso followed his legs and he sprawled into the passenger seat beside her.

"I would have pulled off."

He pulled his shirt down and smoothed it straight. "No need. The early crash investigation results are pretty clear. There was no altercation during the flight, no terrorism attack. The cause was a mechanical failure."

She nodded.

"Okay, Calvaruso's a retired laborer. What's the theory? He somehow sabotaged the mechanical system and then, what, got on a plane he knew was going to crash? No way."

"Maybe he sabotaged it mid-flight," she hinted.

Connelly shook his head. "You don't understand. The onboard computer suddenly locked in with the wrong coordinates and couldn't be manually changed. He couldn't have accessed those systems during the flight."

She'd given him the opening. If he'd known RAGS had been installed on the plane, he would have walked through it. Metz was right. The feds didn't know.

He cranked back the passenger seat and closed his eyes. She figured he was catching a nap, which was smart. Sleep was a weapon. In her case, though, it always seemed to be in short supply.

One of her nephews had become obsessed with fish after she'd taken him to see *Finding Nemo* and bought him a clownfish. Liam had spouted fish facts at her for months afterward before he'd moved onto a fascination with the planets. According to Liam, fish didn't really sleep. They had periods of restfulness, but they were still alert during those times.

She focused on the ribbon of road and her sweet coffee drink and tried to think of herself as a restful fish.

Apparently, her passenger was also part fish. With his eyes still closed, he asked, "Were you and Peterson involved?"

She kept her eyes on the road and her voice even. "No. Why?"

"I need to know if your emotions are going to be a problem here."

"Noah was a colleague and a friend. We were never intimate—that would have broken two of my dating rules. No married men and no lawyers. Of course, I'm upset that he's dead, especially if he was murdered. But, I'll be honest, I'm also concerned about what it'll mean for my career. Noah had a lot of juice and he was backing me for partner. Now, who knows if I'll make it?"

She surprised herself by how cold she sounded. Connelly just grunted, like he expected nothing less.

She drove on, eating up the miles as fast as she could. It was not quite four in the morning when they reached the Pittsburgh exit. Connelly opened his eyes as they went through the toll plaza.

"Where do you want me to drop you?" She asked.

Depending on how far out of the way he was, she could be home within the half hour. She'd have time for a nap and a shower before she headed into work.

He blinked and cleared his throat a few times. "I think I should keep you in my sights."

"I can take care of myself, Agent Connelly."

He gave her a half-smile, "That's obvious. But, if Collins or Irwin or both killed your boss, you may be a target. I can't jeopardize my investigation by leaving you vulnerable."

She just stared at the road ahead, too tired to argue with him.

17

Sasha parked in her reserved spot behind the condo building. The predawn sky was gray and the air was cold when she left the car. Connelly joined her on the sidewalk and they hurried into the building.

In the hall outside her unit, Connelly took out his gun and motioned for her to unlock the door. After she turned the key, she stood back. He eased the door open and stepped inside, gun drawn.

Two minutes later, he poked his head out. "All clear." Then, "Nice place."

She shrugged. It was a nice place. The building was an old paper warehouse that had been renovated into condos with new wiring and plumbing and high-end finishes. It was in a great location. She still missed the drafty Victorian house she'd rented before she'd bought the place. But the allure of original woodwork, pocket doors, and a clawfoot tub couldn't compete with convenience. With the hours she worked, homeowner tasks like using her hairdryer to thaw the frozen pipes under the kitchen sink in the morning and going from room to room to bleed the air from the radiators had become too much of a chore. The condo was almost maintenance free. An investment.

Once inside her soulless home, the first thing she did was take off her heels. The second was to head to the kitchen to grind coffee beans. As she set up the filter, Connelly started randomly opening cabinet doors. Then, he pulled open the refrigerator.

"Can I help you with something?" she said over her shoulder.

He stared at the contents of her refrigerator. Skim milk. A shriveled lemon. A jar of wheat germ. Olives. A six-pack of beer.

"Don't you have any food?"

"Uh . . ." She opened the pantry. A bag of rice and a jar of cashews stared back at her. "Nuts?"

He just shook his head.

"Sorry, Connelly. I've been working on an appellate brief. Haven't had time to shop."

It was true. It was also true that Sasha never had much food in her house. She didn't really spend any time there. Keeping groceries on hand just meant she'd have to throw them away after they went bad. For the same reason, she had no pets or plants. Her brothers always said her place looked like a builder's model or a hotel room, as if no one actually lived there.

As the coffee machine came to life, she looked at Connelly. He was wrinkled and rumpled. His change of clothes was a bloodied dress shirt and a suit that had been shoved into a duffle bag.

"Do you want to take a shower?"

"Thanks, but there's no point. I don't have anything else to wear. I'm thinking I'll drop you at your office and then go to my place and clean up. Get something to eat. You know, food?" He pantomimed eating. "I'll check in at my office and then come to yours. I assume you'll be safe there."

She smiled an apology for the lack of food.

"Could you turn the rental car in at the airport and pick up my car for me?" If she was going to be stuck with a bodyguard, at least he could make her life easier.

"Anything else? Do you want to give me a shopping list?" His tone was light.

"I guess that depends on how long you plan to stick around."

She left him with a steaming mug of coffee

and headed into the bathroom to shower and change for work.

She emerged from a very hot, very long shower feeling almost rested. She dressed in a charcoal gray suit dress and a warm black sweater. Then she dried her hair and headed out to the kitchen, a pair of black pumps dangling from one hand.

Connelly sat at the breakfast bar, looking out the window at the parking lot. She slipped her feet into the shoes and took a coffee mug from the cabinet.

He turned. "A silver Camry has cruised through your parking lot twice."

"Okay?"

"It has Maryland plates."

Sasha's heart skipped. She put the mug down and went over to the window. The lot was almost full. Most of the cars had been sitting all night, and a light frost covered their windows. Not the rental car, though. Its engine was still warm. It sat there, with its Nebraska license plate, like a big arrow pointing at Sasha. *Here she is*, it yelled to the world. She pulled her sweater tight across her chest and turned away from the window.

~

Irwin's men were tired and hungry. They'd made good time on the trip from Maryland but the bitch attorney wasn't even home. Gregor, the older of the two, had driven the first leg of the trip, so now Anton was driving around Shadyside.

Apparently, he was hoping they'd find her just walking through her neighborhood at five in the morning. Anton was just muscle. It fell to Gregor to supply both muscle and brains.

Anton palmed the steering wheel and turned left on Walnut Street, which was some fancy-looking commercial strip. It was like someone had dumped an upscale mall out onto the sidewalk. Pricey brands like Banana Republic, Williams-Sonoma, Anne Taylor, and an Apple Store were scattered among ethnic restaurants and little boutiques. Nestled in among the hulking chains were a stationery store, a Thai restaurant, a jewelry store, a sushi joint, an art gallery, a coffee shop, a Chinese restaurant, and a martini bar—nuggets of local flavor to break up the mall vibe. Gregor also noticed some clear holdover establishments that must have predated the yuppification of the street. He counted a card store, a dive bar, and a bakery that looked like they hadn't been updated since they'd opened.

"You sure you got her make and model right?" Gregor asked.

Anton rolled his eyes. "Yeah. I was sure last time you asked. I'm still sure. I'll be sure next time you ask. It's a 2009 Passat. The coupe, not the wagon. It's dark gray. Usually dirty, the security guy said."

Security guys. In their line of work, Gregor and Anton had found security guards to be the most reliable source of information. Easy, too. Half the time, they didn't even have to bribe a security guard. He'd start talking right away, just to show how observant he was or some shit.

"The reason I'm asking," Gregor continued, ignoring the eye roll, "is that on our last two passes of the lot, there was a new car there. Midsize, blue, Nebraska plates."

"Not her ride, Gregor. She must be spending the night at a boyfriend's or something."

Gregor nodded. Finding her was going to be the hard part. The helpful security guard had described her for them. Under five feet tall, under a hundred pounds. If he'd have known that, Gregor would have sent Anton out here alone. Two of them was overkill.

The car crept past a joint called Pamela's. Gregor peered through the windshield, spotted with bug guts from the long drive. A banner hanging over the door bragged that the place had Pittsburgh's best breakfast. He squinted at the menu posted in the front window. Pancakes.

"Pull over. I gotta piss. We'll get breakfast. Irwin's treat."

Gregor hated that uptight, nerdy asshole. He was going to get the biggest breakfast Pamela's had to offer. Maybe two of them.

18

The rental car was idling in front of her office building. The sun was doing its level best to light the slate gray sky. The early risers were streaming into the lobby, collars turned against the morning chill. Some people had already broken out their scarves and hats. Connelly was looking at her. Waiting for her to get out.

Sasha had been quiet on the short drive downtown. She'd been thinking about Peterson's wife, wondering if he had talked to her last night. If Laura knew he was planning to take her to France for a year would that make it better or worse?

She couldn't even hazard a guess. Her longest relationship hadn't outlasted a container of milk.

She knew this for a fact because, for maybe a week after she'd broken up with the guy, she was still drinking the milk she'd bought on her way home from her first date with him. Neil. Emergency room resident.

He'd taken the news stoically, until she got to the part where she was just too busy at work. "I save *lives*," he'd protested. "I work twenty-four hours at a time and am *on call*. If I'm not too busy for this relationship, how can you be?" Remembering poor indignant Neil, she thought maybe she should add another rule: No doctors.

Connelly drummed his fingers on the steering wheel.

"Sasha?"

"Sorry. I was just thinking about Peterson's wife. Yesterday she was married, today she's a widow. Just like that."

"That's how it happens sometimes."

"Mmm. I suppose it happened to a lot of people yesterday, all those crash victims . . ." She trailed off and turned to look at him. "Oh my god, Rosa Calvaruso. What if Mickey Collins or Irwin went after her? She probably knows something. I'm sure she knows something about her husband's job. You have to check on her, Connelly. Make sure she's okay."

Sasha's pulse throbbed in her ear. Noah had thought she was going to visit Mrs. Calvaruso.

What if he told his killer that? The old lady's death would be on her hands. Just like Warner's.

Connelly's eyes told her he was worried, too, but he tried to calm her down. "I'm sure she's fine; but you're right, we should check it out. I'll go this morning, after I return the car."

She breathed out. "Okay. Call me after you see her."

"Sure. I'm going to call your office number, not your cell phone. Do you know why?"

This again. He'd insisted on laying out his ground rules before they left her apartment. She wasn't to leave the office. Not for lunch, to go to the coffee shop in the lobby, not to go for a run.

"Ass in chair" was how he'd put it. All day long. Or at least until the package from Warner arrived. Then, she was to call him and they'd figure it out from there. It wasn't much of a plan, in her opinion, but he only seemed to care that she stay put.

Now, she said, "Yes, Connelly. I'm not going to leave my office."

She was going to spend any down time in her day figuring out how to rid herself of Connelly. He was getting on her nerves and in her way.

She rolled her neck and reached for the door.

"Be careful," he said as she shut the door and headed for the plaza.

Across the street, Gregor elbowed Anton in

the gut. "There she is. Getting out of a car with, well look at that, Nebraska plates." He strained, but he couldn't see the driver.

Anton rubbed his side. "Must be the boyfriend. Whatever. We got a bead on her now."

Gregor leaned forward and watched her enter the building. She looked like a child compared to all the other office drones around her. He was glad he'd thought to stake out the office building after the pancake place had turned out to be closed. Now, they just had to wait for her to leave and grab her up.

"How long do you think we can park here?" Anton was worried about a sign posted high on a wall warning parkers that the lot was for visitors to the Frick Building only. He'd been hesitant to pull in, but Gregor had instructed him to follow the Aston Martin that they'd been behind on Grant Street into the lot, so he had.

Gregor just shrugged and chewed on the stale bagel he'd picked up at a gas station. He watched the lawyer's boyfriend pull out into traffic and disappear into the sea of cars.

SASHA HADN'T EXPECTED to see many people in the office at this hour. Someone must have called some trusted secretaries to come in early because a tight cluster of veterans gathered in front of the reception desk. The room was heavy with their shock and sadness. Lettie caught her eye as she walked by and freed herself from the hushed conversation.

"Sasha, wait." Lettie's eyes were red and puffy. Sasha felt like crying herself just looking at her.

"Lettie."

Lettie rubbed Sasha's arm, "Are you okay? I know you and Noah were ... close."

Sasha ignored the unasked question about her relationship with Peterson. "It's unbelievable. His poor wife."

Lettie nodded. "Listen, Mr. Prescott asked me to help out with contacting Mr. Peterson's clients and getting his files in order. He gave Jenny the day off."

That sounded like something Charles Anderson Prescott, V,—Cinco, behind his back, and to his friends, too, for all Sasha knew—would do. Cinco had inherited his place in the world, despite a complete lack of legal talent. He was the chair of the firm, responsible for managing more than eight hundred lawyers and staff. That was his excuse for not practicing law. The truth was Cinco couldn't find a persuasive legal argument with both hands and a flashlight.

This bad fact was compounded by his regal bearing, which had an unfortunate tendency to enrage judges, who were the only kings in their courtrooms —even the female ones.

It worked out, because Cinco busied himself with running the operations and dealing with the staff. He left dealing with the lawyers and their demands to the various firm committees on practice development, professional development, business development, and whatever other kind of development could be identified and governed by committee. The staff seemed to like him fine, probably because he did things like give a secretary the day off when her boss of twenty-some years died.

Sasha figured he was at least partially responsible for the free coffee, so he was okay by her, too. Even though he had introduced himself to her at no fewer than four firm events, to the point where she was thinking she might give him a fake name the next time she "met" him.

Losing Lettie for the day was not going to work, though. Peterson's death would throw the Hemisphere Air team into disarray, not to mention the other cases Sasha was handling with or for him.

"I can't . . ."

Lettie cut her off, "I got Flora to sit for you. I

left very detailed instructions for her. It'll be fine."

Lettie's gray eyes were set. Sasha could see this was a matter of loyalty to the firm for her secretary. There was no point in arguing with her. It was only one day.

"Okay. Thanks for getting me coverage." She turned to leave.

"He told me to have you come to his office when you arrived."

"Who?"

"Mr. Prescott."

Cinco had summoned her? That was not how things worked at Prescott & Talbott. There were several layers of insulation between Cinco and someone like her. Her stomach tightened and she wondered what he wanted.

Only one way to find out. Out of habit, she headed for the stairs instead of the elevator. She used the time hoofing up the eight flights to gather her thoughts.

She stopped in the hallway outside his personal secretary's office and realized she was not sure exactly how one announced oneself for a meeting with Charles Anderson Prescott, V.

She rapped on the walnut-paneled door.

"Come in," called a refined voice with a hint of a English accent.

Sasha pushed open the door. Caroline

Masters, Cinco's secretary, had her own small but tasteful office outside his. It was decorated in warm colors. A pair of formal, striped chairs sat in front of a burnished walnut desk. Classical music played, just barely audible.

Caroline smiled, "Good morning, Ms. McCandless. Mr. Prescott is expecting you. Can I offer you a drink?" She waved a manicured hand, weighed down by an emerald ring, over a tray that held a tea service and a coffee carafe.

She looked exactly like a secretary to a man like Cinco would look. Trim, pretty, and ageless, not flashy or memorable. Sasha realized the description also fit his wife.

Sasha resisted the impulse to hide her own unpolished, unadorned fingers behind her back. "No, thank you."

"Very good." She pressed a button on her telephone and announced, "Sasha McCandless is here, sir." She waited a moment and then said, "Please go in."

Sasha eased open the door to Cinco's inner sanctum and stepped through. She blinked. Prescott & Talbott lore had it that Cinco's office was over the top and had to be seen to be believed, but she had never gotten a description. She had expected to walk into a moneyed attorney's office, full of dark, gleaming wood, oriental carpet, loads of bookshelves and gold-framed certificates, diplomas, and pictures of the neglected family. Something in keeping with the décor of Caroline's space and the rest of the firm.

But Cinco's office was one of a kind. The walls were painted bright orange and there was not a diploma, certificate, or family portrait to be seen. A single piece of art hung on the long wall to the right of the door. It was an enormous black and white print of a nude woman's backside. It focused on the curve of her hip, the rise of her butt, and a long tangle of hair streaming to the small of her back, nothing graphic.

She turned from the picture to where she expected Cinco's desk to be. But, instead of sitting behind the standard-issue hulking executive desk, Cinco stood behind some sort of lectern or podium. Two enormous white leather captain's chairs flanked it. She saw no computer, no books, and no phone, although his secretary had just buzzed him, so he had to have a phone hidden somewhere in the office.

"Sasha, please have a seat." He moved out from behind the podium and sat in the chair to the right of it, waving her into the one on the left.

She complied. The seat was so high that her feet dangled several inches above the floor.

They looked at each other.

"You wanted to see me?" She didn't know what else to say. Obviously, he wanted to see her;

associates didn't just pop in for a visit with the chair of the firm.

"Yes. While the partners are still grappling with the loss of our friend, our duty to the firm and its clients means we need to put aside our grief and take care of Noah's caseload." He nodded, as if to say, and that is that.

Sasha found herself nodding along, her feet swinging as she did.

"At the risk of seeming. . .," he paused and pursed his lips, "crass, I note that you will be a candidate for partnership in the spring."

She nodded faster, keeping time with her heartbeat now. Jesus, these guys were shameless.

"You're highly regarded by the litigation department. Not only did Noah trust your judgment, but others speak well of you also."

He glanced at his lap and she noticed that he was holding a notecard. "Mmm. Kevin Marcus called you a rising star."

He met her gaze and then the eyes went back to his notes. "Several clients, including UPMC and Myron Construction have shared glowing reviews of your work."

None of this was news. Marcus was the deputy managing partner for the litigation department. She'd worked with him on several matters, and he was responsible for giving the associates their annual reviews. The in-house attorneys in the clients' legal departments—big firm refugees who knew how the system worked —had blind copied her on the laudatory e-mails so she'd have a set when the partnership decision was made. She waited for him to get to the point.

He frowned. "In fact, Hemisphere Air has asked that you take over responsibility for the crash litigation."

That *was* news. "Bob Metz asked for me?"

"No." Another frown. "Vivian Coulter asked —no, insisted—that you take over."

Viv? Sasha turned that one over in her mind as he went on.

"As a former partner, Vivian well knows that it is simply not done here. Associates, no matter how senior and valued they may be, do not run large cases like a multidistrict litigation without partner supervision, guidance, and oversight." No need for his notes for this part, she noticed. "This policy is out of concern for associate professional development, not to mention malpractice exposure."

He fixed Sasha with another long look, then he stressed, "We would never do that."

She remembered a conversation she'd overheard between two of her brothers when they were in college. She couldn't have been older than twelve, maybe thirteen. She'd passed by the door to the bedroom they shared when they were home on breaks and heard Ryan laughing at Patrick.

"Ry, you don't get it. She says she never does that."

"No, Patrick, *you* don't get it. Lydia does give blow jobs. She gave you one."

Sasha had frozen in the hallway, her stomach fluttering at the news that sweet Lydia, Patrick's girlfriend was *that* kind of girl.

Now, she focused on keeping her expression neutral while Cinco worked to convince both of them that he really wasn't a slut.

"But, Hemisphere Air is a very important client, so we've decided to honor their request. You need to understand that the firm will be watching closely. This case will impact your prospects—for good or for ill."

He flashed a tight smile.

In the past twelve hours, she'd beaten up a federal agent, found a corpse in a dumpster, learned that her mentor and friend had died, and driven two hundred and fifty miles, give or take. She was being stalked. There was a good chance whoever had blown up Flight 1667 would strike again. And she was pretty sure the plaintiff's attorney across the street was responsible for all or most of it.

Now, Charles Anderson Prescott, V, from the comfort of his captain's chair, was telling her she was going to run a multimillion dollar class action defense and the firm would use it as an excuse to deny her partnership if anything went wrong.

She wondered if the job description for Cinco's secretary included protecting him from bodily harm. She gave herself a minute to imagine delivering a solid palm heel strike to his chin.

Then she smiled back and said, "Thank you for the opportunity, Mr. Prescott."

He waved the gratitude away, "I'm sure you'll acquit yourself well."

It sounded like she was being dismissed. She slid off the chair. Cinco stood to see her out, checking his notecard one last time to make sure he'd covered everything.

"Oh, yes. There's a class certification hearing this morning in another of Noah's cases. The caption is *Jefferson v. VitaMight, Inc.* My understanding is Noah and plaintiff's counsel had reached an agreement in principle to settle. You just need to appear to let the court know about Noah's death, assuming news has not already traveled, and explain that the parties are working out the details of the settlement. Noah had apparently been intending to file papers to that effect yesterday afternoon but never got to it."

"Got it." It sounded pretty simple.

He walked her to the door and said, “Good luck.”

Caroline had the *VitaMight* file ready to hand to Sasha as she walked through the outer office and returned to the real world.

19

Connelly made his way down a narrow, two-way street cut into the side of a hill. Parked cars lined both sides, making the passage so tight that he'd had to back Sasha's Passat into an alley to make room for a car traveling the other direction. He pulled over and squeezed the car into a space four doors down from the Calvarusos' house.

He felt stiff as he got out of the car. Getting his ass kicked by a tiny attorney, staying up all night, and the mad dash to return the rental car, pick up the Passat, shower, eat, and check into the office had taken a toll on him. Not to mention his broken nose had bloomed into a bruise, and he now sported two black eyes.

He stopped on the cracked sidewalk in front of Rosa Calvaruso's house and looked up at it. It was a modest brick house with a small neat lawn, set close to the houses on either side. The house looked tidy, unimpressive, and closed up tight.

Motion caught his eye behind what he imagined were the living room drapes. The heavy fabric was swaying. He saw a shadowed face peering out from behind. As he tried to see in, the drapes fell shut again and the figure disappeared.

He walked up the front steps to the porch and stooped to pick up the newspaper. Tucked it under his elbow and rang the door bell with his good hand.

Waited.

He was getting ready to ring it again when he heard movement on the other side of the door. Then a burst of rapid Italian. It was a woman's voice, angry.

"Mrs. Calvaruso? I'm Agent Leo Connelly with the Department of Homeland Security. I need to speak to you, ma'am."

The same voice, in English this time, said, "You get the hell off my porch!"

"Ma'am, I'm afraid I can't do that. I am very sorry to bother you right now, but I need to speak to you."

Silence.

Connelly sighed. "Mrs. Calvaruso, I have reason to be concerned for your safety. If you don't let me in, I am going to have to break your door to confirm that you are unharmed."

"I'm fine. Go away."

"I can't do that."

Connelly shifted his weight and eyed the door. It didn't really fit with the house's simple brick façade. It was ornate, with frosted glass sidelights and a transom window, and it looked solid.

He raised his voice. "I'm going to count ... "

The door swung open.

"Come in, then." Her voice was flat and resigned.

He stepped forward into the dim hallway and right into the path of the widow Calvaruso. She was about Sasha's size, with stooped shoulders and steel gray hair cropped close to her head. And she was wielding an aluminum baseball bat.

He was beginning to hate Pittsburgh. And its tiny, aggressive women.

He thought about reaching for his identification but instead just raised his hands. The newspaper thudded to the floor.

"Mrs. Calvaruso, I'm not going to hurt you."

She fixed him with her fierce brown eyes. Took in his conservative suit and his busted nose.

"What do you want?"

What he wanted was a kindly, mourning

Italian grandmother who would offer him tea and maybe some biscotti.

"Put the bat down, Mrs. Calvaruso."

He kept his hands up but made a patting motion, encouraging her to ease the bat down.

She lowered the bat, and all the viciousness leaked out of her. She was just a sad, little old woman.

"You can come into the parlor." She leaned the bat against the wall behind the door and turned into the room to the left.

He followed her into the small room. It had a threadbare couch, two red velvet chairs, and a glass coffee table. Pictures of kids and grandkids lined the mantle. A gilt-edge crucifix hung over it. No television. No bookshelves. A Bible and a paperback novel sat on the coffee table. A tasseled lamp sat on an end table between the two chairs. That was it.

He stood there, awkward, waiting for her to shuffle over and lower herself into one of the chairs. Then he took a seat on the couch across from her. He stretched his legs out under the coffee table and waited.

The room was still and too warm, the way old people kept their houses.

She spoke first, "I'm in trouble?"

"No, you're not in trouble. I was worried about you."

"Why?"

He could see in her eyes that she knew why. "Because the men Angelo was working with are bad men. But, you already know that, right? That's why you have the bat."

She nodded, her mouth set in a line.

"Can you tell me about them?"

"I don't know anything," she said. "Nothin'. Angelo, he didn't tell me. Just came home one day and said he had a new job."

"When was this?"

"Last month, I don't know. He was at the clinic and . . ."

"The clinic?"

She nodded.

"What clinic?"

"Hillman Cancer Center."

"Your husband had cancer?"

Another nod. With the fingers of her right hand, she worked a slim gold band on her left ring finger, turning it back and forth as she spoke. "Bone cancer. He kept going for treatment. I made him go, but he was dying."

Connelly gave her a minute, but she didn't tear up.

She crossed herself. "He said it was a good job, a lotta money. He was worried that his pension would run out on me. I never worked outside the home." She tilted her head to the family pictures. “I raised the kids, kept the house.”

“How did Mr. Calvaruso get the job?”

She shrugged. “He met someone at the clinic. They hired him and another man.”

“Who?”

Her hands came up, helpless. “I don’t know a name.”

“Did he tell you anything about the man? Young? Old?”

She shook her head. Then, she slapped a hand on her thigh, remembering, “Single.”

“He was unmarried?”

“Yes.”

“Anything else?”

“Single. And sick. That’s all I know.”

He tried a different tack. “What were your husband’s job responsibilities with Patriotech?”

She gave a short laugh. “He was a, what do you say, consultant. He knew nuthin’ about anything but gardens and landscaping. But they gave him a big title, big check, fancy phone. I told him, Angelo, this isn’t right. He didn’t wanna talk about it.”

The words were rushing out now. “Then, he gotta go to Texas. No reason. Just fly to Washington D.C., then fly to Texas. And now he’s gone.”

Connelly’s phone vibrated in his pocket. He

pulled it out and checked the display. Sasha's office number. He was almost done here; he'd call her back.

"A phone like yours," Rosa Calvaruso said.

He looked at the smartphone in his hand. "Patriotech gave your husband a smartphone? What for?"

"Who knows what for? He couldn't even figure out how to turn it on," she barked out a laugh. That's why he hadda fly to Washington first before Texas. To get a lesson to use the smart phone." She said it as two words.

"Has anyone from Patriotech contacted you since the crash?"

"Mr. Warner. He called twice. Once to confirm that Angelo was on ... that plane. Once to tell me about the insurance benefits. And they sent flowers." She sniffed.

Connelly looked around and realized there were no sympathy bouquets at all in the house. She followed his gaze.

"I take all the flowers to the church."

He nodded. "Do you have somewhere you can stay for a few days, Mrs. Calvaruso? A relative, a friend from church?"

She looked at him, "I'm not goin' anywhere."

"Mr. Warner's been killed."

She repeated it, slowly, like maybe he hadn't heard her the first time. "I'm not going anywhere.

This is our ... my ... home." She set her jaw and held his gaze.

He stood up. "Then, I'd keep that bat handy if I were you, Mrs. Calvaruso."

She slowly rose from the chair, using the armrests for leverage to get on her feet. She walked him to the door.

"I am sorry about your husband." He handed her a business card and bent to get her paper from the foyer. "Call me if you need me."

She put a papery hand on his arm. "Did my Angelo crash that plane?"

He didn't have an answer for her. So he patted her hand and opened the door.

He heard the lock clang into place behind him as he started down the steps to the sidewalk below.

20

Sasha hung up as Connelly's voicemail greeting began. It was bad enough she felt compelled to report to Connelly that she had to go out to court; she damn well wasn't going to leave him a message. What he didn't know wouldn't hurt him.

She turned her attention to the file and her fresh coffee. The Hemisphere Air team meeting had been brief—mainly a chance to make sure everyone had heard about Noah and to stress that they were to forge ahead with their assignments in his absence. Grief counseling lawyer-style.

Now she had less than an hour before she was due in court on the class certification argument.

She flipped the pleadings binder open to the

complaint. It was a putative federal class action on behalf of customers who had purchased Slim Down, a diet supplement sold by VitaMight.

VitaMight was one of Noah's newer clients and was headquartered in suburban Philadelphia. Sasha guessed that was why Noah had used Ben Carson—an associate who worked out of the firm's small Philadelphia office—on the case.

The putative class representative, one Warren Jefferson, alleged that, not only had he not lost the promised weight while taking Slim Down, he had *gained* forty pounds. The complaint alleged common law fraud, breach of contract, and violations of Pennsylvania's Unfair Trade Practices/Consumer Protection Act. There was no way the complaint would withstand a certification challenge.

She paged back to the briefing papers. Noah, or more likely, Ben, had written a strong opposition to certification. The plaintiff's response was not compelling.

Why would Noah agree to settle what looked like an easy defense win? She checked the signature block for plaintiff's counsel. Eric Donaldson. She didn't recognize the name, which meant he wasn't a power hitter.

She dialed the interoffice number for the

Philadelphia office and was connected to Carlson.

"Ben Carlson."

She'd met the junior attorney a few times but had never worked with him. "Ben, this is Sasha McCandless in the Pittsburgh office."

"Uh, hi, Sasha. What can I do for you?"

She heard his desk chair roll across the floor. He was probably reaching for a pen, so she gave him a minute.

"Well, first, in case you haven't heard, Noah Peterson was in a fatal car accident last night." She had no idea how Cinco and his band of managers was planning to spread the news to the satellite offices.

"Noah's ... dead?"

"I'm afraid so."

They sat in mutual silence for a moment.

Ben spoke first. "I'm so ... sorry."

"Me, too. Listen, I have to be in court at 9:30 on your *VitaMight* case. Just to let the court know about Noah. I have the file and I understand you guys were working out the details of a settlement with plaintiff's counsel."

"Right."

"Why?"

"Why?" he repeated.

"Yeah. I read the briefing. You slammed him.

There's no way class cert would get granted. Do you know why Noah was settling the case?"

Ben forced out a little laugh. "The judge."

She flipped to the civil cover sheet. The case was assigned to the Honorable Cliff Cook.

"I'll confess I don't know much about Judge Cook." He was an Obama appointee and Sasha hadn't had any cases before him.

"I only attended one status conference," Ben said. "But it was clear that the judge hated Noah — really hated him. I asked Noah about it at lunch. He said Cook had a bias against all big firms, but especially ours. I don't know, though, it sure seemed like personal animosity to me. Anyway, Noah advised the client that, given the hostile judge, the safe business decision was a cheap, early settlement. And they agreed. I think Donaldson is going to take somewhere in the neighborhood of thirty grand to go away, so Noah was probably right."

She could hear in his voice that he had wanted to fight this one out. It was a hard lesson for young Prescott & Talbott lawyers. They weren't trial attorneys, they were litigators—working hard to litigate the case away before it got to trial.

"Ok, well, thanks for the background. I'll be in touch after the hearing. I assume you're working on a settlement agreement?"

"Yep. I'll forward you a draft. And, Sasha, will you let me know about the ... uh, arrangements for Noah? I learned a lot from him. I'd like to pay my respects."

"Will do."

She put the receiver back on the base and looked out the window. Why would Judge Cook hate Noah?

She smelled cinnamon. She turned to see Naya in the doorway to her office, balancing a slice of coffee cake on a small porcelain plate.

"You look like shit, sister," she said pulling the door closed behind her. "When's the last time you ate?"

Sasha couldn't remember. It was probably when she had the sushi. She took the outstretched plate from Naya and put it on the desk in front of her. She started to pick at it with her fingers. It was still warm.

"Where'd this come from?"

"The Westinghouse conference room. Noah's clients have started sending over food and flowers. It's like a corporate wake or something."

The coffee cake was good. Moist and fresh. Plus, she was starving. Sasha nodded, her mouth full. Swallowed and washed it down with some coffee.

"Thank you."

"No problem. You looked a little faint at the

meeting."

That was not good. She couldn't afford to appear weak; not now. "Eh, I was probably still recovering from my meeting with Cinco."

Naya's left eyebrow shot up. "You met with him?"

"Yeah. They're gonna let me run the crash team."

Naya's right eyebrow joined its mate high on her forehead.

"I know, right? Get this, Viv insisted."

Naya looked as baffled as Sasha felt. Sasha scooped the last of the cake into her mouth, then went on, "I don't know. Anyway, I have to go into court on another one of Noah's cases this morning. I just got off the phone with the associate in Philly and he said the judge has some kind of personal animosity for Noah."

Naya interrupted her, "Cook. Gotta be."

"It is. Do you know the story?"

Naya pulled the guest chair over and had a seat. "How much time you got?"

Sasha checked her computer display. "A few minutes."

"The short version is, back when he was a partner at Bristow & Baines, Judge Cook was the first African-American invited to join Noah's country club, North Heights or whatever it is. It was pretty much a done deal. The guy who sponsored him had lined up all the votes in advance. Then, on the day of the actual vote, Noah backed out. He had agreed to support Judge Cook, but he voted against him. A few other old white dudes joined him, but it didn't matter. The vote had to be unanimous, so Cook has had a hard on for Noah ever since."

Sasha stared at her. "Are you saying Noah was a racist?"

"Hell, no, Noah was a capitalist. He didn't care about black or white, just green. What's his face, the CFO of Steel Bank, told Noah he'd throw him his business if he voted against Cook."

"How do you know all this?"

"Noah told me. We were having drinks one night after a jury trial and Judge Cook walked into the bar. He saw Noah and the temperature dropped about twenty degrees."

"Great."

Naya pushed her chair back, "Knock 'em dead, counselor."

"Thanks. Hey, can you have someone pull old deal files on Hemisphere Air? Have them go back ten years. I want copies of all the due diligence memos."

"I'll do it myself. Everyone around here is either crying or running around urgently for no real reason. What are you looking for, Mac?"

"I'm not sure. Anything that seems off."

Naya nodded and left. Sasha slid the file into her trial bag and shed her sweater to shrug into the spare suit jacket that hung on the back of her office door.

She stopped at Lettie's work station on her way out. Flora hurriedly hit the X to close out her internet browser, but not before Sasha saw that she was searching for images of a mermaid.

Realizing she was caught, Flora laughed to cover her guilt. "I'm getting a new tattoo this weekend," she explained. "A mermaid on the small of my back."

Sasha closed her eyes briefly. Wrestled control of her temper.

"Great. Listen, Flora, I have to go to court. I should be back in an hour, probably less. I'm expecting a *very* important package. As soon as it arrives, please bring it in and put it on my desk."

"Got it!" Flora answered a little too brightly for Sasha's comfort.

"Okay, thanks." She checked her watch. She didn't have time to stop up and see Lettie, ask her to make sure Flora understood. It wasn't rocket science. She'd have to trust the fill-in secretary.

As Sasha hurried through the building lobby, she noticed two large men in wrinkled suits talking to Ron, the creepy security guard. She did not notice the silver Camry with Maryland plates parked across the street.

21

Sasha walked the four blocks to the federal courthouse at a rapid clip. The sky had clouded over and the morning air was cold. She ran up the large stone stairs to the lobby and pushed the heavy brass-framed doors open with her shoulder, digging in her bag for her cell phone.

By court rules only lawyers were permitted to carry cell phones into the courtrooms of the United States District Court for the Western District of Pennsylvania. Civilians had to check them at the security desk.

Before the 9/11 attack, lawyers had to turn them over, too. Evidently, the inability of attorneys to reach their offices and families from court on the morning of the attacks had added to the chaos, as they mobbed the security guards to retrieve their phones.

Now, attorneys were permitted to have them in court, but there was no mercy for the lawyer whose cell phone rang while a judge was seated on the bench. Sasha had seen it happen more than once: a seasoned trial lawyer would be in his groove, telling his story, and his cell phone would ring in open court. Invariably, the intrusion would whip the judge into a rage and it would be all downhill from there.

She stopped in the vestibule to mute her Blackberry each time she went to court. She made it part of the pre-security routine in the hope that she would never find herself on the receiving end of a ringtone-induced tirade.

As she stood just inside the door, soaking in the warmth and turning off her ringer, an obese, slovenly, middle-aged man lumbered through the door. She stared in open amazement. It was 9:20 a.m. and he was shoving what was unmistakably a Primanti's sandwich into his mouth.

Primanti Brothers was a Pittsburgh institution. The original restaurant—and in Sasha's view, still the best of the ever-expanding Primanti Brothers empire—was a run-down sandwich shop in the Strip District. Primanti's sandwiches were enormous, with generous portions of both meat and cheese. But Primanti's true claim to fame was the addition of both coleslaw and perfectly crisp French fries right on each sandwich.

The story was that the truck drivers who delivered fresh produce to the Strip District wholesalers wanted sandwiches they could eat on the road. As it could be difficult to steer a big rig with a sandwich in one hand and a container of fries and coleslaw in the other, Primanti's just slapped them between the two slices of bread.

The sandwiches were great. To end a long night of bar-hopping. Or to enjoy during a baseball game. But, Sasha, a Pittsburgher born and bred, had never seen anyone eat one for breakfast. The guy walking past her was doing so with gusto. He crammed the last bite into his mouth and headed for the metal detectors, tucking his shirttails in as he went.

Sasha dropped the phone back into her bag and lined up behind him. He worked his jaw, still chewing the last of his sandwich, while the elderly security guard handed him a basket for his keys and wallet. He walked through the detector and gathered his things.

She swung her briefcase up onto the conveyor.

"You're at Prescott, ain't cha'?" The security guard was squinting at her.

She smiled at him. "Yep. I had a long employment trial in front of Judge Dolans last year."

The elevator chimed and the door opened to let the sandwich eater on.

The security guard nodded. "With Mr. Peterson."

"That's right." Her smile faded.

"I was sorry to hear he passed. Mr. Peterson was a good lawyer. Good man, too. Never blew by us with an attitude."

The second security guard bobbed his head in agreement from his perch on a stool beside the scanner.

"He was a good man," she agreed.

Sasha scooped up her bag and headed for the bronze-doored elevator. At the federal courthouse, she usually broke her rule of taking the stairs. All the stairways were thick with stale smoke. Every stairwell had a posted "No Smoking" sign. It usually hung right above an ashtray overflowing with butts.

She passed the short elevator ride to the fourth floor thinking about Peterson. She couldn't believe she'd never again walk into a courtroom with him by her side.

She replayed his standard pre-court appearance pep talk in her head. *Mac, only a moron could lose this argument. Just don't be a moron and you'll be fine.*

It hardly qualified as inspirational but it always helped to remind her that an argument was not a life-or-death proposition. At least for her. Friends of hers who specialized in death penalty appeals probably wouldn't find the mantra very helpful.

The elevator stopped on the fourth floor. She stepped out on to the gray marble floor and headed for Judge Cook's courtroom. Just outside the courtroom doors, a tall man, not thin, not fat, was looping a tie around his neck. Based on the pile of legal-sized folders jammed into the redweld at his feet, she assumed he was plaintiff's attorney.

She hesitated. Ordinarily, she would introduce herself to plaintiff's counsel before a court appearance. But, ordinarily, plaintiff's counsel would be fully dressed at the time. She nodded at him and headed toward the doors.

"Are you from Prescott & Talbott?" he asked.

She turned. "I am. Eric Donaldson?"

He walked over, straightening his knot. He buttoned down his shirt collar, buttoned closed his suit jacket, and then offered her his hand.

"The one and only."

"I'm Sasha McCandless. I assume you heard about Noah?"

"A tragedy."

She waited a beat. "My understanding is that

you and Noah reached an agreement on the terms . . ."

He cut her off. "We can talk about that in court. I'm just waiting for my client. He's in the restroom." His eyes flashed from her face to the men's room door over his shoulder. "Let me gather up my files. See you inside."

He headed back to his overflowing redweld and she walked into the courtroom. She thought it was kind of strange that his client was here for this. But, maybe individual litigants showed up for every appearance. The in-house attorneys for her corporate clients usually had to be dragged to court under threat of sanction or contempt.

She walked past the empty benches in the gallery and swung open the waist-high bar (knee-high to taller attorneys) that led to the counsel tables. She claimed the table on the right, further from the jury box. Some old school lawyers insisted that the defendant always sit further from the jury box. Others said whichever party had the burden of proof should sit closer to the jury. Here, Noah had filed the motion opposing class certification, so she supposed, technically, she had the burden of proof. But, there was no jury and there would be no hearing. Just an appearance to let the court know they had worked out an agreement.

Sasha had been around long enough to

understand that most of trial practice was theater. So, she took the table on the right anyway.

The door leading from the judge's chambers opened and his deputy clerk walked in. He stacked some papers on the bench then turned to Sasha.

"You here on *VitaMight*?"

"Yes. Sasha McCandless for the defendant. Noah Peterson, uh, died last night in a car accident."

"We heard." The deputy clerk was a young-looking guy, except for his spiky gray hair. He smiled. "I'm Brett Waters. Judge Cook's deputy."

"Nice to meet you."

"You seen plaintiff's counsel lurking around anywhere?"

"He's in the hallway, waiting for his client."

"Good deal. I'll call down to the court reporter and tell her to come on up."

"I don't know that we'll need to go on the record for this," she said.

"A class cert hearing? That's on the record, kid."

She cringed at the *kid*. "I think we're just going to be informing the court that the parties have reached an agreement in principle."

He looked at her then, his expression almost sad. "I'll just give her a call in case."

Sasha shrugged and turned to organizing her files on the table. Her blood was starting to rush. She got keyed up before every court appearance, no matter how minor. As long as she focused her excitement, it helped her performance.

The door swung open behind her. Eric Donaldson entered first, followed by the Primanti's sandwich guy.

Sasha swallowed a laugh.

She waited until they had settled at their table and Donaldson had dumped the contents of his files into an uneven pile. Then she walked over and extended a hand to the plaintiff.

"Mr. Jefferson? I'm Sasha McCandless. I represent VitaMight."

He clamped his hand around hers and pumped it. His palm was moist. "Call me Warren."

"No, you go right ahead and call him Mr. Jefferson," Donaldson interjected with a fake laugh.

Sasha raised an eyebrow and withdrew her hand. "As I mentioned to your attorney, Mr. Jefferson, I understand we've agreed on the terms of a settlement and just need to let the judge know. It shouldn't take long. Perhaps the three of us can meet after this to work out the details?"

Jefferson opened his mouth to speak but his lawyer beat him to it. "Perhaps." Then

Donaldson leaned in and started whispering in his client's ear.

ANTON AND GREGOR were choking on the stench of smoke that permeated the stairwell. Waiting.

The security guard at the lawyer bitch's office building had said she always took the stairs.

She blew past them in a hurry in the lobby, so they'd left the car and trailed her on foot to the courthouse. She was moving pretty fast, so they were almost a whole block behind. Close enough not to lose her, far enough not to be noticed.

When they got to the courthouse vestibule, she had already gone through the security set up. Gregor hated to draw any attention to them, but he had to know where she went. While he was filling out the paperwork to check their cell phones in the public cubbies, he asked the guard as casually as he could manage, "Which courtroom is Ms. McCandless in?"

The guard raised his hands, palms up. "Beats me."

But the older guy running the scanner said, "Must be Judge Cook. On the fourth floor. He's got a nine thirty hearing on a case of Mr. Peterson's, rest his soul."

The old guy read every court calendar every

morning. Had done so for as long as he'd been working the lobby.

"Fourth floor. Got it. Thanks." Gregor and Anton strolled over to the elevators. Anton hit the button.

They got off on three and headed for the stairwell. Coughed on the smoke stink and lumbered up one flight of wide marble stairs. Anton had cracked the door to the fourth floor hallway open and stuck his head out.

"All clear."

"Find out where the courtroom is."

Anton had slipped through the door and shoved his hands in his pants pockets. He strolled past the men's room to the courtroom that had Cook's name above the door, then wheeled around and hurried back to the safety of the stairwell.

"This is the closest stairwell."

Gregor had nodded, satisfied. He positioned himself at the landing on the fifth floor. Anton walked back down to the third floor landing.

They waited.

22

Brett returned with the court reporter, who set up her equipment at a table just in front of the judge's bench. Sasha walked up, careful to avoid the well, and placed a business card in front of her machine.

She glanced up at Sasha, "Thank you. Party?"

"Defendant."

The woman scribbled that on the card then peered over the top of her square glasses at Donaldson. He was pawing around in his mounds of papers.

"Does plaintiff's counsel have a card I can use to set up the caption?"

Donaldson's head snapped up. He patted himself down, breast pockets first, then pants pockets. Shook his head.

"Sorry, I guess I'm all out. The name is Eric,

E-R-I . . ." He stopped when his client elbowed him and handed him a business card from the table in front of them. "Oh, I do have one after all."

As Donaldson crossed the well to hand up his card, Sasha caught the court reporter shoot Brett a look like *can you believe this guy?*

"Don't traverse the well!"

Brett's tone left no doubt Judge Cook was one of those jurists who did not appreciate any break in protocol. Hardliners insisted that attorneys never enter the well—that space between the counsel tables and the bench—without asking for and receiving permission to approach.

Donaldson stopped mid-step. "But the judge isn't even on the bench."

Brett shooed Donaldson to the side with an impatient wave of his hand. "Stay out of the well."

Donaldson scuttled to the side of the room and shoved his card toward the court reporter. His face was red.

Sasha really couldn't believe Noah had convinced the client to settle with this clown.

Immediately, she emptied her mind of Eric Donaldson's apparent incompetence.

More times than she could count, she had flattened a sparring partner at her Krav Maga class. Usually a newcomer. Someone who looked at her and saw a tiny girl. Someone who had not yet learned that Sasha was as vicious as she was small.

It was never smart to underestimate an opponent. Just look at poor Connelly, roaming around town with two black eyes, a broken nose, and a broken trigger finger. It wouldn't do to end up like him.

And then she almost did.

The judge swept into the room from his chambers. With his black robe flapping behind him and his bright, close-set eyes, he looked like a crow. Or maybe a hawk.

Everyone except the court reporter rose and Brett opened the session. "This Court is now in session. The Honorable Cliff Cook presiding."

Judge Cook ascended to his bench and sat. Sasha, Donaldson, and Warren Jefferson bent their knees to return to their seats as well. Only Donaldson and his client made it.

"Counsel for Defendant! Did I tell you to sit down?"

Sasha straightened. "No, Your Honor. You did not."

"Very good, counselor. I'm glad to see your time at Prescott & Talbott hasn't so dulled your wits that you can no longer play Simon Says."

Sasha's pulse thumped in her ears. It seemed the judge's grudge hadn't died with Noah.

"We're here on your motion, counselor. Let's get started."

She stared up at him for a minute then shifted her gaze to Brett. The deputy clerk didn't meet her eyes. Could Judge Cook not know?

She drew herself up and said, "May it please the court, Sasha McCandless for VitaMight, Inc. Your Honor, if I may, this motion was actually made by my colleague—or former colleague, rather—Noah Peterson. Mr. Peterson was killed last night in a car accident and, for that reason, I ask the Court to continue this hearing . . ."

The judge cut her off. "Oh, come now, Ms. McCandless. Surely you don't mean to suggest the late Mr. Peterson was the *only* attorney at your *venerable* law firm capable of handling this matter against the hapless Mr. Donaldson over there, do you?"

Donaldson's smirk faded. But the judge was just getting warmed up.

"Your Honor," Sasha started.

"Don't you tell all your old money clients the reason your rates are so high is because of the *depth* and *breadth* of your talented cadre of litigators, spread throughout the world, but integrated *seamlessly*?"

He was quoting from the firm's website now. He was also half out of his chair, arms waving.

"Your Honor, in addition to Mr. Peterson's

tragic death, there is another reason to postpone the hearing."

"Oh, do tell." Judge Cook returned to his seat, put his elbows on the desk, and propped his chin on his fists, doing a fair impression of a child anticipating a treat.

"The parties agreed to settle this matter. All that remains is working out the details, which Mr. Peterson had undertaken but, unfortunately, had not finished before his death."

"Oh, really?"

"Yes, Your Honor."

Sasha looked at Donaldson, who was suddenly very interested in his cascading pile of folders.

"Mr. Donaldson, is this true?"

Donaldson stood, one hand clamped around the knot in his tie, like it was his security blanket. "Your Honor, um ... Mr. Jefferson objects to Vita-Might even ... uh, raising the subject of a confidential settlement agreement. But, um, the fact is no agreement was finalized and, uh, as I informed the court this morning, we are ready to proceed with the class certification hearing today. Mr. Peterson's tragic death notwithstanding."

Sonofabitch.

She couldn't breathe. It was like he'd delivered a solid blow to her diaphragm. Judge Cook had set her up. Donaldson couldn't possibly have planned this ambush. At least not without some guidance and suggestions from someone whose synapses actually fired.

"Excellent. Ms. McCandless, it is, as they say, show time. Unless you'd like to withdraw your motion?"

Forget the Hemisphere Air case. If Sasha messed this up, her partnership prospects were over. She took a moment to hope Noah had really enjoyed the incremental increase in his millions that he'd probably gotten by screwing Judge Cook over at his country club.

She squared her shoulders. "VitaMight is ready to proceed, Your Honor. VitaMight has moved for a denial of class certification at this early stage for all the reasons set forth in our papers. But, I'd like to focus on the very simple point that class certification is not appropriate unless the same issues of law and fact apply to all the members of the proposed class. Here, those issues of fact would require all class members to have taken VitaMight according to directions and, not just failed to lose the desired amount of weight, but to have actually gained weight. To prove this up would require mini-trials for each class member to determine that there were no other factors, such as a health problem, responsible for the weight gain."

She paused and poured herself a glass of ice

water from the cut-glass pitcher on the table. She was pleased to see her hands weren't shaking. She took a sip. Then she looked over at Donaldson and his slovenly client and smiled.

She picked back up, her voice stronger now. She was about to decimate Donaldson's case and he had no clue it was coming.

"Indeed, these issues of fact illustrate why Mr. Jefferson cannot possibly serve as the class representative. To that end, we are seeking not just a denial of class certification, Your Honor, but a finding of summary judgment in VitaMight's favor and the dismissal of this case."

Donaldson turned to stare at her and Judge Cook's fuzzy eyebrows shot up.

"Oh, you are?" the judge said.

"Yes, sir. Because Mr. Jefferson failed to follow the Slim Down weight loss plan, he cannot represent a class of plaintiffs who did follow the plan."

Donaldson stood. "Your Honor, I object. There is nothing in VitaMight's papers that establishes Mr. Jefferson did not follow the plan. Of course he did. That's the crux of our complaint!"

He was right. The papers didn't allege that. But, Sasha figured Donaldson wouldn't stand on that point. He'd be eager to prove Jefferson was a good class rep. Otherwise, he would never be approved as class counsel. Some moderately competent attorney would swoop in with a suitable representative and he'd be left with nothing.

She baited him. "Mr. Jefferson is here today, I see. Why don't you put him up on the stand and let the Court make that determination?"

He bit. "We would be more than happy to."

Jefferson looked less than happy to. He wrung his meaty hands together. Then he nodded.

Judge Cook narrowed his eyes and pursed his lips. He looked at Sasha for a long moment.

"Okay. Here's what we're going to do. Mr. Donaldson will put his client up on the stand and question him. Ms. McCandless will have the opportunity to cross-examine him. Then Ms. McCandless can continue her argument on class certification."

Donaldson nodded his agreement.

"Provided there's a need to continue the argument, right, Your Honor? I mean, if you don't grant my two motions after my cross."

Sasha said it just to rattle Donaldson. He didn't seem like a guy who would perform well under pressure.

The judge's eyebrows were ready to shoot right off his forehead. "Of course, Ms. McCandless. In the unlikely event I grant your motions from the bench after Mr. Jefferson testifies, your work here will be done." He smiled. "Call your client, Mr. Donaldson."

Warren Jefferson shuffled toward the witness box, taking great care to avoid the well.

Brett swore him in and Jefferson arranged his bulk on the narrow chair.

"Good morning, Mr. Jefferson." Donaldson walked his reluctant client through the warm up questions—name, address, occupation.

Sasha half-listened while she plotted her cross.

"When did you begin taking Slim Down?" Donaldson asked his client.

Jefferson shifted in his seat and thought back. "Maybe, uh, January 2009?" He turned to look at the judge. "New Year's resolution."

"And, if you don't mind my asking, what was your weight at that time?"

"A little over two hundred and fifty pounds."

"And, how much weight did you lose?"

"Actually, I gained weight."

"You *gained* weight on VitaMight's Slim Down product?" Donaldson feigned surprise, playing to some imaginary jury.

"Yes sir. About forty pounds. I'm just shy of three hundred now. Two ninety-seven."

"And you took it as directed?"

Sasha gritted her teeth. Starting every sentence with "and" was a lazy trial attorney's way of developing a rhythm. It drove her up the wall.

"Hmm-mmm, yes. Three times a day. With three reasonable meals. Water to drink."

"And how do you know what's a reasonable meal?"

"They had a little booklet with the capsule bottle. It had menu recommendations. Like fruit, yogurt, and a piece of dry toast. That was a recommended breakfast. In fact, that's what I had today."

Jefferson was doing her work for her. She jotted down his breakfast on her note pad.

Donaldson looked at the judge, hands spread open. "Your Honor, I don't see any point in belaboring this. I will make a proffer that Mr. Jefferson closely followed the meal recommendations."

The judge glared at Sasha. "Do you have any objection, counselor? Do we need a blow-by-blow account of Mr. Jefferson's meals?"

Sasha stood. "Defendant accepts Mr. Jefferson's proffer that he followed the recommendations for breakfast, lunch, and dinner."

Donaldson turned and squinted at her. Wheels turned slowly in his head. She could see him trying to figure out why she worded her response that way. He'd know soon enough.

"I have nothing further." Donaldson sat down.

Sasha glanced one last time at her notes. "I just have a few questions, Mr. Jefferson."

In a jury trial, she would typically stand between counsel's table and the witness stand to draw the jurors' attention away from the witness. Today, she wanted Judge Cook's focus and, with any luck, his ire to be entirely on Warren Jefferson.

She stood behind her table and tried to keep her voice even and her gestures minimal. No easy task for an Irish-Russian-American from a big family.

"You said you follow Slim Down's recommended meal plan for breakfast, lunch, and dinner, correct?"

"Yes."

"Does Slim Down also provide snack recommendations?"

A yes or no question. If Donaldson had prepared his client, Sasha would have gotten a one-word answer. Instead, Jefferson started explaining.

"Well, I'd say they're more like, uh, suggestions. The pamphlet said you could have light snacks and it listed examples of snacks, like almonds, or fruit, popcorn, like that."

"So, let me make sure I follow you. The meal

ideas are recommendations and the snack ideas are suggestions?"

"Right."

Tap, tap, tap. Judge Cook was drumming his pen against the decorative gavel in front of him.

"What's the difference?"

Jefferson shot his lawyer a desperate, panicked look. Donaldson, busy straightening his papers, missed it.

"Um, for one thing, the snacks aren't required. If you aren't hungry between meals, you don't have to snack."

"Do you snack between meals?"

"Sometimes."

"When you snack, do you follow VitaMight's *suggestions* in choosing your between meal snacks?"

He stared at her. She stared back. He dropped his gaze to his lap.

"Not always. Sometimes I'll substitute, like, I'll have cottage cheese instead of hummus."

Judge Cook appeared to be doodling now.

"Did you have a mid-morning snack today?"

"Yes."

"One of the suggested snacks?"

"No, I substituted."

"What did you have?"

No response.

"Mr. Jefferson, on your way into the courthouse at about 9:15, what were you eating?"

"A sandwich."

"What kind of sandwich?"

Jefferson spoke in a whisper. "A Primanti's sandwich. Capicola and cheese."

The court reporter recoiled. Judge Cook looked up, mild interest in his face. Donaldson stopped shuffling his papers.

"With fries and coleslaw, I imagine?"

"Well, yeah." Jefferson said it like he couldn't conceive of holding the fries and coleslaw on his mid-morning snack.

Sasha let that sink in, then took a stab. Violated the rule that you never ask a trial witness a question you don't already know the answer to.

"Did you have an after dinner snack last night?"

"Yeah." Jefferson's hands were balled into fists.

"From the list of suggested snacks?"

"No. Peanut butter chocolate ice cream." His face was red.

She'd made her point. No need to further humiliate the man.

"Thank you, Mr. Jefferson."

The judge leaned forward, "Do you want to try to rehabilitate your class representative, Mr.

Donaldson or can we finish up here so he can go get his before-lunch snack?"

Donaldson winced. "No redirect, Your Honor."

Judge Cook turned to the witness. "You can step down, Mr. Jefferson."

Sasha was silent until he had climbed down from the box and returned to his seat next to his lawyer.

Then she addressed the judge. "At this time, VitaMight respectfully renews its motions for summary judgment and denial of class certification. In light of Mr. Jefferson's admitted deviations from a healthy diet, he cannot establish that his weight gain was caused by VitaMight's supplement nor could he serve as the named representative of a class of consumers who *did* take Slim Down as instructed."

Donaldson didn't even bother to respond. He was busy trying to calm down his client, whose angry whispers threatened to veer into an outburst.

Judge Cook sighed theatrically to communicate his disgust.

Sasha waited.

The judge flipped his pen onto the desk in front of him and exhaled loudly, his nostrils flaring. "Ms. McCandless, I do not approve of your tactics, but it is evident that Mr. Jefferson's case has serious weaknesses. I will issue an opinion in short order." He leaned forward. "Mr. Donaldson, you might want to revisit that settlement."

He stood and left the courtroom through the door to his chambers. Brett trailed behind reluctantly. Sasha was sure he'd bear the brunt of the jurist's displeasure at not succeeding in his efforts to screw over Noah's client.

She slipped her notes and files into her bag, trying not to listen as Warren Jefferson yelled at his attorney. She stood to leave.

Donaldson broke free of Jefferson and grabbed Sasha's arm as she passed by.

"Sasha, is the thirty grand still on the table?" If he had tried to keep the desperation out of his voice, he failed.

Sasha swallowed her initial response, which was to laugh in his face. She'd love to tell him what he could do with his settlement demand, but the sad truth was VitaMight would probably still pay him to go away. There were two types of corporate clients: those that made litigation decisions based on business factors and those that would not settle ever, no matter what. Almost all clients claimed to fall in the second category. Almost none did.

"I'll have to talk to my client."

"Of course. Can you let me know, maybe this

afternoon?" Donaldson cut his eyes toward his pissed off client.

"I doubt it will be this afternoon, Eric. I have a lot on my plate, especially with Noah's death. I'll call you after I've had a chance to consult with VitaMight."

Donaldson reddened at the mention of Noah, briefly chastised, but then engaged in a final bit of theater for his client's benefit.

"You do that. But, you're on notice, we won't wait forever. If we don't settle this soon, our number goes up."

Sasha didn't bother to hide her laughter this time. "Noted," she said, as she shook his hand off her arm.

She walked out into the hall and decided to take the stairs. Running a gauntlet of illicit smokers would be better than riding in an elevator with Donaldson and his client.

23

Sasha pushed open the heavy door to the stairwell, thinking about her courtroom performance. Noah would have been proud of her. The client and the firm would be pleased by how she handled today's hearing.

If she could convince VitaMight not to settle before Judge Cook wrote an opinion, she figured she might even deliver a dismissal. That would be a nice card to have in her pocket when the partnership vote came up.

The door swung closed behind her with a quiet thud.

She started down the stairs and two things happened.

One, heavy footsteps hurried down from the landing above her. And two, a big, young guy rounded the corner from the landing below at full speed.

She locked eyes with him and he yelled up the stairwell, “Gregor, it’s her!” The footsteps from above quickened.

She wasted a precious second berating herself. The fundamental rule of Krav Maga was to be ready, be aware of your surroundings. Walking around lost in thought invited an attack.

Then she began the calculations that were second nature. At least two of them. Not complete amateurs, because they had spread out to trap her between them. Not total pros, because the downstairs guy should have waited until she rounded the corner going down and ambushed her then.

Multiple attackers meant she was going to have to hurt the first guy badly enough to incapacitate him for a while. Unless she could get back to the door and the fourth floor hallway before they reached her.

She wheeled around and headed back to the door. The guy coming up from below made it to the landing before she got there.

He grabbed her from behind by her hair, pulling her back and down.

She let her briefcase drop from her right hand to the floor.

He’d be expecting her to pull forward, away

from him. So, she arched her back, leaning into the backward momentum.

She turned and planted her left foot as a base, stopping the fall. As she swung around, she drove her right hand into his groin.

He doubled over and she grabbed his shoulder with both hands, pulling him forward and into two fast groin kicks.

His friend appeared in the stairs above. Another big guy, older. She searched his face. Didn't recognize him.

No, her brain screamed at her. She'd seen them before. They were the guys from the lobby of her office building who'd been talking to the security guard when she'd walked by.

The young guy straighten up, panting, "Lady, just give me the files. I won't hurt you. Irwin just wants his files back."

Tim Warner's bloodied, smashed-in face flashed in her mind.

"Go to hell."

His fist shot out. She bobbed left, and he caught her off-center with a glancing blow to the right corner of her mouth. She felt her lip burst and tasted warm, metallic blood.

Sasha rolled with the momentum pushing her to the left and dropped her left elbow. She pulled back and drove the elbow into his chin.

His head bobbled back from the force and his

mouth fell open. She thought she might have cracked his jaw from the way his mouth was hanging.

She smacked her left elbow into his chin again. Followed it with her strong side, her right elbow. Smashed it into his cheekbone. He howled.

Once more, she brought her elbow up, crashing into his shattered cheek. Then she grabbed him by the shoulders and kneed him hard in his groin, stomach, groin again.

He was bent forward, panting and cursing now. She dropped him and he crumpled to the floor. Didn't move again.

His friend had reached the landing now and was lunging toward her, his eyes darting from her to the heap at her feet.

He grabbed her by the throat. She plucked at his wrists and pulled his hands loose.

Once she was free, she bent to pick up her briefcase. As she stood, the guy brought his hand up, swung from the side, and smacked her cheek hard, open handed. Her eyes watered from the sting.

He shuffled back a step, raising his arm to hit her again. She ducked the wild swing and ran.

She skittered down the stairs, heels flying across the slick marble and her hand sliding down the brass railing. She covered the four floors to the lobby in under thirty seconds.

The old guy had grabbed for her as she went, but missed and tripped over his friend. He toppled hard down the stairs and landed with a thud on the third floor landing, bounced off the marble and then fell still.

She listened for sounds from above, but the men were not moving.

When she hit the ground floor, she turned into a back hallway and left the building through the connected post office. She wanted to avoid the guards and any colleagues who might be in the lobby.

She could feel her cheek swelling. Bruises had probably already bloomed on her face and her throat. Blood from her split lip was dripping down her chin. She wiped her mouth with the back of her hand and ran a shaking finger across her teeth. They all seemed to be intact.

She wished she could just sit down on the wide stairs outside the post office and cry. Let great heaving sobs shake her body until they ran out. But, she didn't have that kind of time. The guys in the stairwell weren't down for good. She needed to get back to the office, call Connelly, and figure out what to do next.

She ran the length of Grant Street at full

speed, dodging between office workers and crossing against the lights.

24

Bethesda, Maryland

Jerry Irwin shut his office door in an effort to drown out his receptionist's hysterical wailing.

He had done the decent thing and broken the news of Warner's death to his employees in person. It had made the papers, so he'd figured he might as well. He took the opportunity to suggest that he'd been in contact with the police and they'd hinted that Warner's murder may have been a gay lovers' quarrel gone bad.

That was partly true. The D.C. police had

called him, but he was the one who'd implied that Warner had a boyfriend with a violent streak. He imagined chasing down that false lead would keep them busy for awhile.

Now, his employees, who hadn't seemed particularly attached to Warner when he was alive, were wandering around his office, keening like they were bereft.

He squeezed his fingers against his temples to stave off a growing headache.

One of the cell phones was ringing, cutting through the high-pitched sobs still emanating from Lilliana.

He dug it out of his pocket. Pittsburgh was calling.

"Yes?" he answered.

"Do you have your files back?" No niceties this morning.

"I should have them soon. My guys in Pittsburgh haven't checked in yet."

"For the sake of argument, what's in them?"

"The files?"

"Yes, Jerry. The files." His partner was irritated.

"The name of Calvaruso's replacement and his travel arrangements for Friday." Irwin saw no reason to sugarcoat it.

"So, if the lawyer gets those files, she'll know which plane is in play?"

"If she gets the files. Which she won't. At least not long enough to do anything with them. Don't worry."

"*I'm* not worried. But you better be."

25

The offices of Prescott & Talbott

At last! Flora smiled in triumph at the mermaid on Lettie's monitor. It was perfect. Long, dark curly hair like her own. And a gorgeous shimmery pink tail.

It had taken her forever to find the right picture. It hadn't helped that Sasha's phone had rung off the hook all morning. Clients who had heard about Mr. Peterson's death and wanted to know what it meant for their cases, attorneys calling to gossip about it, and a totally rude federal agent dude who called like a zillion times and acted like he didn't believe her when she told him Sasha was in court.

Well, she finally had it. This was definitely what she wanted for her tattoo. Now, to print it out in color. Only problem was, they weren't supposed to tie up the good color printers with personal jobs. Those printers were for trial exhibits and stuff.

But her printer at home was kind of crappy. And a crappy picture would mean a crappy tattoo. She looked again at the image on the screen. It was so sharp. And detailed.

Screw it, it was only one page. Who would even know? She opened the print menu and selected the high-speed color printer on the third floor as the destination.

She snuck a look at Janet, the secretary at the next work station over. "Hey, Janet, I'm gonna run down to the supply room and get some, uh, pens. Do you need anything?"

"There's pens in those cabinets behind you. Lettie keeps her supplies stocked pretty good."

"Yeah, but I like those micro point ones. Anyway, I won't be long. Can you cover Sasha's phone for me?"

Janet put down the time entries she was trying to decipher. "Look, Flora, I couldn't care less if you want to use the color printer. Just come straight back. Lettie and I have a deal. I eat lunch first and it's almost time. You need to cover my desk. So make it fast."

Flora didn't want to admit she'd been caught in a lie. She said nothing. Just closed her browser, hung her purse over her wrist, and walked out to the elevator lobby.

She pressed the down call button. As she waited for the elevator, she remembered Sasha was expecting an important package. She considered going back to ask Janet to look out for it then thought the better of it. She wouldn't be away from Lettie's desk that long. And Janet was kind of bitchy.

The elevator doors opened and she stepped in for the short ride down to the third floor to get her printout.

She grabbed the mermaid from the printer and hurried back so she wouldn't keep Janet waiting. But Janet was ready to go when she got there. She had touched up her lipstick, and her chenille scarf was already knotted around her throat. As soon as she saw Flora, she put her coat on and sailed past her.

"See you in an hour."

Flora was busy in Janet's absence. Sasha's phone continued to ring like crazy, and one of Janet's attorneys needed help with edits to some kind of pleading. All that typing made her break a nail, so she needed to do a quick repair job right there at the desk. She was glad Janet wasn't around to complain about the acrylic glue smell.

Whenever she got a free second, she snuck a peek at her mermaid, just for the little thrill she got each time. It was going to be such a cool tattoo.

She didn't notice the thin UPS envelope the mailroom staff had delivered while she was gone. It was under a thick stack of periodicals the library staff had also delivered in the short time she was away from the desk.

Flora finished the edits for Janet and started thinking about her own lunch.

Sasha hurried through the lobby and shot up the stairs to her office. Her goal was to make it to her desk chair without being seen and assess the damage to her face in private.

She charged past Lettie's desk at a near-run and didn't stop when Flora called her name. Once inside her office, she slammed the door shut and pulled out her makeup mirror for a look. It was about as bad as she had imagined.

Her split and swollen lip would be back to its normal size within a day or two, and she could cover the break with lipstick. But the bruises on her cheek would last longer on her pale skin. Much longer, probably. They would fade to green, then linger for a while as pale yellow smudges. Finally, they would turn brown and then disappear. She'd have to put her makeup on with a trowel if she wanted to cover those.

She worked her way down. There were distinct finger-shaped marks, already black, on her throat near her collarbone.

The intercom on the desk phone beeped, interrupting her survey of her injuries.

She jabbed the speaker button with a finger. "Yes?"

"Uh, Sasha? An Agent Connelly called four times for you while you were gone. He said to call him as soon as you got in. He sounded kinda mad."

"Anything else?"

"Um, Naya Andrews called and said to please let her know when you were back. So I just did that, okay?"

"Sure. Fine. Is that it?"

"Everyone left messages. I put them by your phone."

Sasha glanced down at her desk. There was a thick stack of pink message slips beside the phone's base. But no overnight package.

"Did the mailroom come around with deliveries yet?"

"Um, I think so? But, nothing came for you."

"Are you sure?"

Sasha could hear her shuffling through

papers. "I'm sure. The only thing here is a bunch of legal journals."

"Okay. If anything comes in later, bring it right in, please."

"Will do. Uh, do you mind if I take off a little early for lunch? Janet should be back in about twenty minutes. I can forward your phone to reception."

"That's fine." The only thing she really trusted Flora to do was to bring her mail in. Since she apparently hadn't gotten any, she had no immediate need for the fill-in secretary.

She hit the button to disconnect harder than she needed to.

Where was Warner's package? And where was Connelly?

She picked up the phone to try him again. Put it right back down because there were two quick raps on her door.

Without waiting for an answer, Naya plowed into the office and pulled the door shut.

"Mac, how'd it go with...oh, sweet lord, what happened to you?" Naya's hand flew up to her throat.

"I was attacked in the stairwell at the courthouse."

"What!?"

"You should see the other guys."

Naya didn't laugh. "Mac, are you okay? Did you call the police?"

"I'm fine, Naya, really. And I have a call into a federal agent."

"What the hell's going on, Mac?"

Sasha rubbed her eyes. They burned from lack of sleep. Maybe also from the tears that had threatened to escape all day. She yawned, and the motion stretched the skin on her lip, breaking open the wound. She tasted blood.

"Shit." She found a napkin from her takeout order the night before and held it to her lip while she considered how much to tell Naya. She waited for the bleeding to slow.

"Okay. This is between us," she said. She folded the napkin in half, then in half again, and pressed it back against her lip.

Naya nodded her agreement.

"The plane crash wasn't an accident. Someone overrode the controls and deliberately flew that plane into the mountain."

"What? Terrorism?" Naya asked.

"No, I don't think so. I mean, I don't know, but I think it's just about money."

Naya waited for Sasha to convince her.

"It's crazy that Mickey didn't contact Calvaruso's widow, right?"

"Beyond crazy. She's like a guaranteed payday. Very sympathetic class rep."

"Right. So, why would any plaintiff's attorney, let alone one as savvy as Mickey Collins, pass her up?"

"Maybe he didn't know about her, Mac."

"I have it on authority that he knew about Mrs. Calvaruso within hours of the crash."

Naya thought hard. "The only reason he wouldn't use her as his representative would be if it was somehow more lucrative to him not to."

"Right."

"But, how could that be?"

"I'm not sure on the details, but here's the way I think it works: Patriotech—the company that hired Calvaruso as a consultant—developed an application that would allow someone to remotely control the flight computer. They tried to sell it to the government, but the feds passed. So, the CEO and Mickey Collins hatched a plan to crash a plane, then sue the airline. Hemisphere Air settles; and I guess Mickey splits his attorney's fee with Patriotech."

"But, it's a violation of the ethics rules to share fees with a non-attorney."

"Really, Naya? You think Mickey would conspire to commit mass murder, but the ethical prohibition on fee splitting would stop him?"

Naya laughed. Sasha joined her. Gallows humor. Employees of a big law firm almost universally found it funny.

Their laughter died as quickly as it started.

"Anyway, I think Calvaruso was a patsy. Or maybe he was in on it. I don't know. Patriotech used him to crash the plane. And, I think they might do it again."

"Why?"

"Because Noah is dead. Patriotech's human resource director agreed to send me Calvaruso's personnel file, and he's dead, too. And the two goons who beat me up this morning were looking for the file. I mean, it's possible they're just covering their tracks, but why not keep crashing planes and holding up airlines until you run out of people willing to do it for you?"

They looked at each other.

"Well, shit." Naya said.

That about summed it up.

Sasha jumped, as her office door swung and Connelly stormed in, already yelling.

"I thought I made myself clear. Ass in seat. Remember? Stay in your damn office?" He stopped when he saw the damage to Sasha's face.

He walked around behind her desk and cupped her chin in his good hand to get a better look. He tilted her face toward the light. His hand was warm.

"What happened to you?"

Naya got up and closed the office door, clearing her throat.

Connelly's hand dropped from Sasha's chin, and he turned and focused on Naya for the first time.

"I'm Special Agent Leo Connelly, Internal Affairs, Department of Homeland Security." He raised his bad hand and waved at her in lieu of shaking her hand.

"Nice to meet you, *Agent* Connelly. I'm Naya Andrews. I'm Sasha's legal assistant. What happened to *you*?"

"I got on your boss's bad side."

Naya arched an eyebrow. She was one of the few people at Prescott who knew about Sash's Krav Maga training. "Nice work, Mac."

Connelly turned back to Sasha. "Why did you leave your office?"

"I have a *job*, Connelly. I had to cover an argument Noah had scheduled in federal court."

Sasha moved to the other side of the room to put some space between them. Her anger scared her. She felt like it might take control of her.

Connelly frowned but said nothing more about their deal. "So, you got beat up in court?"

"The stairwell. Two big guys. They were asking about Irwin's files. But I remember seeing them here in the lobby, talking to the security guards."

Naya's eyes flashed. "Right after we talked this morning?"

"Yeah."

She leaned forward, tense with energy. "Okay, I went out for a smoke break right after we talked. Don't even say anything, Mac. With my mother, I need a stress reliever. I know, okay? So, I was on the side of the building facing the lot by the Frick Building and these two linebackers got out of a silver car in the lot and went into the building. When I came back in, they were standing at the security station talking to that pervy security guard—you know the one."

Connelly went to the window. "Can you see the lot from here?"

"No, other side of the building. You don't think the car's still there, do you?"

"I don't know. How badly did you hurt them?"

Sasha considered the question. "The first guy, pretty bad. I figured I had to incapacitate him to deal with the second guy. I definitely shattered his cheekbone. Might have broken his jaw. Knocked him unconscious. The second guy took a tumble down the stairs while he was chasing me. I imagine he's banged up, but nothing too serious."

Naya's expression was a mixture of awe and disgust.

Connelly nodded, satisfied. He said, "If I'm them, I don't go to a hospital in town. But that first guy, he's pretty much out of commission. I bet they check into the closest hotel. The first guy holes up and the second guy comes looking for you."

"Gregor. The first guy called the other one Gregor."

"Here's what we're going to do. You are going to stay here." He pointed at Sasha. "You," he said, pointing at Naya, "are going to make sure she stays here. I'm going to check and see if the car is still in the lot across the street."

Connelly headed for the door. Sasha remembered the widow.

"Wait, did you talk to Mrs. Calvaruso?"

"I did. She doesn't know much. Her husband met someone at the Hillman Cancer Center who gave him and another man jobs at Patriotech."

"The Cancer Center? Did he have—?"

"Yeah. It was terminal, from the sounds of it."

"So, Patriotech hired a man who knew he was dying? And, who they likely knew was dying?"

"Yep."

"Did she give you a name?"

Connelly shook his head. "All she knows is he was a single guy with cancer. That should narrow it down, right?" His laugh was short and bitter.

"They hired two men," Naya said.

They're going to crash another plane, thought Sasha. Now, she could tell Connelly about RAGS. Ethically.

"I think you better sit down, Leo. I have a story to tell you before you go."

Connelly gave her a look and took the guest chair next to Naya. "Let's hear it," he said.

She started at the beginning, with Metz's revelation about the RAGS link. Then she told him how Peterson was supposed to get Hemisphere to agree to tell the NTSB. How she believed that Peterson's car ended up wrapped around a tree, not because he'd finally run out of drunk driving luck, but because he knew about the RAGS link and was going to go to the authorities.

Connelly's voice was tight with anger. "Do you know how much time we've wasted because you didn't tell me this last night?"

"I couldn't. I had an obligation."

He exploded. "Your obligation to save your client money was more important than saving lives?" He slammed a hand down on her desk.

She stood and stepped back, assumed a defensive posture but kept her voice calm. "Lower your voice. And step back." Her tone conveyed the rest of the message.

Naya's eyes widened.

Connelly ran his hand through his hair, leaving a trail of black spikes in its wake.

"I was out of line. Sorry about that." His voice was soft.

She relaxed her stance. "Apology accepted. I think everyone's under pressure."

He cracked a small grin. "You think?"

CONNELLY WENT to check the Frick Building's parking lot for the attackers' car.

As soon as the door shut behind him, Naya said, "What's the deal with this guy? You trust him?"

Sasha thought about it. He pissed her off, but he seemed trustworthy. "I do. I think. Why, does he give you a bad vibe?"

Naya shook her head; her braids snapped against her shoulders. "Not at all. He comes across pretty stand up. It's just . . ."

"What?"

Naya could read people. She'd take one look at an expert witness and know whether he was going to be brilliant or fall apart on the stand. She was a dangerous poker player, as Sasha had learned during a trial in St. Louis. Whenever there'd been downtime, Naya had dragged her to some riverboat casino where Sasha had nursed watered-down drinks and watched Naya clean up at low-limit hold 'em.

If Naya told her Connelly was sketchy, she would believe it.

"I don't know, Mac. He seems decent. But, where's his partner? I mean, this is an official government investigation he's running? And, it's just him? And you? No offense, woman, but I wouldn't go around investigating a mass murder plot with no backup except a mini-lawyer, fierce as you are."

Naya had a point. Connelly had balked at calling the police when they found Warner's body. And Sasha was sort of surprised that he hadn't suggested reporting the attack at the courthouse. Was he a rogue agent, working outside his authority? And, if he was, then what?

Sasha massaged her temples. Pressed hard with both hands. Counter pressure for the pressure building inside her head. Filled her lungs with air and exhaled slowly.

Naya's smooth forehead wrinkled in concern. "Know what, Mac? Forget I said anything. Really. I'm gonna get you a cup of coffee, okay? Then, I'm gonna call my mom's aide and tell her to stay until midnight. That's as late as she'll go and I really can't afford the overnight shift, but I'll help you all evening, as long as it takes. Okay?'

She leaned over the desk and rubbed Sasha's arm. "It's gonna be okay."

Sasha nodded. "Thank you. I don't know what we're getting into though, Naya. I'm not sure it's safe to get involved."

"Listen, your federal agent man does have a gun, right?"

"Yes."

"And you have your karate moves or whatever the hell they are. And, I'm mean as a snake. No fear, baby."

Sasha surprised herself by laughing.

"Really, Naya, thank you."

"No problem. Let me get you that coffee. And maybe a sandwich. You look even worse than this morning. Which is saying something, sister."

She left, and Sasha stared out the window. She had no plan, no direction. Just a vague goal: prevent another plane crash without getting killed in the process. What she needed was a list.

By the time Naya returned with two mugs of coffee and the news that she'd ordered up some lunch, Sasha had drafted a task chart, setting out their perceived next steps in order of priority. Next to each task, she had jotted a set of initials —hers, Naya's, or Connelly's—to indicate who was responsible for completing it.

Connelly followed Naya through the doorway, with a Prescott & Talbott mug of his own.

Naya put the coffee on Sasha's desk. When she saw the chart in front of Sasha, she smiled. "A Sasha McCandless task chart. Now we're in business."

She tossed her head in Connelly's direction,

"And I ran into Agent Connelly. I asked reception to get him a visitor's badge, so he can come and go."

"The car's still in the lot. I gave the valet fifty bucks not to have it towed and told him to call me if anyone gets in it." Connelly said, raising the mug to his lips.

Sasha frowned. "Couldn't you have someone from your office sit on the car?"

"I'm internal affairs, Sasha. People don't trip over themselves to work with me. I'm working out of the local field office right now, but it's just a base. A place to have a desk and a phone."

Sasha met Naya's eyes over his shoulder. She shrugged.

"Okay. I made a list of tasks." She took a long swallow of coffee. "Let's find an empty conference room, so we can spread out and eat lunch while we work."

THEY CAMPED out in the Heinz Conference Room. Heinz was the smallest conference room, but it was Sasha's favorite.

It had a view of the side of Mt. Washington. Sasha had passed the time in many meetings watching the Duquesne incline cars travel from Grandview Avenue atop Mt. Washington down to

Station Square and back up again. Slow, unyielding, constant.

In addition to the view, the Heinz had the benefit of being warm. Probably because of its size, the small conference room was the only one that didn't have the ambient temperature of a meat locker. Given that the thermostat boxes in the conference rooms were, as far as Sasha could tell, decorative and not functional, this was no small point in the Heinz's favor.

But, there was no denying, it was a tight work space. Naya and Sasha had fanned out diligence files going back a decade, and the small oval table was covered.

Connelly, who couldn't help review the files without violating Hemisphere Air's attorney-client privilege, was relegated to the corner. He sat with his long legs outstretched and resting on a second chair and Sasha's laptop balanced on his thighs. His task was to query various government databases for information about RAGS.

They'd been working in near silence for about forty minutes when the star-shaped conference phone bleated. Sasha snatched a folder off the top of the thing and pressed the speaker button.

"Conference room."

Anne at the reception desk said, "I have Bob

Metz on the line for you, Sasha. And your lunch order is here. Should I send it in or hold it?"

"Thanks. Naya and our guest will come out to reception and pick it up."

Sasha looked at Naya and tilted her head toward the door. Connelly couldn't be in the room while she talked to her client.

"C'mon, agent man," Naya said to Connelly.

He shot Sasha a look but put her laptop on the chair and followed Naya out the door.

"Go ahead and put him through," Sasha said.

The connection was terrible. Metz sounded like he was trapped in a snare drum during a rainstorm.

"Sasha?"

"Bob, I'm here. Can you hear me?"

"Barely. Damned monsoon out here."

She could hear the wind behind him. She looked out the window again. Calm and dry.

"Where are you?"

"At the cabstand at Sea-Tac."

"You're in Seattle?"

"Came out here on the first flight this morning. At least the jet stream was calm, gained some time. Miserable."

She didn't know if he meant the weather, the flight, or the connection. "What's going on? Why are you in Seattle?"

"Some sexual harassment case. I don't know

why Viv is so worked up over it, but last night after she talked to Noah, she told me she'd take over the crash and sent me out here. Where is Noah, anyway? He hasn't returned any of my calls." Annoyance crept into Metz's voice.

"Noah's dead." She figured she'd just say it.

"Dead?"

"There was a car accident last night. Noah spoke to Viv?"

"I guess so. Viv called me around eight o'clock last night to tell me she needed me to come out here. She said she'd talked to Noah. She agreed we needed to tell the feds about the RAGS link and said she'd take care of it. I can't believe he's dead. Was he...driving?" Metz's tone said everything his words did not.

Sasha just said, "The cause of the accident isn't known yet."

"Well ... I'm flummoxed, to be honest." There was a long pause. "Has Viv been in touch with the partner who's taking over?"

"Actually, Viv called the firm and asked that I run the defense without another layer of supervision."

Silence.

"Bob, did I lose you?"

"I'm here. I'm ... I have always liked you, Sasha. You have a great deal of promise, so please know I'm saying this out of genuine concern for your career—you should be careful. You don't know Vivian."

Sasha looked out the window, watching the incline's red wooden cable cars climb and descend the hillside as they'd done for more than a hundred and thirty years, and considered her response.

"I appreciate that, Bob. More than you know. But, I worked very closely with Noah and I think I . . ."

He cut her off. "You're not Noah. He's the only outside counsel we have that she hasn't fired at least once in a snit. And it's not that she has any loyalty to her former firm, because she doesn't. If it weren't for Laura, she would have pulled the business a long time ago."

"Laura?"

"Laura Peterson. She and Viv went to college together. They were in the same sorority at CMU."

Hemisphere Air remained a Prescott & Talbott client because one of the partners' wives had passed a candle around a circle in some bastardized Greek ceremony with the Vice President of Legal Affairs. Sasha thought the old boys' club that still ran the firm would find that to be an appropriate sort of progress.

"Sasha?"

"Sorry, Bob. I was thinking. I understand, really."

"Okay." He sounded unsure. "Have you talked to Viv, then?"

"Not yet. I didn't realize you weren't running this on the inside anymore. I guess I should give her a call."

"Do not call her." He said each word as if it was its own sentence. "Do not. When she wants to talk to you, she'll call you."

"Got it." Sasha felt her shoulders tensing. "Well, thanks for the call, Bob. Good luck out there."

"Wait . . ."

"Yes?"

He said nothing. She could hear him breathing, trying to decide how to phrase something.

"Bob?"

"Um. If you can, will you find out if my return flight was modified with the RAGS link?" His voice dropped. "I didn't want to ask Viv. But, I thought about it all the way across the country today. Waiting for someone to run the plane into a mountain or a skyscraper or to plunge it into a lake." His voice was shaking. "I can't do that again."

Sasha closed her eyes and remembered the helplessness and panic that had flooded her when she'd had the same thought during the approach to Reagan National the night before. She'd held her breath as they'd swooped over the monuments and hadn't exhaled until the wheels touched tarmac.

"I'll try, Bob. What's your flight number?"

"Uh," she heard him clawing through papers. "1480. The Friday night red eye."

She wrote it on a legal pad. Circled it. "Okay. Hang in there, Bob."

"Thank you, Sasha. You, too."

She pressed the button to end the call.

She sat thinking about Metz's cross-country flight until Naya and Connelly returned. He carried a tray of assorted wraps and a plastic bowl of pasta salad. She held the door with one hand and a plate of cookies with the other.

"Oh, good, you're off." Naya put the cookies down on the window sill and stacked up the files on the end of the table to clear a space for the food.

Sasha picked out a vegetable sandwich in a spinach wrap and filled a glass with water from the pitcher on the credenza. She focused on chewing with the uninjured side of her mouth.

She wasn't sure what to do about Metz's news that the NTSB and TSA had known about the RAGS link since the night before.

The TSA and the Federal Air Marshal Service were both pieces of the Homeland Security monolith. The NTSB was independent, but it worked hand-in-hand with the TSA on crash investigations.

If any one of the three agencies knew about the RAGS link, it would have shared the information with the other two right away. Which meant Connelly had known all along and was trying to keep her in the dark, so his outburst when she told him had been staged. Or he really hadn't known, which meant. . . what? His investigation wasn't authorized? Someone at the government was in on the plan with Irwin and Mickey Collins?

She wasn't sure. She *was* sure that they were both bad scenarios. Time to find out which was in play.

"Hey, Connelly?" she said. She thought she'd kept her tone neutral, but from the way Naya's attention shifted from her plate of pasta salad to the air marshal, it looked like she hadn't.

"Mm-hmm?" he answered around a mouth full of turkey and swiss cheese.

"I know no one likes the rat squad, but why didn't anyone at DHS tell you about RAGS?"

Naya mouthed, "rat squad?"

Rat squad. Nick Martino, a narcotics detective she'd met in the corridor at the courthouse and dated for a few weeks, had told Sasha he'd turned down a promotion because it would entail a transfer to internal affairs, also known as the rat squad. Nick had explained he preferred to associate with drug dealers and gang bangers than with the scumbags on the rat squad who investigated their fellow officers.

As it turned out, Nick's strong opinions had extended beyond his views on his workplace. After a heated discussion about the merits of legalizing marijuana that ended with Nick calling her a moron, Sasha volunteered to handle a series of depositions in Wichita and informed him that she'd be gone for at least a month. That was the last she'd seen of the good detective.

She waited for Connelly to swallow and answer.

"Presumably because no one at DHS knows about it." He wiped his mouth with a paper napkin and reached for a cookie.

"According to my client, the NTSB has known since yesterday evening. I thought you said the agencies were getting better at sharing information."

Connelly chewed his cookie, unperturbed. "They are. You must have bad information."

Naya looked from Sasha to Connelly and back. She folded her napkin in a square and picked up her plate and empty soda can. "I think I'll check on the trial team."

She tossed her plate in the trash and the can

in the recycling and hurried out of the room before it got any uglier.

"I doubt that," Sasha said. "Are you lying to me or are your bosses lying to you? Which is it?"

"Maybe your client is lying."

"Why would anyone at Hemisphere Air lie to me? They can tell me anything, remember? Attorney-client privilege."

"Which you violated by telling me about RAGS, remember? Maybe they thought if you believed the government already knew, you'd back off. They don't know you told me."

They glared at each other. She was pretty sure he hadn't lied to her. Sasha wasn't quite the mind reader Naya was, but she'd questioned enough witnesses to have a sense for when she was being lied to. Connelly was far too calm.

"It's possible. Unlikely, but possible," she conceded. "But, if they did tell the NTSB and someone is sitting on it, we have a big problem."

"Yes, we do," he agreed.

"That means Irwin or Collins has help from inside, right?"

"It would have to be someone pretty high up the food chain, though. What do you know about Collins?"

"Not much. He's a very successful plaintiff's attorney. Used to be married to a federal judge. Drives an Aston Martin. He's a local kid made good. I think he went to Carnegie Mellon for undergrad and Pitt for law school."

Connelly looked blank. "I don't know, Sasha. Let's table it for now. You need to somehow find the modified planes in that mountain," he said, pointing to the piles of binders and folders that Naya had gotten out of file storage, "and I have my own fruitless search to finish." He tossed his plate in the trash and picked up the laptop.

Sasha knew he was right. Identifying the modified planes was her first priority. The second priority was to find the second guy. Dealing with Collins, Irwin, and their goons was a distant third at this point.

She opened a closing binder. She and Naya had agreed the best course was to review all the deal documents they had on hand for Hemisphere Air. It was the likeliest place to find something out of place.

Whenever a company sold or bought another company or expensive assets (like airplanes), merged, or entered into any sizeable investment arrangement (stock purchase or offering, venture capital deal, private placement, or commercial loan), the zombie hordes otherwise known as junior corporate associates had the thankless task of reviewing all the underlying documents and drafting a diligence memo. It was a tedious, soul-crushing, and vital job.

Based on the due diligence review and resulting memo, the client would decide whether to go forward with a transaction, how much to pay, and which assets or liabilities to include or exclude.

From Sasha's vantage point, a due diligence review was just about the only task that made a privilege review look pleasant. She'd also heard from friends that preparing a Hart-Scott-Rodino filing to get antitrust clearance was pretty much hell on earth. But, for her money, nothing could be worse than a diligence review.

In a due diligence review, if the associate did her job properly, there was no recognition, no credit, no bonus. If she missed the smallest detail, the ramifications could be huge. Lawsuits, firings, delisting from the stock exchange. As far as Sasha was concerned, it explained why corporate associates tended to be anal, short-tempered, and prone to stomach ulcers.

The *only* time she had broken her no lawyers dating rule had been to date a corporate associate. It went against her better judgment, but her law school roommate had vouched for the guy. When she called it quits, Joseph had presented her with an itemized schedule of expenses he'd incurred in the course of their three dates and a suggested formula to divvy up the costs based on their respective incomes, who had suggested each date activity, and who he determined had enjoyed it more. Her old roommate had laughed so hard when Sasha showed her the schedule that she'd snorted beer through her nose. She picked up the tab that night, too.

Sasha was certain if evidence existed to show which planes had been modified, some dead-eyed corporate associate had found it.

26

The federal courthouse

Anton was in bad shape. Gregor wasn't feeling too hot himself, but he was worried about his younger partner.

Once he was able, Gregor had crawled over and rested against the cool, pink marble wall. He figured he'd catch his breath and wait for Anton to regain consciousness.

The first part was proving to be a problem because his fall had fractured a couple of his ribs. Every time he took a breath, fire spread across his torso.

The second part was a problem because Anton wasn't coming around.

Gregor made his way over to Anton, rolled him onto his back, and winced. From the stabbing pain and from looking at Anton's face. The little bitch had really done a number on him. In fact, he didn't look much better than that kid they'd killed by mistake the night before.

He leaned in and listened. Anton was breathing.

Now what? Gregor tried to think. The pounding in his head made it hard.

He stared at Anton.

In a dim corner of his brain, he thought he remembered that a shattered cheekbone could kill a guy if pieces of bone got driven into the brain. Was that true? Gregor sighed. If it was true, it wasn't like he could do anything about it.

He needed to get Anton out of here before someone had a nicotine fit and snuck into the stairwell for a cigarette.

He pulled Anton up and draped his body over his left arm, ignoring the screaming heat in his ribs. He half dragged, half carried his partner down the stairs.

It was slow going. He had to stop on the third floor landing to rest. He leaned Anton against the wall, braced his palms on his knees, and took some shallow breaths, riding the wave of pain in his ribs. Then he slung Anton over his shoulder and resumed his creeping descent.

When they hit the second floor landing, Anton started to moan.

"I got you, Anton."

Gregor pushed on. He stopped at the door leading out to the lobby to catch his breath again. Panting and sucking in air.

Anton was getting louder.

"Listen, we're almost out. Be cool."

Gregor squared his shoulders as best he could and pushed the door open. He led Anton to the wall across from the security station and propped him up, trying to turn his face away from the desk.

He hurried over to the guards. "Hi, can I get these two cell phones back now, please?" He handed the older guy the ticket stub, very glad he'd checked both phones together.

The guy took the stub. He ambled over to the wooden box behind him and reached into one of the slots. Pulled out the phones. Took his time checking the numbers on the two halves of the claim ticket.

Gregor jiggled his leg.

The old guy peered up at him as he handed over the phones. "You and your buddy okay, sir?" His head tilted toward Anton slumped against the wall.

"We're fine. Fine. My friend is diabetic. He went into insulin shock and took a tumble down the stairs. Lucky me, I broke his fall." Gregor forced a chuckle.

The guard didn't look convinced, but he didn't look like he cared too much either way.

"Okay, well you take care of your friend."

"Yes sir, I will."

Gregor collected Anton before he fell over, then he shouldered his way out the courthouse door.

27

The offices of Prescott & Talbott

Naya found it.

They'd been working for several hours with no breaks and none of the empty chatter that usually accompanied a document review. Connelly had struck out with his database queries. He'd fielded a call from the valet, but it was nothing exciting: the guy was going to leave for the day; the car was still there; and he'd put an overnight ticket under the windshield wiper so it wouldn't be towed.

He agreed to pay another fifty dollars for the same arrangement if the car was still there in the morning then hung up with the valet.

"It's getting close to five. Why don't we work until seven and then get some dinner. Maybe go out and grab something quick?"

He'd been fidgeting for the last hour or so; now, he paced around the small room in a loop. Sasha imagined he didn't spend much time trapped behind a desk. She was stiff from her encounter on the stairwell and could use a brisk walk and some air.

She was about to agree, when Naya slapped a binder down in front of her.

"Look at this."

Naya had the closing files from an asset purchase agreement from 2007. Hemisphere Air had sold off eight older 737s from its fleet to Blue Horizons, one of the budget carriers. The binder was open to a draft of the agreement, which, if Sasha understood the firm's document retention policy, should have been shredded, not hole-punched, placed in a tabbed, three-ring binder, and sent to storage.

A deal, any deal, goes through multiple negotiated revisions. She knew from sharing a printer with a corporate partner that the lawyers for the parties exchanged their proposed edits as redlines. Each side's lawyer would make changes to the file, save the changes, and generate a redline version that showed the additions as underlined bold text and the deletions as text with a line struck through it. Along with the substantive changes, formatting changes would show up, as well as any comments or questions posed by the reviewer. The result was almost always unreadable.

Trial attorneys engaged in a similar process to negotiate confidentiality agreements, stipulations, and settlement agreements. But their work product usually involved a much lighter edit. Adversaries in a courtroom battle were more likely to look at a wall of text indicating lots of changes to their proposed terms and to tell one another to go pound salt than were partners in a financial transaction.

Sasha skimmed the draft and immediately got lost in all the strikeouts and inserts.

"Help me out here. What am I looking for?" she asked Naya.

Naya flipped to the schedule of assets purchased. She leaned over Sasha's shoulder and pointed at a series of strikeouts.

"See these five planes? They were originally part of the deal, but in this version all five were removed."

Connelly came and stood behind her. He craned his neck to see over her shoulder. Sasha knew she should tell him not to try to see the documents, but she ignored him.

"Okay. Do we know why?"

Naya flipped the pages forward. "There's a reviewer comment here that they were taking out five planes that didn't conform to Boeing's standards."

Sasha looked up at her. "You think they were modified with the RAGS link?"

Naya said, "I know one of them was." She flipped back to the schedule. "Look at the tail number on the third one."

The tail number was a plane's aircraft registration number. It functioned like a car's license plate, and every civil aircraft has one. And the tail number for the third deleted plane did look familiar.

"You're sure that's Flight 1667?"

Naya nodded. "I'm sure. But, we can check."

Connelly grabbed the laptop and opened the browser to the Federal Aviation Administration's N-number/tail number lookup. All planes registered in the U.S. had a tail number that began with the letter *N*. And the FAA was kind enough to make public a database that cross-referenced planes with their N-numbers.

"Give me the number."

"N-247AA."

Connelly typed it in. They waited. Sasha realized she wasn't breathing. She went ahead and breathed.

"Boeing 737, registered owner, Hemisphere

Air Lines, Inc., out of service as of two days ago." He looked up.

"Go to planespotters," Sasha said.

Several websites existed that would spit out a list of flight numbers that a given plane had flown under, along with cities of origination and destination. All they needed was the tail number.

Connelly went to the site and typed in N-247AA. A list of flights, in reverse chronological order by date, appeared. N-247AA's last recorded flight was Flight 1667 from DCA to DFW, the night of the crash.

"How did you know about this website?" Connelly asked.

"There are several of them. Some frequent travelers like to see where their planes have been, how often they've been taken out of service, and for how long," Sasha said.

She had once deposed a plaintiff who'd been on a Hemisphere Air flight when a bird had gotten sucked into the engine. The pilot had executed a textbook emergency landing; no passengers were injured. Undeterred, the plaintiff claimed the incident had left him shaken and emotionally scarred. He maintained, however, he had no choice but to continue to fly because his job entailed heavy travel.

In response to a document request, his lawyer had provided the guy's meticulous logs of his flights—complete with printouts from the planespotters website showing the flight histories of all the planes he'd flown on after the incident. Sasha had noted that almost all of the guy's flights were short hauls on regional puddle jumpers.

She'd spent most of his deposition asking him questions about why he frequently flew from Pittsburgh to places like Cleveland, Philadelphia, and Baltimore if he was so terrified of flying. California or Texas, sure. But Pittsburgh to Wheeling, West Virginia, was an hour-long drive tops. She'd waved those logs around in front of him like she was a matador.

He ended up settling in exchange for two free round-trip tickets, completely putting the lie to his emotional distress claim.

Connelly tensed his jaw. "These websites could aid terrorists. Just like those real-time flight tracker websites. Why don't people think before they make this information accessible?"

Sasha raised an eyebrow. It was news to her that terrorists had time machines. "Connelly, the information is *historical*. You know what, never mind. Go back to the FAA site, okay? Naya read him the other four tail numbers."

She didn't have time to argue with him about access to information or indulge his Patriot Act-induced delusions.

Naya read them off and Connelly typed them into the search box, one by one. All registered to Hemisphere Air. All still in service.

Sasha called Metz and got his voicemail. She hung up without leaving a message and contemplated her options.

Four planes currently in service almost certainly had been outfitted with the RAGS link. Four vulnerable planes. Hundreds, if not thousands, of passengers.

With Metz's warning not to call Vivian in her ears, she left Naya and Connelly in the conference room to map out the itineraries of the three compromised planes. As an afterthought, she handed off Metz's flight information and asked them to check it out.

She plunged down the hall to the stairwell and raced to her office. She passed Flora, who was putting on her coat.

"Oh, Sasha, I thought you had left for the day. Um, do you still need me?" Flora stopped with one arm in her coat sleeve; the other sleeve flapped around, red and manic.

"No," Sasha called over her shoulder. "I have an important call to make. Good night, Flora."

She raced into her office and pulled the door shut.

Flora shrugged and slipped her other arm

into her coat, sending the pile of legal journals flying off the ledge behind her.

"Shoot!"

She bent to gather them up. As she squared them into a stack, she saw the slim UPS envelope alone on the ledge. She closed her eyes for a minute. Opened them. The package was still there.

Flora looked at the phone. Sasha's line was already lit up; she was on her important call. She could wait a few minutes, see if Sasha hung up. She checked her watch. But, if she left now, she could catch an earlier bus, change into jeans, and meet her girlfriends for happy hour.

She peeked at the phone again. Still lit up. She chewed her lip for a minute, unsure. Then she put the envelope on top of the neat stack of journals so Lettie would see it first thing in the morning and turned off the desk lamp.

Having made up her mind, she hurried past Sasha's closed door on her way to the elevator.

Inside, Sasha stared at the phone on her desk, shocked into silence and wishing she'd listened to Metz.

Vivian Coulter's anger was booming through the phone's speaker.

"Do I make myself clear? We are not going to ground four perfectly safe planes because you have some wild theory that they might have been outfitted with the RAGS link. We are working to determine which planes actually have the RAGS links installed, of course, but it's going to take some time. Right now, we have no reason—*none* —to believe that any of our planes pose a danger of any kind to the flying public. And even if these four planes do have RAGS on board, there is no basis for thinking someone would or could attempt to access the system. The cause of Monday night's crash remains unknown. I will *not* jeopardize the economic health of this company and the interests of our shareholders unless and until someone in the federal government gives me a reason why I should. And, by the way, I note no one from Homeland Security or the NTSB has suggested any such thing."

Either the tirade was over or Viv was taking a breath.

Sasha took the opening, "I understand your position, but the government appears to have no record of Hemisphere Air reporting that the RAGS link was on Flight 1667."

No response. A few seconds later, a dial tone. Apparently, her client had hung up on her once her venom had run dry.

There was a light tap on the door, and then Naya cracked it open. Connelly loomed behind her in the hallway.

"How'd it go?"

"Not well."

"Viv didn't agree to ground the planes?"

"In a word, no. And then she hung up on me."

"Well, this is gonna make it worse: Metz's red eye on Friday is on the list. It's one of the four."

Sasha closed her eyelids and pressed her fingers hard against her tired eyes for a minute. Then she stood, picked up her purse, and put on her jacket. "Let's go."

"Food?" Connelly asked, hopeful.

"We'll get food later. We're going to see Mickey Collins."

They took the elevator down in silence and crossed the empty lobby in silence. Their shoes on the gleaming floor and the hum of the building's mechanical systems were the only sounds. The security guard gave them a bored half-wave and went back to his Sudoku puzzle.

After the revolving door spit them out on the sidewalk, Naya finally spoke.

"Do you have a plan?"

Sasha pulled her wool suit jacket close to keep out the wind and checked the street for traffic.

"Nope."

28

Hoping the element of surprise would work in the absence of an actual plan, they breezed past the front desk in the Frick Building like they belonged there and made a beeline for the elevator. Connelly jabbed the up button and they hustled into the waiting elevator before anyone could stop them.

When they reached Mickey's office suite, the receptionist was gone for the day. Her station was empty and her computer monitor dark.

Naya grabbed the arm of a paper-laden associate passing through, and he pointed them toward Mickey's office.

They marched down the uninspired hallway. Mickey might have spent his cut of his verdicts on an expensive car—and maybe alimony for Judge Dolan, considering an Article III judge, appointed by the President of the United States, earned less per year than a first-year associate at Prescott & Talbott (before associate bonus)—but he definitely did not spend it on interior decorating. Unless he was going for a drab motif. Tan carpet that was worn and dull, blank walls, save for some scuff marks, and fluorescent lighting that made everyone—even Naya—look a little green.

It was all part of the game. Just as Prescott & Talbott's clients expected their attorneys' offices to be well appointed and refined, Mickey's clients expected his office to be a barebones, threadbare operation. He was their champion, a fighter for the little guy. The fact that he belonged to Oakmont Country Club and sent his kids to Shadyside Academy was his dirty little secret.

The door to his office was ajar, so they sailed right in.

Mickey was packing up to leave for the day. When he saw Sasha, he put down his battered leather satchel and gave her a big smile that faded into a look of concern as he remembered the news about Noah.

He came around the front of his walnut desk and grabbed both her arms, more than a handshake, but not quite a hug. "Sasha, I'm so sorry about Noah."

Then he focused on her bruised face. Flicked

his eyes to Connelly's injuries. "What happened to you?"

"Mickey, we need to talk."

He gestured for them to have a seat on the worn green couch along the wall. Naya and Sasha sat, while Connelly shut the door and Mickey dragged over an extra chair from in front of his desk.

He ran a hand through his slightly too long, wavy silver hair. The criminal defense attorneys tended to wear ponytails in an effort to appeal to their clientele. The big firm lawyers were all clean shaven with haircuts that conformed to military regulations to appeal to theirs. The plaintiffs' bar straddled the middle. Some had beards. Others, like Mickey, grew their hair until it touched their collars.

"What's going on?" He cut his eyes back to Connelly.

"Mickey, you remember Naya, I'm sure. This is Special Agent Leo Connelly with the Department of Homeland Security." It was technically true and sounded scarier than air marshal.

Connelly extended a hand but didn't smile. "Mr. Collins."

Mickey shook it with clear reluctance. "Agent Connelly."

Then he turned his charm on for Naya. "I'm

glad to see your gorgeous face doesn't have a scratch on it."

Naya gave him a tight smile.

"Listen, Mickey," Sasha said, watching his face for a reaction, "Agent Connelly is investigating the crash and Noah's death. He came to me for information about you. He wants to take you into custody as a material witness. I told him there must be some misunderstanding, and I know you can clear it up."

Not bad for no plan, she thought.

Mickey blanched gray under his perpetual tan. His eyes grew wide. "What?!"

Sasha said nothing. She hoped Naya and Connelly would follow suit. If Mickey had one weakness as an attorney it was his inability to stand silence.

She'd seen Noah get him to negotiate against himself simply by remaining silent. Mickey couldn't take it; he would lower his settlement demand to try to get a response.

Mickey spread his hands wide, "Why? I don't understand."

He looked from Sasha to Connelly and back.

She waited.

Mickey's eyes filled with understanding and he slumped in his chair. "It's Irwin, isn't it?"

"Why don't you tell us about your relationship with Mr. Irwin?" Connelly said.

"We were roommates in college," Mickey said. "At CMU." He shook his head. "Freaking Jerry Irwin."

"Did Mr. Irwin approach you with the plan or did you approach him?"

"Approach? What plan?"

"Mickey," Sasha said, "we don't have time to play around. We know you and Irwin crashed that plane. Which one of you killed Noah?"

Mickey's head snapped back. "What the hell are you talking about, Sasha?"

"Seriously, Mickey. I went out on a limb for you. Tell Agent Connelly what you know already."

"What I know? What I know is Jerry Irwin is a goddamn psychopath. I would cross over and work with you assholes before I would get in bed with Irwin."

"That's not a very nice thing to say about your old college buddy," Naya observed.

"Irwin is no buddy of mine." Mickey was tugging at the buttons on his white-collared blue dress shirt.

He struggled with them and ripped open the shirt. He wore no undershirt.

"Look at this! You see this scar? Irwin did that." Mickey pointed to a jagged line that ran diagonally across his chest from his clavicle to his rib cage.

Connelly leaned in for a look. "How?"

"With a broken beer bottle." Mickey started to button back up. It was slow going because his hands were shaking. Sasha looked away.

Naya asked in a soft voice, "Why?"

Mickey met her eyes. "Because he's crazy. We were roommates our freshman year. Assigned, not by choice. I was taking political science classes and he was in the engineering school. He was a typical nerd—awkward, analytical, humorless. I made a lot of friends pretty quickly. Irwin, not so much. I felt bad for him. So, during Tech Fair . . ."

"What Fair?" Connelly asked.

"Tech Fair," Sasha said. "It's like a spring carnival, with booths and rides. The engineering school is really strong at Carnegie Mellon, so they design amazing stuff. But there's bands and partying, too."

"Right. Anyway, I was a pledge in a fraternity and I had been invited to a bunch of parties."

Sasha nodded. Beginning in high school, she and her friends had been able to wander away from the games and into the fraternity parties. Back then at least, there was an unusually high male-to-female ratio at CMU, so just about any girl over the age of fifteen could walk into a party, but guys had to know someone. Although the eager fraternity brothers had discriminated on the basis of gender, they didn't do so on the basis of age. Her first taste of alcohol had been warm grain punch served in a plastic cup at one such party when she was a sophomore in high school.

Mickey continued, "I had one invite for this party, so I took Irwin along. You know, to be nice." He pulled a sour face at the memory. "And Irwin got really drunk. He had been trying to talk to some girl all night and the more he drank, the more he pestered her. The brothers were starting to get pissed off, so I tried to talk to him. Told him we should go get some air. He agreed right away. Like, no problem. Brought his beer bottle with him. Once we were outside behind the house, he smashed it against the wall and just lunged at me. He was a madman, slashing at me, screaming that I was trying to move in on his action. To this day, I've never seen anything like it. Some of the fraternity brothers ran out and wrestled him off me. Got me to the hospital. I needed forty-two stitches. Lost a ton of blood." Mickey shook his head like he was trying to dislodge the memory.

"Did you press charges?"

"No. I slept at the fraternity house for the rest of the semester. Stayed away from him." His face was etched with fear and hatred at the memory.

Sasha and Connelly exchanged a look. Then

Sasha glanced at Naya, who nodded. They all believed Mickey was telling the truth.

"That's why you didn't sign Mrs. Calvaruso up as your class rep after you heard Irwin had made her husband's reservation?" Sasha said.

Mickey cocked his head at the information. Sasha watched him consider asking who in his firm had been yapping and saw him decide to let it go.

"That's right. I don't want anything to do with Jerry Irwin."

"Someone does, though. He's behind the crash, Mickey. And behind Noah's death, I think. But he has a partner. Someone local. Any ideas?"

Mickey shook his head. "Not really. Did he do that to you?" Mickey waved a hand at Sasha's face.

"Yes."

"And you?" He pointed to Connelly.

"No. That was her." Connelly pointed at Sasha.

Mickey took that in.

"But Irwin did have one of his employees killed."

Mickey nodded, "So, what's the plan?"

And this time, Sasha had one.

"We think there are at least four more planes that he has the ability to crash," Sasha said, skimming over the details. "All owned by Hemisphere

Air. If *someone* filed a temporary restraining order tomorrow morning seeking an injunction to ground those planes, thousands of lives will be saved." She stared at Mickey.

Mickey stared back. "Hemisphere Air's your client. Why doesn't Bob Metz just ground the planes? Hell, ground the entire fleet."

"Metz is off the case. Vivian's running it."

Mickey groaned. "Let me guess, Viv Coulter won't take those planes out of service because she has a *duty* to her shareholders to maximize their profits?"

"If she said something amazingly similar to that it would be an attorney-client privileged communication," Sasha said.

Connelly was getting antsy again. He stood up and paced over to the window behind Mickey's desk. He pressed his forehead against the smeared glass and stared down at the parking lot below. He zeroed in on the silver Camry with Maryland plates parked next to Mickey's ride.

Mickey shook his head, "I don't have the manpower to draft up a TRO tonight. Not to mention, I don't have any factual basis for one. Judge Cook would laugh me out of court."

"Cook?"

"Yeah, Judge Cook is hearing them tomorrow. I have a friend in the clerk's office call me at the end of the day to let me know who's up for emergency motions the next day. Some emergencies, they can wait a day or two for the right judge." He smiled.

Naya sat up a little straighter. Sasha knew she was making a mental note to talk to her own friend at the courthouse about getting that same advance information going forward.

"Cook is perfect," Sasha said. "I can guarantee you'll win."

Mickey looked like he didn't want to know any details. "I do want to help you, but I'm not kidding, I can't draft a TRO overnight."

An emergency temporary restraining order, or TRO, wasn't the sort of document an attorney could just dash off. The standard for obtaining one was very high because the effect of a TRO was to immediately restrain or enjoin a party from taking some action.

Under the rules of procedure, a federal judge could actually grant a temporary restraining order *ex parte*, or without notice to the defendant. But, in the Western District of Pennsylvania, the practice was to provide notice to the other side when it was feasible. Often, the parties would work something out without court involvement after notice of the motion for a temporary restraining order. In this case, Sasha would show up and argue against the restraining order. She had no doubt that once he heard Hemisphere

Air's position, Judge Cook would trip over himself to grant it.

"No worries. What's in your bag?" She nodded at the leather case he'd dropped on the desk when they barged in.

He didn't answer.

"Nothing, right? Maybe some legal magazines, some administrative paperwork? Just enough to weigh it down so the underlings think you're taking work home when you cruise out of here early?"

Partners were all the same. Didn't matter if they were plaintiff side or defense. They wanted their associates to feel like they were rolling up their sleeves, too.

Mickey gave her a wry smile. "More or less."

"Give me your bag. I'll have it messengered out to your house before midnight with a motion for a TRO ready for your signature. All you'll have to do is file it when the courthouse opens in the morning."

Mickey looked at her for a very long time. "We could both lose our licenses."

"We could. Or we could just agree that you lost your briefcase and, nice girl that I am, I found it and returned it. And I'll lose an argument on a motion for an emergency TRO tomorrow. That's it."

Mickey traced the path of his scar through his shirt. He swallowed, then he nodded

"Sasha, I'm not so worried about me. Hell, a temporary disbarment would be great advertising for me—Mickey Collins puts his client's interests before his own or something. But, you could tank your career at a place like Prescott."

Sasha didn't want to talk about it. "We'll get the motion to you as soon as we can, Mickey."

Connelly picked the bag up from the desk and Naya and Sasha stood to leave.

"Good night," Mickey said.

"See you in court," she replied, mainly because no one ever said it in real life and she'd always wanted to.

When they reached the ground floor, Connelly said he had some business of his own to attend to. He didn't say what it was.

Sasha and Connelly agreed to split up and meet back at her place for a very late dinner and to work out their next steps. She gave him her spare key.

Connelly walked them back to their building. At the entranceway, he told Naya he needed to speak to Sasha alone, so Naya went in and called the elevator.

Sasha shivered. It was almost dark now and the wind had picked up. A discarded fast food wrapper whipped against her ankle. "What's up,

Connelly?" she demanded, hopping from foot to foot to stay warm.

"You can't let your guard down," he said.

"I *know*." She was annoyed.

"I'm worried about those guys who jumped you. They have to be somewhere nearby. The car's still here."

"They're probably holed up in a hotel room near the courthouse, like you said," she answered. "That first guy is in no condition to travel."

"Even so," he said. He was staring at her.

"Connelly, it's cold out here. Give me Mickey's bag. I'm going in."

He held the bag out to her. As she reached for it, he wrapped an arm around her waist and pulled her tight against his body. Anyone watching would have thought they were lovers saying good night.

He bent down and put his mouth to her ear. His breath was warm. "I'm putting my gun in your purse right now," he whispered. The strap tugged against her shoulder as her bag took on the extra weight. "The safety's on."

She pulled her head back and craned her neck to see his face. "I don't want your gun."

"Just humor me, Sasha."

"Whatever, Connelly. Fine." Her back was getting tight from the cold.

He tightened his grip on her waist. "Why don't you ever call me Leo?"

"Okay, *Leo*, let go of my waist *right now*."

He dropped his arm abruptly, and she stumbled. She caught her balance and headed for the door without looking back.

Naya was holding the elevator door open. "You okay?" she asked, as Sasha hurried into the elevator car.

"Fine. Why?"

"You're shaking."

"It's just from the cold."

29

Leo crouched by the silver car. He felt nervous. It was an unfamiliar, but unmistakable, emotion. The pit of his stomach was squeezed tight by it and his heart hammered in his chest.

He couldn't remember when he'd last felt this way. Not when Sasha had pointed his own gun at him; not when he'd confronted a dirty air marshal in a back alley; and not when he'd traveled alone as a teenager to Vietnam to track down his father and tell him he was his son.

But, now, he was definitely nervous. He was, after all, about to break the law. He had dug around in the loose gravel on the side of the parking lot, hoping for a brick, willing to settle for a large rock. Found nothing suitable.

He eyed the door lock. As he'd suspected, it

wasn't pickable. Not without a set of tools and a lot of time. He knew how to pop a lock with a pocketknife, or scissors, or even a tennis ball. But, those skills were fast becoming party tricks, as newer model cars became more sophisticated.

It'd be handy to have his service weapon right now. He could shoot out a window or just crash it into the glass. Everyone said the Sig Sauer was a big, heavy handgun. But he was a big guy with huge hands and hadn't ever really noticed. Not until Sasha had been clutching his gun in Warner's apartment. It had looked cartoonishly large in her tiny hands.

He paused to wonder why he had given it to her. She didn't have a license to carry. He could be fired or even prosecuted for lending his weapon to a civilian. Especially a pain-in-the-ass, argumentative civilian. Even a little tiny one whose hair smelled like ginger and honey when he bent over to whisper in her ear.

He didn't fully understand it, but he felt a strong urge to protect the woman who had assaulted him just one night before. When he'd walked into her office and seen her battered face, he'd been flooded with worry, rage, and shame. As though he had failed her.

He needed to get the drop on the guys who wanted to hurt her. Step one was to get into their car and see if he could find out who the hell they were. He felt better leaving her with a weapon.

He swept the lot with his eyes. The five p.m. crowd had trudged into their cars and joined the sea of taillights heading home to make dinner and fight with the kids about doing their homework. A handful of cars remained in the fading light. No people. The attendant's hut was closed up for the night.

He checked the street. No foot traffic. Pittsburgh had one of those downtowns that rolled up the sidewalks in the evening.

He stood, ducking low, and took off his jacket. Went down into a squat and wrapped it around his bad hand. No sense hurting the other one. He made a fist and rocked back on his heels.

Do it. Now.

He shot to his feet, putting as much force as he could behind his fist, and collapsed. A wave of pain swelled across the back of his head. He fell headfirst into the car door, bounced back, and landed in a pile on the ground.

GREGOR LOOKED DOWN at the guy who'd been about to smash his car window. Big guy, Asian. Suit, preppy striped tie. Twin shiners and what looked to be a broken nose. He looked to be in his late thirties. He'd never seen him before.

He bent over the guy and felt around in his pockets. No gun, no car keys. A wallet and a cell phone. He took both, left the house key. Flipped open the wallet to an identification card claiming the Asian guy at his feet was Leonard Connelly, United States Air Marshal.

The picture looked like the guy, but Gregor figured the badge was a fake. As far as he knew, federal air marshals didn't prowl around public parking lots after dark, looking for cars to break into. And Leonard Connelly wasn't even close to this dude's name. No chance.

Maybe he was a gang banger dressed to blend in with the worker bees. Did Pittsburgh have any Asian gangs? Hell if he knew. Or maybe he was a worker bee. Some pervert who spent his days shuffling paper and his nights scoping out downtown parking lots looking for women to attack. Whatever he was, he was a problem.

Gregor tried to decide what to do about him. He did not make it a habit to kill people for free. Fact was, he didn't kill too many people for pay, either. Mostly, he was hired muscle.

Got his start in with the Russian mob in Baltimore. But, the gamblers had all gone online and the johns usually paid up front. So, there wasn't so much work anymore. He'd branched out. Freelanced.

Everyone understood a man had to feed his family, and the old guys still called on him once in a while. But, mainly, Gregor worked for other freelancers—small-time bookies, a couple drug pushers, the occasional loan shark.

Business was good enough that he'd hired his sister's son Anton. And they started marketing themselves to a higher class of criminal. Some clients just wanted him to threaten a guy who was making noises like he might back out of a deal. Most wanted him to rough somebody up over a business transaction gone bad. Then there were guys like Irwin. Irwin wanted his files back *by whatever means necessary*. He'd said it like that, all intense and meaningful. Irwin was paying them a boatload. So he'd get his damned files.

Gregor popped the trunk. He really wished Anton wasn't out of commission. This guy looked heavy. Gregor braced himself for the pain he knew was coming. Then he hoisted the man over his shoulder and dumped him into the trunk.

30

Jerry Irwin's house

Jerry Irwin was packing his overnight bag when the cell phone rang. He looked over at the nightstand to see which of his disposable phones it was. Pittsburgh. Where the hell was Gregor? He hadn't even called in with a progress report.

He folded his long-sleeved polo shirt and put it down on top of the bed.

"What is it?" he snapped.

"Don't take that tone with me."

Irwin sighed. *Two more days*, he told himself. Just two more days of suffering this insufferable bitch.

"I apologize. I was hoping to hear from my guys. What can I do for you?" he said through gritted teeth.

"You can tell your guys to get their asses in gear!"

He held the phone away from his ear as Vivian Coulter shrieked.

"That little bitch figured out which planes have the RAGS installed and called me, asking me to ground them. Take care of her, Irwin. Do it right this time. And get that damn personnel file back. I will not have all my careful planning ruined by your ineptitude. You have no idea how . . ."

This time, Irwin hung up on her.

He stared at the phone in his hand. Then in a fluid motion, he hurled it at the mirror hanging opposite his bed. It bounced off and the glass shattered in a waterfall of shards.

Irwin returned to his packing. He counted his outfits, then smoothed out the blazer on top and added his shaving kit to the bag. He did a final sweep of the room to make sure he wasn't forgetting anything. He wasn't. It occurred to him he would likely never come back to this house.

He zippered the bag closed and slung it over his shoulder. Then he picked up the cell phone from his nightstand, stooped to get the one he had thrown, and stepped over the glass.

In the doorway, he stopped and reached into his pocket to retrieve his third cell phone, his real one. Hit the button to dial the only preprogrammed number it held.

"I'm on my way" was all he said.

Irwin shut out the light and headed to Pittsburgh, humming to himself.

31

The offices of Prescott & Talbott
8:30 p.m.

One of the main benefits of working for a big law firm was the repository of documents the attorneys could draw on. Whatever you needed to file, someone had already done one. And because the document had been drafted, revised, and vetted by fellow Prescott attorneys, you could be confident that it was done properly. Cases were Shepardized, citations conformed to the Blue Book, and local rules of procedure were followed.

Despite this wealth of material, however, a diligent Prescott & Talbott attorney never filed papers without double and triple checking that everything was in order, which meant that—in the end—the client paid just as much for its recycled documents as it would have had the attorney drafted them from scratch.

With all those resources at their fingertips and with time at a premium, Sasha and Naya wanted to copy a motion for an emergency TRO from the database to use as their starting point. Creating one from whole cloth seemed so inefficient. But they both knew they'd leave their electronic fingerprints all over the network if they logged in.

It occurred to Sasha that she knew Noah's login and password information. So they accessed the database as a dead man.

Dozens of people had been using Noah's login all day long in an effort to get their arms around his cases. If someone really wanted to, they'd be able to match up the times that the database was accessed with the names of lawyers and staff who were signed in at the reception desk after hours.

The results would be imprecise, though, because signing in was not policed and Sasha and Naya had paused at the register when they returned from Mickey's office but had not entered their names.

Cinco had resisted efforts to install card

readers throughout the office. Prescott & Talbott employees and guests simply flashed their badges as they walked through the reception area. It was more or less an honor system. And Sasha and Naya intended to exploit it.

They entered Noah's attorney number and the name of his boat, *"Res Ipsa Loquitur."* Latin for "the thing speaks for itself." Then they searched until they found a recent TRO filed in the jurisdiction.

Sasha copied it, changed the caption, customized the facts, updated the law, and drafted the affidavit. She printed and then closed the document without saving it, but she didn't kid herself. Someone who knew where to look would find a trail that led right back to her.

She read it over. It was solid. Much better than what Cook would be expecting from Mickey's shop. It hit all the elements.

To obtain a temporary restraining order, a movant must show four things: One, he is likely to win on the merits of the underlying argument. Two, he will suffer an irreparable harm if the TRO is not granted. Three, it will be less harmful to the defendant if the court issues the TRO than it will be to the plaintiff if the court doesn't issue the TRO. Four, any public interest weighs in favor of issuing the TRO.

Sasha tried to think of a harm more irreparable than death. She couldn't.

She had Naya review the facts. They had to give Cook enough to hang his hat on but not so much that it would be obvious Mickey had access to Hemisphere Air's privileged information.

Naya agreed they'd walked the line safely.

"I think we're done," Sasha said. And it wasn't even nine o'clock yet.

She left a voicemail for Lettie, asking her to check first thing in the morning with the mailroom, UPS, and FedEx to try to track down a package from either a Tim Warner or Patriotech that should have been delivered to her attention but hadn't.

"Let's call a messenger and put this to bed," she said to Naya, slipping the emergency motion into a manila folder. She slid the folder into Mickey's well-worn bag and fastened the buckle.

"I'll deliver it, Mac." Naya's eyes were tired but her mouth was set. "Carl's picking me up. He can run me over to Fox Chapel. It's just across the bridge."

Faithful Carl. He'd been Naya's next door neighbor for years and had been open about his attraction to her. Naya'd been equally open that she didn't have the same feelings for him, but Carl was undeterred. He'd do anything Naya asked of him. To her credit, Naya didn't abuse his infatuation. She did accept his help when he offered it. She seemed to consider him a friend.

Sasha was glad Naya wouldn't be going home alone. She couldn't see how Naya would be a target, but then she never would have expected to be attacked in the stairwell of the federal courthouse at eleven o'clock in the morning, either.

"Okay," she said, "that'd be great. Tell Carl I'll reimburse his mileage."

Naya waved the offer away with a hand.

"And thank you for your help tonight. I promise if this goes south I'll keep your name out of it."

"I know you will, Mac. That's why I stayed. Do me a favor and be careful."

"I'll be fine."

"Where's your car?"

"Connelly left it on four."

Naya frowned.

The fourth level of the garage was shadowy, and the elevator bay was obscured by a wide column. She never parked on four if she could avoid it. No one did. Which was why there was a spot available when Connelly returned her car to her at lunchtime.

"Naya, I'll be fine."

"I hate that elevator. That blind spot freaks me out."

"I'll take the stairs. I'll be *fine*. Now, go. Carl's

probably waiting in the fire lane and you need to deliver that bag and get home to your mom."

Naya came around the desk and surprised Sasha with a quick, light hug. "Good night, Mac. You take care and don't stay too late."

"Good night."

Naya hung Mickey Collin's bag across her chest diagonally and left.

Sasha watched her go. She would wade through her e-mails then cut out. Another thirty minutes, tops. Then she'd pick up some takeout and meet Connelly to plan for tomorrow.

Connelly. Funny how he'd become a fixture so quickly. An annoying fixture, to be sure. But, still. She called up his cell phone number. Four rings. No answer.

"Connelly, it's me. It's quarter to nine. I should be home before ten. I'll bring Thai food. Let me know what you like."

She dropped her phone into her bag and it thudded against Connelly's enormous gun. Just having the gun in her purse made her feel queasy with responsibility.

She stared at the computer screen. Her inbox was devoted to Noah's death; e-mails provided information about the arrangements, expressed sympathy, and discussed the transition of his various matters.

An image of Laura Peterson, alone and grieving, flashed in her mind, and, on an impulse, she dialed the Petersons' home number.

Laura answered on the third ring. "Peterson residence." Her voice was strained, but still elegant.

"Laura, it's Sasha McCandless."

"Sasha."

"I am so sorry about Noah, Laura. I just wanted to call and see if you need anything. Is there anything I can do?"

"That's very kind of you, Sasha. I have a friend coming over to stay with me. I'll be fine."

Laura sounded drained.

"Okay, well, please. If you think of anything . . .," Sasha trailed off.

"Thank you." Laura paused, and then she said, "Sasha, I hope you know what high regard Noah held you in. He respected you very much as a lawyer and liked you a great deal as a person."

Sasha's eyes filled. She blinked back the warm tears, afraid if she started crying, she might not stop.

"That means a lot to me, because I felt the same way about him."

Sasha decided to tell her, not about her belief that Noah had been murdered—she couldn't do that until she had some answers—but about the trip to France.

"I don't know if Noah got a chance to tell you

before ... before he died, but he was planning to take a sabbatical and take you to the French countryside for a year."

Sasha hoped she'd made the right decision. Laura wasn't saying anything.

"Laura?"

"Are you sure about that, Sasha?" Laura's voice was soft.

"Yes. We were having a dri. . . talk. He seemed distracted and I asked why. He definitely was planning to tell you the last time I saw him."

Laura's response came slowly. "But, why would he do that? Take a year off from the firm?"

Now it was Sasha's turn to hesitate. She'd started this. She had to be honest; she just hoped the truth wouldn't cause Noah's widow more pain. "He was afraid you were going to leave him."

Sasha heard Laura's sharp intake of breath. "He was right."

"Pardon me?" Sasha must have misheard.

"I was going to leave him. After all, he left me years ago. For the firm."

The two women sat in mutual silence. Sasha didn't know what Laura was thinking. Sasha was thinking she was glad Noah had died not knowing.

32

Sasha pushed all thoughts of the Petersons' marriage and the day's events from her mind. She gathered her things —wallet, keys, a slim file related to the emergency temporary restraining order—and slipped them into her bag. She hesitated, then pulled Connelly's gun from the bottom of the bag and put it within easy reach on the top of the pile. She closed her bag and turned out the office light.

She walked a loop around the floor, hoping to run into someone else getting ready to leave, but the rooms were dark. Only the hall lights were lit, and those would switch to motion detection status at eleven o'clock.

She imagined most people in the litigation

group had taken Noah's death hard and had gone home early to be with their families.

She took out her car keys and pressed the button to pop the ignition key out from the casing. She held them in her fist, pointed out. Ready to be jammed into an eyeball or nostril, if need be.

Sasha had made the mistake of inattentiveness once. She did not intend to make it again. She walked down the internal staircase. Her heart clamored. She was afraid she might not hear footsteps over it, the noise was so loud.

Get it together, she told herself. She could have taken the elevator, but she needed to prove to herself that she was not cowed.

She quickened her pace and burst out into the lobby, her pulse like a trapped bird.

As she past the security station, the dozing guard stirred. "Ms. McCandless, want an escort to your car?"

The guards were required to offer an escort to every woman leaving after eight p.m. It was building policy. In six years, Sasha had never taken a guard up on it.

She slowed and considered it. Certain of her answer, he was already back to sleep.

She shook her head. She just needed to focus.

She walked across the lobby to the entrance to the attached garage. She eyed the door to the stairwell, then the elevator bay. No way out, she thought. Being trapped in an elevator with an assailant was worse, way worse, than being ambushed on the stairs. Plus there was that column. If she emerged from the elevator on the fourth level, she was a sitting duck until she got past that damn column.

She pushed open the door to the stairwell and started to trot up the stairs. As the door closed behind her, she bumped her purse against her side to feel the comforting thump of the gun against her thigh. The exposed light bulb hanging over each landing provided the only light, and the concrete walls magnified the sounds of her footsteps. Her heart was banging in her chest now. She went faster. Like she was running the steps on the South Side Slopes.

She stopped at the fourth floor landing to gather herself before she pushed open the door. Connelly had just said he'd parked on four. She wasn't sure exactly where her car would be. It wouldn't be hard to find, given the late hour. But, she didn't want to spend any more time wandering around the garage than was absolutely necessary.

She pushed the door open hard. It banged against the cinderblock wall with a crack that echoed in the still garage. She rushed through and hit the lock button twice. Unlock, lock.

Listened for the chirp, chirp of her car and walked with purpose in that direction.

Connelly had parked against the wall, two in from the corner. Hers was the only car in the row, and the shadows from the corner fell over the space.

Just keep moving.

She reached the car. Looked behind her. No one. Crouched and peered under the car, with the keys ready in her outstretched hand. No one. Stood and hit the button to unlock the door. Peered into the back seat when the dome light came on. No one.

Sasha pulled the door open, hurried into the car, and pressed the button to lock the doors. Put on her seatbelt and started the engine. Her hands shook. She turned the radio on. Loud, to drown out her thoughts. Connelly must have messed with her stations. Classic rock blared out. Songs from before she was born. She didn't care.

She threw the car in reverse and sped for the ramp. She laid her purse on the passenger seat beside her—open, so she could grab the gun if she needed it.

33

Leo came to. The back of his head throbbed. He sat up to rub it and whacked his forehead against something hard.

He was someplace quiet, dark, and small.

He touched the surface beneath him. Thin, rough carpet. Raised his arms bit by bit until they hit metal. Spread them wide, trying to get a sense of the contours of the area. Slightly curved, smooth.

He shook his head, tried to summon his memory through the dull pain permeating across his skull. Panic was not an option. Survival followed calm thinking. *Think.*

He'd walked Sasha and Naya to the building, given Sasha his gun, and was about to punch out the side window of the thugs' car when something or someone hit him from behind.

The car.

His eyes began to adjust to the blackness. He could make out the luminescent paint on an emergency trunk release, added to newer cars by manufacturers who didn't want to be sued when some kid crawled into dad's trunk during a game of hide and seek and couldn't get out. He was in the trunk of a moving car.

And Sasha had his gun. He inventoried his pockets. Cell phone and wallet were gone. He had his keys and Sasha's spare condo key. Nothing else.

He needed a weapon. He searched every inch of the space with his hands. He didn't know how much time he had. He wanted to hurry, but he forced himself to making slow, small passes so he wouldn't miss anything. The trunk was empty.

The car careened around a bend, throwing him sideways. He braced himself against the bottom of the trunk and his hand scraped against the fastener on the cover to the spare tire well.

He rolled onto his stomach and folded his legs as best he could into the space behind him, his feet touching the outer wall of the trunk on the driver's side. He propped himself up on his elbows, braced his feet against the trunk, and scrabbled at the fastener with both hands. He pried the cover open, steeled himself against disappointment, and tossed the cover to the side.

He ran his hands over the rubber of the donut and down into the center. Wedged inside the spare was the thin, metal rod he'd hoped to find. He traced it with his hands to its hooked end. Relief flooded his body in a wave as he popped the tire iron free. He hefted it once, twice, and then set it down to continue his inspection.

In the back right corner of the well, Leo felt a hard plastic rectangular object. It had a handle. Toolbox, maybe?

He hoped so. There were plenty of serviceable weapons in the average tool box. He could do a lot of damage with a hammer or a wrench—even a screwdriver. He swung the box out and up. Placed it next to the tire iron.

The car was slowing. A series of thumps jostled Leo. Up. Then down. Speed bumps. They were in a parking lot.

He fumbled with the clasp to the box. Flipped the top open. It wasn't a tool box; it was a roadside emergency kit. He pulled out a set of jumper cables, three flares, a plastic rain poncho, and a reasonably heavy flashlight. He shoved everything except the flashlight back into the box and returned it to the well.

As the car came to a stop, he turned onto his

side, held the tire iron in one hand and the flashlight in the other. The driver killed the engine. Leo tensed, ready to spring, and waited for the trunk to open. Minutes passed. No car door slammed. The trunk did not open.

Leo waited some more. Still nothing. He listened to his own breathing over the tick of the engine contracting and cooling down, but he heard no other sound. What was the driver doing?

GREGOR WAS SITTING in the driver's seat, grasping the steering wheel as if he could wring an answer out of it. He was trying to decide what to do next.

Before he'd run into the big Asian trying to break into his car, Gregor's plan had been a simple one: drive to the lawyer bitch's condo building and watch the building until she got home. Get the files from her. Go back to that hotel near the courthouse, where he'd had no choice but to stash Anton. Get Anton in the car and drive straight to Baltimore, where Gregor knew a doctor who liked to play the horses. There would be no hospital, no questions, and no charge for Anton's care—the doctor was still working off his monumentally bad showing during the previous spring's Preakness.

Then he'd planned to deliver the files to Irwin and collect his fee. Gregor figured he'd add a surcharge to Irwin's bill. Anton wouldn't be ready to work again for a while and that would cut into Gregor's earnings.

But, now, Gregor's plans were complicated by the guy in his trunk. As he worked through his options, his cell phone rang. He checked the display: Anton.

"Is everything okay?"

Gregor's sister—Anton's mother—was meaner than hell. When Anton was a kid, he'd gotten in trouble over some nonsense and Petra had stormed down to the elementary school with a baseball bat. She had smashed in a row of metal lockers on her way to the assistant principal's office. She was not going to be happy when she saw her son with his jaw wired shut.

Anton mumbled something slow and indistinct.

Gregor thought he was saying the pain medication was wearing off and he was hungry. The only liquid medication Gregor had been able to find in the hotel gift shop had been a small bottle of children's Tylenol. He'd given Anton the entire bottle, hoping it would provide at least a few hours of relief.

"Okay, Anton. I'm at the lawyer's place now. After I take care of her, I'll stop at the liquor store. Whiskey will probably work better to take the edge off anyway. And I'll get you some...applesauce."

He'd been about to say baby food but caught himself. Anton was humiliated enough by having his ass kicked by the girl.

Anton mumbled again, registering his displeasure.

"Just hang in there. It shouldn't be long."

Gregor hung up. He had no basis for saying that. Who knew how long he'd have to wait for the little bitch. Or if she'd even come home tonight.

He drummed on the steering wheel, thinking. Maybe he could make the guy in the trunk work to his advantage.

And he could tell Irwin he'd had to pay the guy. Run up the bill even higher.

Gregor's neighbor was a contractor and he'd told Gregor that most of his clients pissed and moaned about cost overruns, but they paid them nonetheless. Gregor had begun finding creative ways to add charges with his own customers, and they, too, just dug deeper into their wallets.

Gregor stepped out of the car and into the parking lot. He went around to the trunk and stood back about a foot and a half. Popped the trunk with the button on the key fob and waited.

As the trunk lifted up in a slow smooth

motion, the guy sprang up and shined a flashlight right in Gregor's face. He blinked and took a step back.

The guy climbed out and advanced toward him. Gregor saw the tire iron in his raised right hand. This guy was resourceful. Good.

"Wait, wait!" he said in a hurry. "I'm not going to hurt you. I have a business proposition for you."

The guy stopped but didn't lower the tire iron. "I'm listening."

"I don't know who you really are, because you sure as shit aren't Leonard Connelly, U.S. air marshal. But, I'm gonna assume you were trying to break into my ride 'cause you need some fast money. Am I right?"

The guy shrugged. Smacked the tire iron against his hand but said nothing.

"So, here's the deal. My, uh, friend is hurt. I need to take him some food and medicine. While I'm gone, I need you to sit here and watch for someone to come home."

"Why?"

"Because I'm a private investigator. I just need to keep track of this woman. Nothing illegal and I'll pay you fifty bucks."

The guy looked like he was considering it.

"What makes you think I won't just take off after you leave?"

Gregor had already thought of that. "You're gonna give me your shoes. I've already got your wallet and cell phone. How far do you think you're gonna get?"

The guy nodded. Then he said, "Who's the woman?" He lowered the tire iron.

Now they just looked like two guys in suits having a conversation in a parking lot. Not that anyone was around to see, but Gregor maintained it was always better not to make a spectacle.

"Some lawyer cu--chick. You can't miss her. She drives a dark gray Passat and she's maybe five feet tall. Can't be but a hundred pounds, if that. Dark hair, green eyes."

"So, what do I do when I see her? If you've got my cell phone, I can't call you."

The guy had a point. "Just watch her. Make sure she goes into the building. I won't be gone long."

"Well, what if she comes back and then leaves again?"

This guy sure had a lot of questions.

Gregor snapped at him. "Then just tell me which way she went. We're wasting time here, *Leonard*. Do you want fifty bucks or not?"

"Yeah, sure. Sure. I just thought maybe if she came home and then made to leave again, I could approach her. Say I had a fight with my girl or something and she tossed me out, no shoes, no nothing. See if I can stall her. That's all." The guy shrugged.

Gregor considered the idea and decided it wasn't half bad.

"Okay, you do that. But, listen, don't try to grab her or restrain her, okay? She's, uh, dangerous."

The guy shot him a look, like how dangerous could a five-foot tall, not-quite-a-hundred-pound chick possibly be?

Gregor ignored the look. He'd warned the guy. "Okay, let's have your shoes."

The guy bent down to untie them, keeping his eyes on Gregor the whole time. Handed over a pair of wingtips. The leather was buffed to a high shine and it was soft. These were expensive shoes, well maintained. Gregor took a closer look at the guy. "And the flashlight and tire iron."

The guy stared at him for a long time first, but he picked both up from the ground and held them out for Gregor.

"I'll be back in a half hour or so. You'd better be here."

"Make sure you bring my fifty," the guy said as Gregor climbed into his car.

34

Sasha remained spooked for the entire drive home. She called ahead to Thai Place Shadyside and ordered the takeout. Connelly hadn't returned her call, so he'd have to live with what she got him.

At the restaurant, she parked directly under a street light to run in and get the bag of food. She repeated her check under the car and in the back seat when she returned. But, she couldn't shake the feeling—irrational, she knew—that someone was in the car.

Her fear was morphing into anger, though. That was progress. She kept her eyes on her rearview mirror as she fished her cell phone out of the center console. She hit a programmed number and her Krav Maga instructor's name flashed on the screen as his number rang.

"Daniel, hi. It's Sasha McCandless."

She glanced over her shoulder at the floor of the rear seat. *There's no one there*, she told herself.

"Sasha, we missed you this morning."

"I was driving back from D.C. I don't think I'm going to make it to class tomorrow either."

"Oh?"

"There's a lot going on at work. But, listen, Daniel, I need to ask you a favor."

"Anything," he said without taking a beat, as she knew he would.

"I need a field trip tomorrow morning. I want someone to try to take me down during my run."

Some of the advanced practitioners had agreed to participate in sneak attacks outside of class, as a way to keep their skills honed. It wasn't a true ambush, because the victim had to arrange it to some degree, but it was a very different experience from fighting in the studio.

Sasha had served as both an attacker and a target in the past, but it had been over a year. She needed to re-center herself now.

Daniel said, "Sure. Let me check around and see who can do it. What's the set up? Rape? Mugging?"

"No, I want you to do it. And, Daniel, I want you to try to kill me."

"Sasha, is everything ok?"

"No. It's not. I'll be running the loop from my

condo to the Cathedral of Learning and back. I'm not running to work tomorrow."

"Okay. When will you be out the door?"

"Six a.m. sharp. I run a six-and-a-half-minute mile."

"See you in the morning."

"Thanks, Daniel."

She hung up as she pulled into the parking lot and eased the car into her assigned space. Finally, home.

She sat for a minute, slowed her heartbeat, and scanned the dark parking lot. She realized she didn't know what Connelly drove. She hoped he was already in her condo.

When she lifted the bag of Thai food from the floor on the passenger side, the pungent, spicy smell and the warmth coming through the plastic bag drove home how hungry she was. She checked that the gun was in easy reach, tossed her phone into her bag, and climbed out of the car.

The wind carried the faint howl of ambulance sirens from Fifth Avenue. Otherwise, the night was silent. As she strode toward the building entrance, she locked the car doors with her remote key and kept the key jammed between her fingers.

Krav Maga principles taught never to fully relax one's guard until one was in one's own home. And, even then, only if appropriate security measures were in place. She was almost there. Twenty more feet and she'd be in the entryway.

She stopped and placed the food on the ground while she used her house key to unlock the entrance door. Each resident's key was keyed to open the front door, as well as his or her own door. Through the glass, she could see that the reception/security desk was unattended. Again.

As she turned the key, someone reached out from the hedges that fronted the building and snagged her by the left elbow.

"Sasha!"

She spun to her left as she grabbed the gun from her bag. She held it on its side, wielding it like a brick, and swung at her assailant's head.

Connelly dropped her arm and ducked. "It's Leo!" he hissed from the bushes.

Sasha peered into the row of greenery. It was, indeed, Connelly. He was in a full crouch with his arms crossed over his head for protection. She squinted. He was also shoeless.

"Connelly, what the hell is wrong with you?! I could have shot you."

He stayed in the hedgerow and said, "Not the way you're holding that gun. Were you going to hit me with it?"

She nodded.

"Sasha, you *shoot* a gun."

"Let's talk about this inside. The food's going to get cold." She moved back to the door then looked at him again. "Did you lose my key? And your shoes?"

"We have a problem."

She turned to the hedges. "What now?"

He stepped forward; the light over the entryway cast a shadow across his face.

"I was checking out the bad guys' car in the lot and the one—Gregor, I guess—hit me from behind. I blacked out. Woke up in his trunk. No cell phone, no wallet. The car was moving. We ended up here. I think the other guy needed something. The one you hurt. So, Gregor took my shoes and left me here. He's paying me fifty dollars to be a lookout for you. He thinks my identification is fake, I guess."

Sasha stared at him while she processed his story. "He's coming back?"

"Yes. Any minute."

"How do you want to play it?" She forgot all about the bag of congealing food at her feet.

"First, give me the gun."

"Happy to."

She handed it to him, butt first, and he stuffed it into the waistband of his pants. Then he pulled his jacket—which looked like it had been rolled up in a ball—smooth over it.

"Let's go," she urged.

"No. If we want this guy, we're going to have to wait for him and take him out here."

She hesitated.

"Look, I get that your training emphasizes avoiding a conflict and using violence as a last resort. But this guy isn't going to stop until he has that file."

"I don't *have* the file."

"I know, Sasha, but he thinks you do. We need to face off with him and be done with it. Besides, he might have useful information."

They stared at each other.

Sasha shook her head. "Forget it. You can come in with me and we can eat or you can stay out here by yourself. Your choice."

Headlights washed over them as a car turned into the lot. It slowed over the speed bump, and the street light bounced off its silver paint.

"Too late."

The sound of Gregor's car door slamming shut and the electronic beep of the lock filled the night.

"No, it's not." Sasha turned back to the entryway door and put her key in the lock. Connelly grabbed her elbow again. Firmer this time.

"Connelly," she hissed, "I'll break your arm if you don't let go."

"Lady, please!" he said in a loud voice, "it was just an argument with my girl. I wanna get in and get my shoes. That's all." Then lower, "Just play along. Please."

The older guy, Gregor, was coming up the walk at a half trot.

"Listen," she said to Connelly, "I've never seen you around here before. I don't know what your scam is, but you need to let go of my arm this instant."

Connelly flashed her the smallest of smiles, as Gregor loomed over his shoulder.

"Thanks, pal. I'll take it from here. Scram." Gregor moved Connelly aside. Sasha could see the excitement in his eyes. He was looking forward to paying her back for his friend.

"Do not touch me," she said. "This is your only warning."

Gregor laughed, twisting his mouth into an ugly smile.

He grabbed Sasha by the shoulders, pushing her back against the door.

Connelly removed the Sig Sauer from his waistband and thumbed the safety off. He stepped up close behind Gregor and jammed it hard into the small of his back. With his free hand, he squeezed the scruff of Gregor's neck.

"You weren't going to stiff me my fifty dollars, were you?"

Gregor had tensed as soon as the pressure from the gun hit his back. Now he jerked his head around in an effort to see Connelly. As he did so, Sasha reached up to her left shoulder with her right hand and placed her hand on top of his.

She rotated her arm back and over the top of his hand, trapping it tight against her shoulder. Gregor turned back to her, fast, his eyes full of worry now.

Before he could move, she took a step backward and turned her body, so that she was standing perpendicular to him. She kept rotating her arm, until Gregor's wrist had turned all the way over. She flicked her eyes down to check his hand: his thumb was pointing straight down.

She tucked his hand under her armpit and snapped her arm straight down, bringing the entire weight of her body down on Gregor's wrist, forcing it to bend to the side. Gregor bent his knees, twisting in an effort to ease the pressure on his wrist.

"What are you doing? Is that a wrist lock?" Connelly asked.

"Yeah, I'm going to break his wrist. I'm pretty sure he's right-hand dominant."

They both spoke in a conversational tone, which seemed to concern Gregor more than his physical predicament. Sasha read in his eyes that he thought they were psychopaths.

She read in Connelly's voice that he questioned her use of the wrist lock. It was technically true that Krav Maga used the move principally to disarm weapons: the preferred method for a shoulder grab defense was a head butt. That seemed like overkill, though, when she had an armed federal agent for backup.

"For Chrissake, Sasha, I might have shot him by mistake with all that wriggling around. Let's get inside already. I'll take our friend here. You get that bag of food. I'm starving."

Connelly hauled Gregor to his feet, and Sasha picked up the bag and held the door open.

Gregor made a half-hearted attempt to wrest himself free as Connelly shoved him through the doorway and down the hall to the elevator.

They got lucky. An elevator was waiting in the lobby, its doors open. Sasha ran ahead, stepped inside, and held the door open button, while Connelly pushed Gregor into the elevator car.

Connelly had him stand facing the mirrored back wall of the elevator and kept the gun tight against him.

"Do you carry handcuffs or anything?" Sasha asked, as she pushed the button for her floor and the elevator started its rise.

Gregor's eyes widened in the mirror.

"I used to, when I was in field. I still have a set, of course, but they're in my car."

"Right, and you hitched a ride over here with old Gregor."

Connelly cracked a smile.

"Listen," Gregor said, making eye contact with Connelly in the mirror, "I wasn't going to hurt her. I just need some files that were stolen from my boss." His voice was strained.

"That's a lie," Connelly informed him. "You were going to hurt her. Or you were going to try, at least. I very much doubt you could take her down. But, let's be honest, you did kill Tim Warner. And Irwin can't be happy with you for failing to retrieve his files, so I don't think you were planning to use a real delicate touch."

Gregor blanched and his face registered his shock and panic that they knew about Warner and Irwin. His shoulders slumped forward.

"Are you going to kill me?"

"Only if I have to."

35

They hurried Gregor inside the loft. Connelly directed him to the seat by the window in Sasha's living room area, pointing to it with the gun. Gregor backed into the chair and sat, glaring up at them.

Sasha's skin crawled at the sight of one of the men who had killed Warner and attacked her sitting in the dark brown club chair where she liked to do her reading. She'd always thought that was just a saying, but her nerve endings were jumping. It felt like ants were racing up and down her arms.

"Do you have any electrical tape or wire? Something to restrain him?" Connelly asked, keeping his eyes on Gregor.

"No."

Then Sasha remembered the rock-climbing equipment. “Wait.”

She opened the closet in the foyer. On the floor behind a never-used picnic basket was a box labeled “Patrick’s gear.” She dragged it out to the foyer and dug through it. She tossed the harness, pulleys, and carabiners out onto the floor. From the yellow rope bag, she removed two lengths of rope, then she rifled through the box until she found the paracord, coiled up on the bottom.

Connelly and Gregor both watched her. Connelly, with open fascination; Gregor, with dread.

“Who’s Patrick?”

“He’s ... was my brother.” Sasha didn’t look up from the box. She put the ropes and paracord to the side and replaced the rest of the items she’d strewn on the floor. Closed the box and returned it to the closet.

“Was?”

She met Connelly’s eyes. “Later,” she said.

Or never, she thought. She was in no mood to pick open that wound.

She stood and walked over to Gregor. Laid the ropes and cords on the kitchen island and looked hard at Gregor.

“Empty your pockets. Do it slowly.”

He dug into the breast pocket of his jacket

and took out a cell phone and wallet. Looked up at Connelly. "These are his." His mouth was dry and it came out as a croak.

"Put them on the table to your left."

He did.

"Are you really an air marshal?" he asked Connelly, worried.

"I really am. You should be relieved, Gregor. We're not going to kill you. Well, I'm not. I guess I can't speak for her. But, me, I'm happy to let the prosecutors decide if you get the needle."

Gregor did not respond. He just kept removing things from his pockets. Another cell phone and wallet, car keys, and a hotel room card went in a pile on the table.

"No gun?" Connelly said.

Gregor was silent for a minute. Then he said, "It's in the car. Didn't think I'd need it with her." He tilted his chin toward Sasha.

"Do you have any weapons on you?"

Gregor nodded. "There's a knife strapped to my left ankle."

Sasha moved in to take the knife, and Connelly ordered Gregor to put his hands straight up while she did so. It was a curved, wicked-looking thing. A hunting knife.

Holding it by two fingers, she put the knife on the island and retrieved the ropes.

She hoped she'd remember how to tie the

knots. She hadn't climbed since college, before Patrick died. They'd started rock climbing together when she was home for the summer after her freshman year.

Climbing was the only common ground they shared. Patrick had been conservative and rigid. Sasha's college-aged liberalism and dabbling in veganism, environmentalism, and every other ism hadn't sat well with her older brother.

But, when they were out on a rock face, counting on one another in a very real sense, those differences had fallen away. They'd come back to their parents' home from a day spent in the wind and sunshine, laughing and joking.

Patrick had dubbed her the Spider Monkey, for the way she scrambled up the side of a mountain. The Christmas before he died, he had found a silver pendant in the shape of a monkey and put it in her stocking.

Sasha blinked away the memory and focused on the ropes.

"Put your arms behind the chair."

Gregor did as he was told, wrapping his arms around the back of the chair. His hands dangled in the approximate middle of the back of the chair.

Sasha moved behind the chair and used the paracord to fashion a Prusik knot around her finger. A Prusik was useful for climbing, because it was a friction knot: it could slide up and down a climbing rope, but when tension, like the weight of a climber, was applied to the knot it would tighten, grab the rope, and lock off. She figured it would be equally good for improvising a hand restraint if she pulled it tight. That was the plan at least.

She wrapped the loop of the paracord around her finger and then wound it again, taking it inside the previous first loop. She repeated the process. Once she had six loops in a loose knot, she slid her finger out.

She eyed the free ends of the cord and Gregor's hands. She had plenty of cord. She passed both ends of the cord through the Prusik knot from opposite ends and pulled them to form a restraint knot. Then she formed two loops and passed the ends through again to tie off the loops. She tightened the loops around Gregor's wrists. The Prusik was pulled taut, clamping down on the restraint knot. She tested it. It was tight.

Working quickly, she moved around to the front and used the nylon climbing ropes to each of his ankles to the feet of the chair with a tight half-bow knot.

"My shoulders are already hurting from this position. You know, with the broken ribs." He looked at her dolefully.

"You've *got* to be kidding. You don't really think I care, do you?"

"Ignore him," Connelly suggested from the kitchen area. "Let's heat this food up and eat." He had rested his gun by the sink and was banging around, taking out plates and opening containers. He put a plate in the microwave.

"Can we decide what to do with him first?"

"Why? He's not going anywhere. Aren't you hungry?"

She was. But, she'd planned on opening a Chilean red and having some wine with her mango curry. Maybe having a conversation with Connelly that didn't involve death. Unwinding after three truly hellish days. Now, instead, she was going to scarf down reheated food while keeping one eye on a man who wanted to kill her.

"Sure, fine."

They ate standing at the island.

She gulped down the mango curry, and Connelly shoveled the chicken prik king into his mouth as fast as he could. He paused between bites once to say how good it was. That was the extent of their dinner conversation.

Sasha poured them each a glass of water. She rinsed the empty plates and loaded them in the dishwasher. Start to finish, the meal took seven minutes.

"Sorry I ruined your date," Gregor said.

They both ignored the crack. Sasha slipped out of her high heels and stretched her feet.

Connelly bent his head toward hers, "I'm going to make some calls. Take the gun. Watch him. Shoot him if you need to."

He snagged his cell phone and wallet from the table beside Gregor. "You be good," he told their captive.

Then he went up the three stairs to her bedroom area. As long as he kept his voice low, Sasha knew they wouldn't be able to hear his conversation.

She picked up the gun and pulled a barstool over from the island, placed it directly in front of Gregor and aimed the gun around where his heart would be. Considered him. He looked tired. And old.

"Are you going to cooperate with the authorities?"

He tried to shrug, but the movement just increased the pressure on the knot at his wrists. He grimaced. "Why not? Irwin is nothing to me. Just a job. If I can cut a deal for me and Anton, sure."

He craned his neck as far forward as he could and said, "Warner was an accident. We didn't mean to kill him, and Irwin didn't care that we killed him. Now, *you*, he wants you dead."

Sasha didn't react.

"Let me ask you a question. What's in those files?" Gregor asked.

"I don't know. I never got them. Either you missed them when you tossed Warner's apartment or they're lost in the mail."

They looked at each other. It was Sasha's turn to shrug.

"Do you know who Irwin is working with?"

Gregor shook his head. "No. I know he has a partner here, but that's it. The partner had that other lawyer killed, far as I know."

Connelly came down the stairs, his cell phone jammed in his ear. He picked up the hotel key card from the table near Gregor and turned it over.

"It's The Doubletree," he said into the phone.

He looked at Gregor. "What's the room number?"

The Russian hesitated.

Connelly muted the phone. "Listen, you know you're going to play ball. I know you're going to play ball, so let's throw out the opening pitch, ok? What room is your partner in?"

"220." He looked down at his trussed legs then up at Connelly. "Can I at least call him? Let him know? He can't go anywhere. He's speed dial two on my phone."

Connelly ignored the question and wrapped

up his call. “Listen, you have what you need? Yeah. Outside the building in ten. Roger that.”

He disconnected from the call and stared at Gregor.

“No, you can’t call him.”

“He’s my sister’s kid.”

“I don’t give a shit. Do you seriously think I am going to let you warn him that the marshals are on their way? You think I’m taking responsibility for an ambush?”

Gregor looked at Sasha as he answered Connelly. “You don’t understand. He couldn’t ambush anybody. He’s in bad shape. Real bad.”

“The answer is no.”

Connelly turned to Sasha.

“I assume you want to keep your name out of this?”

“If at all possible.”

“The TOD—Tactical Operations Division of the Marshals’ Office—is going to handle this. Officially, they are working off a tip from a confidential informant about two men who killed a young man in Washington, D.C. Gregor and his friend will be charged with Warner’s murder. There will be no mention of the assault on you, and they won’t be charged for it. Is that okay?”

Sasha shrugged. “Sure, that’s fine. Aren’t the marshals going to have some questions about Anton’s injuries?”

Connelly turned to Gregor and said, "Anton sustained a broken jaw and shattered cheekbone during his struggle with Warner. Isn't that correct?"

Gregor would agree to anything at this point.

"Yeah, that's right. That kid had a lot of fight in him. But, I'm gonna need to pass a message to Anton so he goes along. Can I call him?"

Connelly shook his head. "Listen carefully. No. I'm sure a businessman like you has a criminal defense attorney on retainer."

Gregor cracked a smile. "Speed dial three."

"Tell the marshals you want your call and talk to your shyster. If he's representing your nephew, too, he can tell him."

Sasha looked out the window, scanning the parking lot below for headlights. It was dark.

Gregor's cell phone, still in Connelly's hand, gave a shrill ring. Connelly checked the name that flashed across the display.

"Client No. 1," he read from the screen. He looked at Gregor.

"I save speed dial one for my current most important client, always," Gregor said, proud of his client relations savvy. "That's Irwin."

"Talk to him," Connelly told Gregor, pressing the speakerphone button and picking up the call.

"Yes," Gregor said. It seemed to serve both as a greeting to Irwin and an agreement with

Connelly that he would play along. To be sure, Sasha waved the gun at him as a reminder.

"What's our status?"

Irwin's voice was hard and nasal.

"I'm in the lawyer's home now."

"Do you have my files, you ape?"

"I haven't had a chance to search the place yet."

Despite herself, Sasha was impressed. Gregor was doing what most witnesses couldn't seem to manage. He was answering the questions asked honestly but without helping the questioner. If only the clients she prepared for depositions could do it half as well.

"I want those files in my hands tomorrow morning. Do you hear me?"

"I hear you."

"Good. One change. I've left Potomac. I'm on my way to Pittsburgh now."

Connelly and Sasha exchanged a glance. Connelly motioned with his hand that Gregor should elicit more information from Irwin.

"Uh, where should I bring the file?"

"I'll call you in the morning with an address. In the meantime, don't call me for any reason. I have something important to attend to."

"I understand."

Connelly hung up the phone and dropped it

in his pocket. "You don't mind if I keep this for a few days, right?"

Gregor understood this wasn't really a question. "I don't mind," he said, eyes downcast.

Connelly eyed the restraints.

"You think we can get him out of the chair with his arms still tied up?"

Sasha tilted her head and looked around to the back of the chair. His arms weren't bound to the chair, just stretched across its back and trussed together.

"Sure. It's not going to feel good."

"Gregor doesn't mind," Connelly replied.

Gregor's face darkened, as if he'd reached his limit of cooperation, but he said nothing.

"Okay." Sasha handed the gun back to Connelly, glad to be rid of it, and picked up Gregor's hunting knife. She removed it from its sheath, knelt by Gregor's legs, and sliced through the lines tying his feet to the chair's legs.

The climbing ropes were thick and she expected to have to saw at them, but it was easy work. Sasha turned the knife in her hand. The blade was at least four inches long and sharp. She thought for a minute about what Gregor might have had planned for her. When she looked up, he smiled at her.

"Stand up," she said, ignoring the growing urge to crack a few more of his ribs.

Gregor tried to hoist himself to standing. He lifted his bottom off the chair about six inches and then collapsed back into it.

"I can't do it. I need my arms free."

"No chance," Sasha told him.

She moved around to the back of the chair. Shook her head.

"He's going to have to stand or we'll never get his arms over the back of the chair," she said to Connelly.

Connelly appraised Gregor and the chair for a long minute. Then he picked the club chair up and heaved it on to its side on the floor.

Gregor's legs were splayed out to either side of him. The weight from the chair put pressure on his injured ribs, and his face turned purple from the pain.

Connelly grabbed the bottom of the chair and pulled it toward him. The motion jolted Gregor, and he yelped. Once the chair had cleared Gregor, Connelly righted the chair and placed it back in the precise spot it had occupied by the window. He dusted it off, paying no attention to the man writhing on the floor at his feet.

"Well, that'll work, too." Sasha said.

She put the knife back into its leather sheath and handed it to Connelly, along with Gregor's wallet and car keys.

"Thanks. I'll be back as soon as I can. You're

going to have to stay put for the night. They'll send a unit for the Camry, but it'll be several hours before they complete all of their testing and move it."

"You're coming back here?"

"I think I should. We don't know if this partner of Irwin's is also after you or if you're the business Irwin has to attend to here."

It made sense. Sasha nodded.

"See you later."

Connelly picked Gregor up from the floor by the paracord, hauled him to his feet, and marched him to the door.

Sasha engaged the lock behind them and went in search of that bottle of wine.

36

She was asleep when Connelly let himself back into the apartment. From the bedroom just steps above the door, she heard him ease the lock into place. He was trying to be quiet. She rolled over and eyed the illuminated display on the alarm clock. *1:47.*

After she had finished reviewing the temporary restraining order papers, she'd made up the pullout bed in the living area. Around midnight, she'd gotten ready for bed. But even though she hadn't slept in forty-three hours, sleep was a long time coming. The two glasses of wine she'd drunk didn't quiet her mind as she'd hoped, and it had taken her an hour or so to fall asleep.

Connelly was walking up the steps to the loft. She heard the soft pat of socks on stairs.

He hesitated in the doorway.

She sat up. "Connelly?"

He whispered back. "I didn't mean to wake you."

"Is everything okay? Do you need something?" She reached over and flipped on the lamp on the bedside table. She strained to make out his face in the weak light but couldn't. She could see that he had changed into sweats and was carrying a small duffle bag.

He walked into the room and stood at the foot of the bed.

"Everything's fine. Gregor and Anton are both in custody; they're spilling every detail they can think of about Irwin. They gave us his address in Potomac and a team's been mobilized to search his home."

"Okay, good. I made up the guest bed. It's actually not terribly uncomfortable. For a pull out."

He cleared his throat. "Actually, I think it's better if I sleep right here."

Sasha was fully awake now.

"Connelly, I don't think . . ."

"Relax. I mean *right* here." Connelly unzippered his bag and took out his gun. Then he lay down on his back across the bottom of her bed, where a dog would sleep, and closed his eyes.

"Good night, Sasha."

She watched him. His eyes didn't open and

he didn't move. His ankles and feet dangled off the side of the bed. He also hadn't slept in almost two days, she thought.

She sighed.

"You can sleep in the bed like a normal person, Connelly. I trust you not to do anything inappropriate. We both know I can kick your ass if you do."

His eyes stayed closed but he let a smile play across his lips. "I'm fine here."

"Suit yourself."

She tossed a pillow down to the end of the bed and he crammed it under his head.

"Want a blanket?"

"Nope."

She reached over and snapped off the light.

"Good night, then."

Sasha closed her eyes and waited for sleep.

"Sasha?"

"What?"

"What happened to your brother?"

Sasha was silent.

"Are you awake?"

Sasha opened her eyes and stared at the ceiling. The street lights threw a scattered web of shadows across the left half of the room.

"Patrick was my oldest brother. He was married to a girl named Karyn. For his thirtieth birthday, he and some of his old college buddies went to Atlantic City for the weekend. The second night there, they came out of a casino at around four in the morning, looking for a place to get breakfast on the boardwalk. They ran into a group of teenagers, acting rowdy. Someone bumped someone and words were exchanged. Patrick's friend, Cole, thought one of the kids had a gun. So, Cole pulled *his* gun."

She closed her eyes again. "Cole'd been drinking—they all had—and he was waving the gun around. Patrick caught his arm, and Cole wheeled around. The gun discharged. Patrick was shot in the head. Close range. He was in a coma, he had brain swelling. My parents are devout Catholics, so he was like that for months. Not dead, not alive. He never woke up, was never responsive. One night, he just stroked out. And that was the end."

Connelly was quiet for a long time. She wondered if he'd fallen asleep.

Then, from the end of the bed, he asked, so softly she had to strain to hear him, "The kid didn't have a gun, did he?"

"It was a cell phone."

Silent tears streamed down Sasha's cheeks. Twelve years later, her memories of rock climbing with Patrick were beginning to fade, but the night he died was as fresh as ever. She took a series of ragged breaths.

"I'm so sorry, Sasha. Try to get some sleep. We need to be ready for tomorrow."

"I know."

The room was quiet. After a while, she heard Connelly's breathing turn rhythmic.

She turned toward the window and stared out, seeing nothing. Her eyes burned with fatigue and tears. She slept fitfully until the dark sky turned gray and the first pink streaks of light filtered through the blinds.

5:45 a.m.

The smell of strong coffee filled the room. She eased herself out of the bed, careful not to wake Connelly, and went through the steps of her morning routine like a robot.

She was tying the laces on her running shoes when Connelly padded down the stairs. A red crease from the pillow crossed his cheek. He headed straight for the coffee.

"Morning."

"Good morning. I'm going for a short run. I'll be back in 20."

Connelly frowned. "Not alone."

"Yes, alone. I called my Krav Maga instructor. He's going to jump me at some point along the way. I need a refresher. And, I don't need any help."

Connelly put his mug down.

"Sasha, you can't . . ."

"I *need* to, okay, Connelly? I need to clear my head, I need to feel competent and secure before I walk into court today and I can't do that with a bodyguard."

She fixed her tired eyes on his, unblinking.

Connelly looked away first. He shook his head but picked up his cup of coffee and drank from it. He wouldn't argue with her.

She held her cell phone out for him to take. "In case Naya or Mickey calls."

"At six in the morning?"

"Just in case."

He reached for the phone and, as he did, he clasped a hand around her wrist lightly.

"Are you sure about this?" he asked with worry in his eyes.

"I'm sure."

"Okay." He released her hand.

She headed for the door.

"Have a nice run," he said to her back as the door closed behind her.

37

A fine, icy rain greeted Sasha when she hit the sidewalk outside her building. She turned up her jacket collar and started to jog. She blocked out the wet and the cold and settled into a stride, taking care to dodge the piles of slick leaves that dotted the sidewalk under the old maple trees.

She tried to focus only on the brisk air filling her lungs and the rhythm of her feet pounding on the pavement, but her attention was split between being present in her environment and trying to predict where Daniel would lie in wait for her.

If she were doing the takedown, she'd get in position behind the shrubs where Connelly had hidden the night before and ambush her as she returned to the building at the end of her run.

That location held two advantages. One, she'd be at her most tired as she finished out the run; she'd be looking to cool down and stretch. Two, it was human nature to let one's guard down close to home. Daniel wouldn't really count on that second factor. A large part of her training was intended to prevent her from doing just that. Still, the hedgerow was the logical place to hide.

She quickened her pace as the rain began to fall harder.

What had been a cold mist turned to a steady drizzle that bounced off her head and ran into her eyes.

She turned the corner at the private elementary school that sat across from her building. As she passed by the wooden fun fort at the school playground, she wiped the water from her brow. With her arm raised to dry her eyes, her vision was obscured for a moment.

She didn't see the man spring out at her from inside the fort.

He dove at her knees and tackled her from behind. She hit the ground hard.

Ground fighting.

In a street fight the most dangerous place to be is down on the ground. Krav Maga taught that you were to avoid ground fighting at all costs. If an assailant did manage to get you down, the goal was to be back on your feet within the first five seconds.

She was annoyed with herself for being on the ground. Daniel would make a big deal of that fact in his critique after they sparred.

She was raising herself on her elbows, when Daniel flipped her from her stomach to her back.

She was face to face with a wiry white man. Taller than her, but not tall. He had shoulder-length, dirty blond hair. It was greasy and thinning and it hung in his face.

Not Daniel. A stranger.

"Where are the files?" He bared his teeth.

He lifted her shoulders off the ground and tried to shake the answer out of her.

She raised her head and cranked her neck to the side. Bit down hard into the tender flesh between his thumb and first finger. Kept biting until she tasted blood.

He yelped and dropped her shoulders. Then he pulled back and punched her, connected solidly with her mouth. Her lip split open where Anton had hit her the day before and blood dripped into her mouth.

The guy smiled at her, showing her the space where he was missing a tooth, and raised his fist again.

She was faster. She wrapped her right arm around his neck; then she clasped her hands and gripped her left hand as hard as she could, palms to her chest. She pulled up on his neck. His head was inclined toward her like she was about to whisper in his ear. She could smell doughnut frosting on his breath.

She tightened her grip. She could focus the pressure on either his windpipe or his carotid arteries. An air choke would cause more pain, but she settled on a blood choke—mainly because it was faster to cause unconsciousness by compressing the arteries than by compressing the airway. She pressed against the arteries in the back of his neck with her forearm, squeezing her hands together like she was wringing out a wet towel.

His marble eyes bugged out and he dug at her fingers with both hands, trying to pry them open. She held tight and waited for the blood to stop flowing to his brain. Saw the telltale flush cross his face and, less than a second later, he was unconscious.

She dropped him and scrambled to her feet. She sprinted to her building and up the stairs to get Connelly.

When they came back outside minutes later Daniel had arrived to set up in the bushes, just as Sasha had expected.

The three of them fanned out and combed the neighborhood for the guy who had attacked her, but he was long gone.

Sasha wasn't surprised. She'd held the choke a little longer than strictly necessary in hopes the guy would stay out longer, but even so, he would have regained consciousness within a minute or two. He was probably disoriented but otherwise unharmed.

They returned to her condo.

Connelly and Daniel, who had sized each other up and seemed to find one another sufficient, sat at the kitchen island, drinking coffee. Connelly filled in Daniel on those details he felt could be made public.

For the second time in as many days, Sasha assessed the damage to her face. It wasn't pretty. Between her old bruises and the new swelling, she looked like she belonged on a poster at a women's shelter. Repair work was beyond her level of expertise.

She took a quick shower, as hot as she could stand, then pulled on a pair of sweats and hurried across the hall to her neighbor's condo, hoping she'd catch Maisy before she fell asleep.

She rapped on the door and heard Maisy's Georgia accent floating through her loft.

"Comin'!"

It always amazed Sasha that Maisy showed

no trace of her accent when she was on television, but, at home, it was as thick as honey.

The door opened and WPXI's early news weathergirl smiled broadly at her. "Hi, sugar!"

The smile faded as Maisy took in Sasha's face. She pulled her into the loft by her arm and shut the door.

"What on earth happened to you, darlin'?"

"It's a really long story and I need to be in court this morning. Can you help me?"

Maisy blinked at her, her violet eyes worked to process this request. "Help ya'?"

"Maybe with some makeup? I mean, do you think you could cover the bruises?"

Maisy appraised her. She took Sasha's chin in her hand and turned Sasha's face to the left, to the right, then back. She pursed her lips.

Finally, she said, "Yup, I do believe I can."

Twenty minutes later, Sasha emerged from Maisy's brightly lit bathroom without a visible trace of her injuries but with a slight headache from the avalanche of chatter that had accompanied the makeup application.

Maisy had performed magic. Sasha was a little disconcerted by the amount of makeup piled on her face. She didn't look like herself. But she did look perfectly presentable. Better than presentable, actually.

Maisy walked her to the door.

"I can't thank you enough. I owe you one, Maisy," Sasha said, as her neighbor leaned in for an air kiss.

"My pleasure, sweet girl. You just remember, drink through a straw, 'cause if that lipstick wears off, your big ole ugly fat lip's gonna ruin the whole effect."

Sasha returned to her place to find Daniel gone and Connelly showered and dressed in a charcoal suit, white shirt, and burgundy tie with a subtle square pattern. He was buffing his dress shoes.

He arched an eyebrow at her makeup mask. "Not bad," he told her.

She ignored the comment.

"Any calls?"

"Mickey called. He said you write like an angel."

Sasha smiled, but the movement hurt her entire face. She went into her bedroom and changed into her favorite suit. A superstitious person would call it her lucky suit. She'd never lost anything—not a motion, an argument, a hearing, or a trial—while wearing the suit.

Of course, today, losing was winning. She shook her head at how upside-down her life had turned in just four days. She stepped into the pale pink tweed dress and put on the matching jacket.

It was just after seven o'clock.

Connelly had planned to spend the morning with the Tactical Operations Division while she was in court. But, after the attack at the playground, he decided to play bodyguard instead.

Sasha was surprised to find she was not annoyed by his insistence on protecting her.

They locked up the loft and left. As they trotted to her car in the misty rain, Sasha was alert but relaxed. She didn't know if she should attribute that to Connelly's presence or her success in warding off her latest attacker.

As she started the car and turned on the heater, Connelly's stomach growled loud enough for her to hear. She twisted in her seat to look at him. He had slept four hours since Tuesday—sleep that had come while he was scrunched on the bottom of her bed—and had eaten next to nothing. Tired and hungry. Not exactly the qualities she was looking for in a bodyguard.

"You like pancakes?" she asked, as she pulled out of the parking space.

He said he did, so she headed for Pamela's Diner in the Strip, which opened at seven a.m. She preferred the Shadyside location, but it didn't open until eight.

She found a spot on Smallman Street, just

around the corner from the diner, and fed the meter. The rain had stopped or—more accurately—paused, judging by the dark clouds. They hurried from the car to the diner before the break in the rain ended.

Inside, it was done up in a retro style, lots of brushed aluminum and vintage posters. It wasn't crowded, but it wasn't empty either. They waited a few minutes before a hostess greeted them and led them to a small formica table.

They asked for a pot of coffee and handed back their menus, saying they wanted to order right away. Their friendly, tired-looking waitress obliged. Sasha ordered the Tex-Mex omelet. Connelly got the breakfast special: two eggs, bacon, and a short stack.

"Have you been here before?" Sasha asked after the waitress left to put in their order with the kitchen.

"No. They put me up at one of those long-term suites out by the airport. I haven't seen much of the city."

She'd forgotten he was just passing through.

"Where's home?"

"Nowhere. Everywhere."

The waitress returned with two mugs, a dish full of creamers, and a white carafe of coffee. They waved off the creamers.

Sasha took a drink of her coffee and waited for Connelly to decide how to tell his story.

"When my mother came back from Vietnam, pregnant and ashamed, her family was eager to welcome her back to the fold and help her raise her baby. Mom had other plans. She signed on with a visiting nurse service. From the time I was born, we moved around. Usually, she'd sign a three-month contract; every once in a while, she'd take a six-month assignment. She said three months was the right amount of time—long enough to get to know a place; not long enough to tire of it."

"What about school?"

"She homeschooled me. She viewed seeing the world as a large part of my education."

"The world?"

Connelly nodded. "Mostly, we were in the states—we spent time in every state except Montana and Louisiana. But, when a foreign posting came up, she always put in for it. We did stints in seven countries, and two U.S. territories."

"Was it hard, all that moving?"

"No, to tell the truth, I liked it. That's probably why I gravitated to the Air Marshal Service after college instead of some other part of the federal alphabet soup. I like to travel. Guess it's in my blood."

"Where's mom now?"

"Dead. Her ashes are scattered off the coast of Maui."

"Sorry."

"It's been a while. She was sick."

Sasha looked at Connelly and tried to imagine how his childhood had shaped him into the man sitting across from her. She decided he'd turned out just fine.

Then, as she watched, he removed the packets of sugar and various artificial sweeteners from the white cube that held them, sorted them by color,—white, brown, yellow, pink, blue—and replaced them in neat stacks. He moved on to the jelly packets. She amended her assessment. He'd turned out mostly fine.

Their food came out fast and hot. The waitress brought a small pitcher of warm maple syrup for Connelly and a bottle of hot sauce for Sasha.

They turned their attention to breakfast and ate in companionable silence. After all, not much of what they had to discuss made for pleasant conversation.

At one point, Connelly paused and pointed at her with a slice of bacon. "Who do you think sent the guy this morning? Irwin?"

"His partner, I hope. If it was Irwin, then he

probably knows Gregor and Anton are in custody. We lose our advantage."

They were both hoping Irwin would call Gregor's cell phone—now fully charged and in Connelly's left pocket.

38

Sewickley, Pennsylvania

Jerry Irwin woke up early on the best day of his life. He was unstoppable. By midnight tomorrow, the demonstration would be complete, the auction would be closed, and hundreds of millions—if not *billions*—of dollars would be flying through cyberspace, headed for his account in the Caymans. But that wasn't even the best part.

The best part was that he'd awoken in the arms of his girlfriend. A most amazing creature. She was soft and refined, loving and supportive. She'd been neglected too long, stashed away in this well-appointed prison, but he was going to change all that.

The double doors leading from the hallway

to the master bedroom swung open, and there she was. She shimmied through the door holding a silver tray that contained a mug of coffee for him and one of tea for herself, two croissants, and some jelly. Her blonde hair was tousled from sleep and she wore a gray cashmere robe over her silk nightgown. She smiled at him.

As she rested the tray on the bedside table, Laura said, "I'm afraid it's typical Pittsburgh weather today. Cold and rainy."

Jerry propped himself up on his elbows, leaned back against the pile of pillows arranged behind him, and patted the bed beside him.

"From what I can see, it's a beautiful day."

She gave him another smile. "I'm sorry we won't be able to spend the day together. I just have so much to do to get ready for the funeral service."

Jerry took her hand. "Stop. I'm here to support you through this, remember? Our new life starts next week, when you wrap up your affairs and hand off Noah's estate to the executor. Then, you'll join me at the villa and we'll put all this ugliness behind us. Okay?"

She turned her blue eyes to his, "Yes."

Jerry smiled back at her, relieved. He'd been worried Noah's death would change everything, make her reconsider her feelings for Jerry, but it hadn't. She'd told him she was sad Noah had died, of course; but, given his drinking problem, it wasn't entirely unexpected. She'd said, in some ways, his death made things easier for her. She wouldn't have to tell him about the affair or suffer the guilt of leaving him.

Laura's pragmatism and ability to adapt to the circumstances encouraged Jerry. The one small loose end in all of his plans was that Laura didn't know about the RAGS application. She believed he was selling his business at a huge profit and retiring. If he could get her out of the country quickly enough, that story would still hold together. If not, well, he just hoped she'd accept the truth.

"Are you going to go to the Cancer Center today?" she asked.

They had met through the Cancer Center. Vivian had used her connection with Laura, who was on the center's board of directors, to get him access to candidates to carry the phones on the planes. He needed men who were terminally ill and had financial worries. Vivian had told Laura that a fellow Carnegie Mellon alumnus wanted to set up a fund to help cancer patients with their expenses.

Laura had taken the prospective donor out for dinner. By the time they'd ordered coffee and dessert, she had a commitment from Jerry to seed the fund with a million dollars. They spent a lot of time together over the next months, setting up the fund and reviewing the applications for financial assistance.

His attraction had been immediate. Hers had grown over time. Her husband was always working and she was lonely. Jerry had been patient and attentive. And, look at him now.

She was waiting for him to answer.

"Oh, uh, no. I think I'll stay here and do some paperwork. If I want to run out for a bite, is there somewhere nearby?"

He didn't want to bring Gregor and that other goon into Laura's tasteful home. He'd meet them out somewhere to get the files.

She gave him the name of a bistro just a few minutes away. Then she went to take a shower.

Her smile over her shoulder as she walked to the bathroom was an invitation to join her in the oversized marble shower. As soon as he finished his breakfast, he intended to do just that.

His ringing cell phone killed his erection. It was the wrong phone. Not Gregor calling to say he had the files, but Vivian.

He kept an eye on the bathroom door as he answered it. He heard the water start to run.

"Good morning, Vivian," he answered as evenly as he could.

"Irwin, why is Sasha McCandless still alive?"

"I'm not sure she is. My guy was in her condo last night, searching for the files."

"Well *my* guy jumped her this morning, as she was going for a run. Unfortunately, she evaded him. Get those goddamn files, Irwin."

He sighed.

"I'm working on it. I'm sure I'll have them by noon." He lowered his voice, "Don't call me again, okay? I'm at Laura's."

Vivian laughed. It was an ugly sound, more like a bark. "Comforting the grieving widow, are you?"

The water stopped. "Jerry?" Laura called out from the bathroom, wondering when he was going to join her.

"Goodbye, Vivian."

Jerry stripped off his boxer shorts and headed into the bathroom.

39

The offices of Prescott & Talbott

There was an actual line outside Sasha's office door when she and Connelly arrived just before eight.

Naya, Parker, Joe, and—for reasons that escaped Sasha—Flora were leaning against the wall in that order.

"Should have installed a deli ticket machine," Naya cracked as she followed them into the office and shut the door behind her.

Sasha could hear the hushed conversation on the other side as the knot of people tried to figure out who Connelly was.

"What's up?"

Naya winked. "This fax came in for you this morning," she said in a too-loud voice. "Looks like Mickey Collins is going to file an emergency motion for a temporary restraining order to ground some of Hemisphere Air's planes."

She handed Sasha a faxed copy of the motion and brief she had written the night before.

"He *faxed* it?" Nobody faxed anything anymore. Everything was scanned and e-mailed as a PDF. Or, if it was really big, put up on an FTP site.

"I guess he wanted word to spread, right?"

"I guess. Okay. I'll take it from here. I don't want you to be involved if it blows up."

Connelly and Naya both winced at her choice of words.

"Sorry. You know what I mean."

"What *can* I do?"

"See what Parker and Joe need. Then, send an e-mail around to the whole team and tell them I have to be in court today, but they can see you if they have any problems or questions."

"I always get the crap assignment. You get to go argue against a motion that you wrote while I babysit."

"Want to trade?"

"Hell, no. Hey, I had the copy center scan those papers. There's a PDF in your e-mail, so you can forward it to Vivian."

"You're the best."

"I really am, aren't I?"

She walked out into the hall and told Parker and Joe to follow her to the workroom.

Flora grabbed the door before it closed all the way.

"Sasha?" she said from the hallway, poking just her head in, "Can I talk to you? It'll only take a minute."

"Come in. Where's Lettie?"

"Uh, she's here," Flora said, shuffling into the room with her eyes down and her hands behind her back. "But, she and I thought, um, I should talk to you about something."

Sasha noticed Flora had left the door ajar. Probably hoping that, with the door open, Sasha wouldn't yell at her about whatever inane secretarial dispute she was coming to complain about.

"Flora, I'm really busy. Is this important?"

It was out of character for Lettie to involve her in the territorial squabbles that arose from time to time amongst the support staff.

Flora wrinkled her brow, confused, and glanced over at Connelly, as if he could help her. "I don't know, I thought it was."

From behind her back, she produced a UPS letter envelope.

"What's that?"

The words poured out of Flora in a rush. "It's the

package you were waiting for yesterday. It must've come while I was at lunch or away from my desk helping someone. I didn't notice it until last night when I was leaving, and you were on the phone."

"You knew this was here last night and didn't tell me?"

Flora appeared to be on the verge of tears. "I'm really sorry."

She thrust the envelope at Sasha, eager to get rid of it.

Sasha was still for a minute, focusing on tamping down her temper. She took the package from Flora's outstretched hand and looked at her, considering her response.

Flora waited.

"Just get out," Sasha said in a soft voice.

Flora opened her mouth to speak.

"Out," she repeated. Louder this time.

Flora got the hint and scurried out the door.

Connelly shut the door and they both stared at the envelope in disbelief.

Sasha used her letter opener to slice the envelope open. On Tuesday, Warner had addressed it to her. Hours later, he was in a dumpster in an alley.

She turned it upside down over her desk and a thumb drive fell out. A handwritten note fluttered out after it. She scanned it. It said nothing of import, but Warner had had neat, even handwriting.

She looked at the clock. *8:10.*

She booted up her laptop and handed the thumb drive to Connelly. "Plug it in and just print everything out, we're going to have to take it with us."

"Can't Naya or one of the attorneys . . ."

Sasha shook her head. "I don't want anyone else to be implicated."

She took a breath and dialed Vivian's number. *Please let it go to voicemail.*

No such luck.

"Vivian Coulter."

Sasha guessed her assistant didn't start until nine.

"Good morning, Vivian. It's Sasha McCandless."

"Oh, hello, Sasha."

The voice on the other end of the phone was polite and calm, in stark contrast to the last conversation she'd had with her client. Sasha knew that would be short-lived.

"I'm calling because I just received an emergency motion from Mickey Collins. He's going to ask Judge Cook to grant a TRO grounding certain of Hemisphere Air's aircraft. Uh, all planes that have the same make and model as Flight 1667 and were put into service within a three-year period of Flight 1667."

That was the best she and Naya could do to include all four of the compromised planes without making it obvious. By their count, the order would affect eleven planes.

Silence.

Sasha plowed ahead. "I'll send you a PDF of the motion. I have to head over to the court right away, but I assume you want to fight this."

Vivian's response was quick.

"Yes, I want to fight it. Why wouldn't I?"

Sasha could hear suspicion in Vivian's voice. After all, just yesterday she'd suggested Hemisphere Air should ground some of its planes. She had to meet that head on.

"Of course, you would. Yesterday, as I am sure you recall, I raised the possibility that you might want to take similar action on your own accord, but this is an outrage. Any decision to keep planes on the ground is a business decision that should be made by the company."

"Do these papers mention the purported RAGS link?"

"No, they simply state that the cause of Monday's crash is unknown but believed to be mechanical in nature."

"Well, that seems like a rather speculative basis for grounding some percentage of our fleet." She pronounced rather the way the wealthy do. *Rah-ther*.

"It looks like eleven planes."

"Regardless, I expect you to shut this down."

"I understand. I have to tell you, though, that, speculative as the papers are, we're probably going to have an uphill battle getting Judge Cook to deny the order."

She figured she might as well try to manage her client's expectations given that she fully intended to lose.

She was about to hang up when Vivian added, "You do realize I fought to have you made the responsible attorney on this matter after Noah died?"

"I do. Thank you for the opportunity, Vivian."

"Don't thank me; prove me right. From everything I've heard, you're a younger version of me, a rising star. Act like it. I'll meet you at the courthouse."

Vivian hung up.

Sasha was left with two thoughts. One, she hadn't considered that Vivian might want to attend the argument. And, two, she wasn't like Vivian. Not at all. Or, at least, she hoped she wasn't.

"Did you print?" she asked Connelly.

"Yeah, it's not that much. Two hundred pages, maybe less. Where's the printer?"

"It's on our way out. We'll grab them and read them while we wait for the argument to start. We need to go now."

"Do you want to bring this?" Connelly gestured toward the thumb drive, still inserted in her laptop.

Sasha considered it.

"No, leave it there. Who's going to notice a thumb drive in a law firm?"

40

Sasha and Connelly huddled in the first row of the gallery in Judge Cook's courtroom, paging through the printout from Warner's thumb drive. Connelly had shown his identification to the security guards in the lobby, who called up the U.S. Marshals Service and confirmed that an air marshal could bring both cell phones and a gun into the courtroom.

They were skimming the pages, looking for whatever was in the files that had Irwin so hot to get them back. So far, it had all been pretty mundane. Calvaruso's job application, the consulting agreement, his benefits package. Sasha flipped the pages in frustration. Nothing worth killing Warner over.

"We must have missed something."

She stacked the papers into a pile and moved up to the counsel table to look over her notes until Mickey arrived.

He hustled in, tossed his briefcase on the table for plaintiff's counsel, and headed straight for her. He gave her a big smile, but she could see the strain wearing through it.

"You okay, Mickey?"

"Fine, fine." His eyes darted around the room and his movements were jerky and frenetic.

She narrowed her eyes. "Are you nervous?"

"What? Nervous? By lunchtime, I'm gonna be the guy who went up against Prescott & Talbott on a long-short TRO and won. I can probably cancel my Yellow Pages ad; I'm gonna be beating off clients with a stick." He grinned at her.

He was right, if everything went according to plan, he'd be the man of the hour and she'd be the associate in over her head who lost an important argument. *That* would do wonders for her partnership prospects, she thought. Strangely, that fact evoked no emotion in her. She simply did not care.

He was also lying. He was nervous, no doubt about it. It occurred to Sasha that Mickey probably hadn't spent much time in court in recent years. He found good, sympathetic plaintiffs, wrote decent papers (for a plaintiff's attorney), and then got defense counsel to the table to settle. She tried to remember the last case Mickey had actually taken to verdict. She drew a blank.

Mickey was out of practice and about to perpetrate a fraud on the court. Of course he was nervous.

The door leading from the judge's chambers opened, and Brett entered, followed by the court reporter, carrying her stenography machine.

Brett placed a stack of papers on the judge's bench, probably copies of the motion, and walked over to the counsel tables.

"Mickey, Ms. McCandless," he said. "I don't suppose you fine barristers have worked out an agreement that obviates the need for the judge to hear this motion?"

"I'm afraid not," Sasha said.

"I'd be afraid, too, if I were you," Brett told her. "The judge is not going to be happy to see your firm in his courtroom two days in a row; but he's really not going to be happy to see you. No offense, of course."

"None taken."

Sasha and Mickey were counting on Judge Cook reacting badly to her.

The deputy clerk fixed her with a look, but he didn't say anything further. Just turned on his heel and retreated to his desk.

Sasha walked over to the bar and beckoned

Connelly with a small wave. He came and stood at the rail, gripping the top with his good hand.

"What's wrong?" he asked, leaning in close so they could whisper.

"Mickey's a ball of nerves."

Connelly blinked. "Is he going to hold up?"

"I don't know. Look at him."

Their fierce whispers drew Mickey's attention and he waved a hello to Connelly, then pointed to himself, seeing if he should join them.

Connelly shook his head no, and Mickey went back to unpacking his trial bag. He dropped his pen and it clattered and rolled across the floor. He chased after it, cursing it aloud.

"He'll be fine once he gets going."

She hoped so.

"Listen," Connelly continued, "I'm going to check in with the Marshal's office. See if anything's going on with their case against Gregor. Will you be okay while I'm gone?"

Sasha looked over at the Special Deputy U.S. Marshal standing against the wall. He was watching Mickey chase his pen with a bemused half-smile.

"I doubt even Irwin is crazy enough to try something in open court with an armed federal agent present," she answered.

"Good point. I won't be long."

The court reporter looked up from her

machine. "Ms. McCandless, I'll just use your information from yesterday. Mr. Collins, do you have a card on you?"

He pulled one from his breast pocket and walked it over to her. Sasha noticed he remembered to skirt the well. Maybe Connelly was right. Once Mickey got going, he'd probably be fine.

She was about to find out. As Connelly walked out the doors in the back of the courtroom, Judge Cook walked in through his private entrance. He looked sour.

"All rise. The Honorable Cliff Cook presiding." Brett sounded like he would rather be anywhere else.

The judge reached his seat but did not sit. Instead, he locked his elbows, pushed his palms against the table in front of him, and glared down at Sasha and Mickey.

"Counselors. The Court is not pleased, not pleased at all, to see the two of you here on an emergency TRO."

He started with Mickey. "Mr. Collins, has Ms. McCandless had an opportunity to review your papers?"

"She has, Your Honor. And it is my understanding that she has read them very closely, perhaps even more closely than I have."

Sasha shot Mickey a look.

"Well, Mr. Collins, they *are* a notch above the usual slapdash job you foist upon the bench. Perhaps she found them a better read than expected."

The judge turned to Sasha. "Ms. McCandless, having read Mr. Collins' papers, are you prepared to tell me your client does not consent to the relief he's seeking?"

Sasha opened her mouth to answer.

Apparently, the question was rhetorical, because Judge Cook kept going. "Hemisphere Air is willing to risk the lives of, hundreds, thousands, who knows how many, Americans rather than ground a tiny percentage of its fleet to rule out a mechanical error that could have caused Monday's crash? Is that what you're saying, counselor?"

"Your Honor, if I may . . ."

"Answer my question. Yes or no."

"Hemisphere Air does not consent to grounding eleven planes with no known or suspected mechanical problems, Your Honor."

Judge Cook glared at her. She braced herself for his reaction, but his attention shifted to the back of the room. Sasha risked a peek over her shoulder, thinking Connelly hadn't been gone for very long. But, instead of Connelly making his way up the aisle, she saw Vivian Coulter slipping into the last row of seats.

She recognized Vivian from photographs she'd seen in the *Business Times* and on the *Post-Gazette* society page. Vivian was close to six feet tall, with a strong, square jaw and broad shoulders. She wore her light brown hair in layers to her shoulders. She reminded Sasha of Kathleen Turner. Old, depraved Kathleen Turner from *Californication*, not young, hot Kathleen Turner from *Body Heat*.

She just hoped Vivian didn't belong to Noah's country club. Sasha didn't mind arguing to an angry judge, but an apoplectic one would be distracting.

The judge returned his attention to the lawyers standing before him.

"I haven't got all day. Let's get started. Mr. Collins, I'd like you to focus on the irreparable harm requirement and its interplay with the public interest prong of the test."

He lowered himself into his chair and nodded at Mickey.

So far, so good. The judge had given Mickey the blueprint for his argument. All Mickey needed to do was follow it and he should win.

Sasha started to sit, too, but remembered the Simon Says rules from the previous day and straightened back up to standing.

The judge held up a hand to stop Mickey before he began. "Ms. McCandless, if you've finished your deep knee bends, kindly sit down. You're distracting the Court with your antics."

Warmth spread across Sasha's face and she sat. The deputy clerk flashed her a quick smile. He remembered, too.

"Your Honor," Mickey began, "the plaintiffs, on behalf of the putative class, seek an order grounding eleven planes until the cause of the crash can be determined or, at a minimum, testing confirms that these eleven planes are free of defect."

Mickey might not have been much of a writer, and his offices may have left something to be desired aesthetically, but he was a master storyteller. He settled into a rhythm right away, and his tone was grave and full of authority.

Sasha listened with one ear as she scanned the printouts from Warner. There had to be something incriminating in the papers. She just had to find it.

"The plaintiffs seek this extraordinary relief, not only to preserve evidence that could explain why their daughter and her fellow passengers died, but also to protect the interests of the flying public. At present, there is no explanation for Monday night's crash other than the plane stopped responding to the pilot's controls and *flew itself into a mountain.*

"Now, Ms. McCandless will argue this was a fluke, a one-off anomaly. Should travelers be required to take that on faith? If she's wrong and another plane crashes, well, the harm will be, not just irreparable, it will be inexcusable, because it is so avoidable. Right now, today, Hemisphere Air can decide to protect the public. The real question, Your Honor, is what is the harm to Hemisphere Air in doing the right thing?"

Sasha looked up. The judge was nodding along with Mickey, who was gesturing broadly as he moved through his points.

She went back to the papers in front of her. Behind Angelo Calvaruso's consulting agreement, there was an identical agreement between Patriotech and someone named Harold Jones. Whoever had created the document had copied it from Calvaruso's and neglected to change the footer, which still read "Calvaruso IC Agreement." Warner's key word search must have tagged it as a hit based on the footer.

Sasha felt a rush of adrenaline. She took the agreement from the stack and put it aside. Harold Jones. With any luck, she had just identified the second cancer patient.

"The relief requested by the plaintiffs is extremely narrow and minimally intrusive to Hemisphere Air's business," Mickey was saying.

"By taking just a small number of planes out of service, they could safeguard the lives of hundreds, if not thousands, of fliers, as well as countless other innocent citizens. Flight 1667 happened to crash into a mountain, but the next plane to crash could collide with another plane or fly right into a building, killing many more people than those onboard."

Mickey paused here to let an image of the September 11th destruction develop in the judge's head.

Sasha pulled a spreadsheet from the stack. It was a draft expense report for the current month, set out in tiny font. She held it up close to her face to read. The equipment category had two entries for smartphone. Each listed a ten-digit number that began with 301, the area code for Bethesda. Presumably, these were telephone numbers. One was labeled Calvaruso; the other one, Jones.

Sasha's heart quickened. She scanned the rest of the sheet. Under travel, there were a dozen or so entries, but two jumped out. The first had Monday's date and the notation *Calvaruso 1667*. The other read *Jones 1480* and had Friday's date. She circled it. Flight 1480 was Metz's redeye back from Washington State. There were two other notations that listed Jones and Calvaruso. Calvaruso's Pittsburgh to D.C. flight and a flight from Pittsburgh to Seattle for Jones on Tuesday morning.

Harold Jones, recently hired as an independent consultant and in possession of a smartphone issued by Patriotech, was currently in the Seattle area with a ticket to travel across the United States on a plane that had been retrofitted with a RAGS link.

Sasha stared at the expense sheet in her hand. The room got very small and her mouth went dry. This was it. She craned her neck to check the gallery. No Connelly.

"Ms. McCandless!" Judge Cook cut through her mounting excitement.

She sprang out of her chair. "Your Honor?"

"I am so terribly sorry to interrupt your daydreaming, counselor. Would you consider deigning to respond to the Court's question?"

"Of course. I apologize, Your Honor." She could feel Vivian's eyes boring into her back. She looked at Mickey in a silent plea for help.

He spoke slowly. "Your Honor, if I may. Before Ms. McCandless addresses the issue of how grounding such a small number of planes could be deemed disruptive to her client's business, I do want to add that, if you grant our order, and subsequent testing indicates the planes are not defective, we would be willing to take into consideration any costs related to the interruption to Hemisphere Air's business later on down the road, when we make a settlement demand in the class action. That's not in our papers, but it seems like a more than fair thing to do."

Sasha got her feet under her, thankful Mickey had hit his stride enough to repeat the judge's question for her benefit.

"Your Honor, while Mr. Collins' offer might seem more than fair to him, it is a complete nonstarter for my client. First, Hemisphere Air is confident that, should this case even proceed beyond the class certification stage, it will be thrown out on a motion to dismiss. Why, then, would Hemisphere Air incur a loss now in the hopes of offsetting it in a settlement that, frankly, is unlikely to ever come to pass?"

She paused to gather her thoughts and the judge jumped in. "You think I'll dismiss it? Why, do you have information that one of the pilots had a Primanti's sandwich before take off?"

He was smiling. Was she supposed to laugh? The court reporter stifled a giggle and Brett chuckled. Mickey, not in on the joke, looked baffled. She settled for a small smile.

Then she continued, "Second, the notion that there's anything wrong with any of Hemisphere Air's planes, including, I might add, the one that crashed three days ago, is pure speculation."

All traces of the judge's smile disappeared, as though it had never existed.

"I think we can go out on a limb and assume that there was something wrong with the downed plane," he said.

"Maybe so, maybe not, Your Honor. The circumstances surrounding Monday's tragedy will come out through discovery. In the meantime, the harm to Hemisphere Air's shareholders, who will lose value; employees, who will lose hours and corresponding pay; and travelers, who will be inconvenienced, are all real."

"Surely, you aren't equating the loss of value to *shareholders* with the loss of human life, Ms. McCandless? I thought even Prescott & Talbott lawyers would have some minimal humanity." Judge Cook's nostrils flared and he leaned back in his chair, recoiling like she was something fetid and unappealing.

"Of course not," Sasha said, moving in for the kill, while he was good and agitated.

"The irreparable harm will come from the public relations fallout that Hemisphere Air will sustain. Imagine the loss of trust the company will suffer when it suddenly takes some, but not all, planes out of service shortly after a fatal crash and then puts them back in service, saying there was never anything wrong with them in the first place, which is, after all, the likely outcome? Travelers will lose confidence in the safety of Hemisphere Air's fleet. Not to mention, they will be skittish about booking flights on Hemisphere Air. They'll worry that the company might pull more planes out of service, they won't want to take the risk of being stranded or delayed. It will be a *nightmare*. The damage to the company's image will be irreparable."

The judge stared at her. Then he said slowly, "The public relations hit to your client's reputation is an irreparable harm that outweighs the loss of human life? Is that your argument, Ms. McCandless?"

"No, Your Honor. The certain harm to Hemisphere Air outweighs the remote and theoretical loss of life. Any plane could crash. Why stop with eleven? Why not ground Hemisphere Air's entire fleet? Or, for that matter, why stop with Hemisphere Air? Why not ground all U.S. commercial flights until we know for sure what happened on Monday night?"

Sasha stood there for a minute, waiting to see if Judge Cook had any more questions. He did not. He just shook his head in a show of disgust.

Sasha felt disgusting. She had spun the argument out to its absurd conclusion. Aside from Mickey, everyone in the room probably thought she was the lowest form of scum. Except for

Vivian. Vivian probably thought she hadn't gone far enough in her defense of the company.

"I've heard enough. Mr. Collins, I am going to grant your motion. Ms. McCandless raised one good point—I'm certain it was quite by accident. Are you sure you want to limit it to the eleven planes you identified in your papers? Speak now or forever hold your peace."

Mickey continued to play the role of World's Most Reasonable Plaintiff's Attorney. "Yes, Your Honor. The plaintiffs believe the planes most likely to share any defect that might have existed on Flight 1667 are the eleven that we have identified on the basis of make, model, and time in service."

The judge leaned forward and pointed at Sasha. "In light of Ms. McCandless' cavalier attitude toward human life, I am going to provide a copy of this temporary order to the U.S. Marshals and ask them to ensure that the affected planes are grounded immediately. I would not normally involve the Marshals Service in a civil matter, but the callous disregard of Hemisphere Air's counsel causes me grave concern that this order will not be taken seriously absent law enforcement involvement."

He arched a brow and scrawled his name with a flourish across the proposed order that Sasha had drafted for Mickey to submit. He motioned for the deputy marshal against the wall to come up and take it.

"Have your office make copies of that, will you?" he said, as he handed it to the deputy. Without further comment, he stood and left the courtroom, trailed by Brett and the court reporter.

Having taken her scolding like a big girl, Sasha was packing up her briefcase and steeling herself to talk to her client, when Mickey walked over and stuck out his hand.

"Well done, counselor."

"You, too." She lowered her voice and said, "I won't forget this. Thank you, Mickey."

He held her elbow while he said, "Just make sure your air marshal friend nails Irwin's ass to the wall. Where is he, anyway?"

Good question, Sasha thought.

"He must have gotten held up in the U.S. Marshal's office."

"You okay facing the music alone?" He inclined his head in Vivian's direction.

She gave a slight shrug. "It can't be worse than what's going to happen when I get back to the office."

She slid the printouts from Patriotech into an unlabeled folder and buried it in the middle of the papers in her bag.

Mickey was still standing there, waiting for something.

"I'm sorry I suspected you were working with Irwin." That had probably stung.

He waved it off. "Forget it. Listen, no matter what happens with those soulless pricks at your shop, you're the real deal. What you did today, that was good."

He suddenly looked embarrassed, like he'd said too much. He clasped her on the shoulder and walked away, past Vivian, and out the door.

She appreciated what Mickey tried to do with his pep talk. She might have been on the side of the angels with this argument, even though her behavior was, without question, unethical, but Judge Cook had her number.

She was nothing but a corporate whore. If Mickey had filed a similar motion in the case, without the backdrop of the RAGS link and the murders, Sasha had no doubt she would have stood in this courtroom and made the same arguments she'd made today. The only difference was she would have meant them.

She pushed it out of her mind. She needed to find Connelly and pass along the information about Jones and the flight from Seattle. Then, she could ruminate on what was left of her career.

Sasha walked over to her client. Vivian had her cell phone jammed in her ear and was hissing at someone. Probably reporting back to the board. She clicked it shut without saying goodbye.

"Vivian," Sasha said, plastering on a smile and extending her hand, "it's nice to finally meet you. I wish the circumstances were different."

Vivian's eyes were gray and cold. They looked like the October sky. And, just like the sky, they held the promise of thunder.

"Sasha." She took Sasha's hand and arranged her mouth into a smile.

"So, not the outcome we were hoping for today. Cook was a bad draw."

Noah had told her to never apologize to a client for a bad outcome. You didn't want them to get the idea that it was your fault.

"Indeed." Vivian said.

"I assume you'll want to file an appeal if we can? I'll get an associate on it when I get back to the office, but the judge's order sounds interlocutory in nature, so we may not be able to appeal."

Final orders were appealable. Interlocutory, or non-final orders, were not. Typically a temporary restraining order was not considered final because it was, well, temporary. But, appellate lawyers rarely let a little detail like that get in the way of a good argument.

Vivian's answer surprised Sasha. "I'm not sure

we do. An appeal may just drag this out and, as you noted, it is a public relations disaster. It might be better to just ground the planes, do the testing, and move on. We'll need to make a formal recommendation to the board, of course. But, that's my current thinking. We can talk through the strategy on the way out to headquarters."

"You want me to attend the board meeting with you?"

"You're our company's lawyer for this matter. Of course, you'll attend the meeting. It'll be a conference call, actually, given the short notice. And we'll also need to issue a press release. Public relations will want to run that by you." Vivian smiled again. Sasha had never seen a smile so devoid of warmth.

"Are you sure you don't want to have someone else . . ."

"Do you want to run with the big dogs or not, Sasha?"

Sasha just nodded, not quite sure what to say.

As they waited for the elevator in awkward silence, Sasha checked her phone to avoid further conversation with the amazon standing next to her.

Connelly had texted her during the argument.

Irwin called. Going to meet him now. Good luck. After argument, GO STRAIGHT BACK TO OFFICE.

No worries there. As soon as she got through this presentation to the Hemisphere Air board of directors she planned to hole up in her office and bury herself in paper. She was glad to be done with the intrigue and drama. She didn't feel like a very big dog.

41

Vivian wasn't much for small talk. They walked in silence to the parking garage in the USX Tower directly across the street from the courthouse. As they crossed, Sasha saw the sign for The Doubletree, just one street away, and wondered briefly if Anton had undergone surgery to reconstruct his face yet.

They pushed through the doors to the lobby in silence and crossed over to the elevator bank that serviced the garage in silence. Waited for the elevator in silence and boarded it.

Not until they exited the elevator did Vivian speak again. She pointed to a shiny, dark red Mercedes SUV parked by itself just to the right of the elevator bank.

"This is me," she said. She aimed her remote key fob at the vehicle and opened the doors.

The SUV was clean inside, too. The burled wood on the console gleamed and the cream leather upholstery was spotless. No change rolled around in the compartments, no empty coffee cups sat abandoned in the cup holders. Everything was orderly.

Vivian started the car, and Sasha strapped her seatbelt across her chest.

Vivian stopped at the booth and handed her ticket and a twenty dollar bill over to a chubby college-age woman, who paid no attention to them, keeping her eyes glued on the small television in the booth while she made change and gave Vivian her receipt.

Vivian nosed the Mercedes out into the street and turned left onto Grant Street. She crept into the mid-morning traffic behind a bus.

Sasha's mind raced as the car inched along. Vivian seemed to be taking Judge Cook's order much better than Sasha had expected. So far, she'd shown no signs of her legendary temper.

Sasha considered the possibilities: maybe Viv was on some sort of mood-leveling medication, or maybe she was relieved the judge had taken the decision to ground the planes out of her hands. Hemisphere Air could do the right thing and she wouldn't have to put herself out on a limb.

More likely, though, Vivian planned to use Sasha as cannon fodder at the board meeting and was just biding her time to humiliate her. Getting reamed out in front of the decision makers at one of Prescott & Talbott's most important clients would make her day complete.

They traveled to the end of the block and then stopped, stuck at a red light. As they sat there, waiting for the light to turn, Sasha tried to think of something to say to her exceedingly quiet client.

The light changed to green. Vivian nudged the Mercedes forward, going slow, still behind the bus. Vivian cut her eyes over to Sasha then pressed the button to lock the car doors.

Sasha cleared her throat. "So, you wanted to talk about our strategy for the board call?"

"We have plenty of time to talk." Vivian inched forward placidly, making no effort to get around the diesel-belching PAT bus.

Vivian's sustained silence was beginning to unnerve Sasha. She reached into her bag and pulled out her phone to check her voicemail and e-mail messages. She had a missed call from Connelly. She frowned down at the display, wondering why her phone hadn't rung.

It was still set to vibrate. She turned the

ringer back on. She couldn't tell Connelly about Harold Jones, not with Vivian sitting next to her, so she settled for responding to his earlier text.

She thumbed away at the miniature keyboard:

"Lost" motion; en route to meet with client. Found something in docs. Need to talk when you can.

Vivian's eyes flicked from the street ahead to Sasha.

"What are you doing?"

"Responding to a message?"

Sasha bit her lip; angry that she'd answered Vivian with a question and not a statement. She needed to project competence, not uncertainty.

Vivian slapped the steering wheel with her palm. "You need to be focusing on this case!" Her voice rose and agitation seeped through.

Sasha wasn't sure how to respond to that. How could she focus on the case if Vivian wouldn't talk to her?

"I mean," said Vivian in a clipped tone, making an obvious effort to control her anger, "you and I need to work together to make this palatable for the Board. If we can smooth this over, it will go a long way toward your partnership evaluation in the spring, don't you agree?"

Sasha stared at her. How did Vivian know she was up for partner in the spring? As far as Sasha knew, no one at Prescott & Talbott had stayed in touch with Vivian after they'd pawned her off on Hemisphere Air.

And, the notion that Vivian would go out of her way to be helpful to Sasha was just beyond belief. The most positive associate evaluation Vivian had ever written when she was at Prescott & Talbott was "this memorandum is no worse than I would expect from a high school dropout."

The associate who had written the memo in question, now a partner himself, was a former clerk to a United States Supreme Court Justice. He kept Vivian's assessment tacked up on his wall over his computer like a badge of honor.

They'd finally reached the end of the street. Vivian crossed the Fort Pitt Bridge to Route 376 West, but instead of staying on 376, she immediately slid across and merged onto the Fort Duquesne Bridge; shot over into the far left lane; and took the exit for Route 65 North.

Sasha twisted in her seat and checked the exit number. They had gotten off on Ohio River Boulevard exit.

The handful of times Sasha had been to Hemisphere Air's headquarters in Coraopolis, she'd taken the 376 West to 22, as if she were going to the airport. Hemisphere Air occupied an ugly office park one exit short of the exit for Pittsburgh International.

Sasha hesitated. Presumably, Vivian knew how to get to her own office.

But, they were definitely on the wrong side of the Ohio River. Not to mention, they were traveling a bit on the fast side, considering this stretch of Ohio River Boulevard was infested with speed traps. Noah had traveled this route every day and complained bitterly about the police cars that dotted the shoulder with radar guns.

She tried to think of a tactful way to mention either or both of these points to Vivian.

Her eyes still on the road, Vivian said, "Isn't it interesting that the four planes you asked me to ground yesterday were on Mickey's list?"

Sasha looked at her. Vivian's face was blank and her tone had been mild, but for all her legendary flaws, the woman wasn't stupid.

"Um ... were they?"

It was feeble, but it was the best she had.

Vivian's right eye twitched.

"Yes, Sasha. They were."

Vivian's knuckles on the steering wheel were white, as she gripped it hard and accelerated.

Sasha stole a glance at the speedometer. Vivian was doing sixty-five miles per hour. Sasha was pretty sure the speed limit was forty.

Sasha cleared her throat and was about to

comment on their speed, when Vivian's key ring caught her eye.

Given their pace and the condition of the road, the SUV was bumping along, and the key ring bounced in time with the car. A small silver ring, hooked onto the larger main ring, dangled from the ignition cylinder. A familiar crystal globe hung from the smaller ring.

Sasha looked away, out the passenger window. They were entering the village of Sewickley. They passed by tasteful, pricey shops in a blur as Vivian increased her speed even more—a holistic book store, the bridal boutique where Sasha's sister-in-law had found her wedding gown, a specialty children's store that sold haute couture for babies to spit up on.

Sasha couldn't figure out where they were going, but she was distracted by that key chain. She leaned forward and craned her neck, straining against the seatbelt across her chest to get a look at the back side of the globe.

As Vivian took a corner too fast, the key chain swung and Sasha spotted it: a small airplane fashioned out of a ruby hovering over North America.

She stared, waiting for her brain to catch up to the input her eyes were sending.

There was exactly one globe like that in the world. Noah Peterson had earned it by defending

Hemisphere Air from a predatory pricing lawsuit filed by United and Delta more than a decade ago.

Sasha looked up as the SUV turned off the street and crunched across a gravel driveway that ran alongside a well-maintained, white colonial house. It belonged to Noah and Laura Peterson.

Vivian killed the engine.

42

Leo sat in the visitor's chair at the U.S. Marshal's Service, willing himself to exhibit patience. He noticed his right leg jittering and stilled it. He knew how this game was played. If he displayed impatience, the inter-agency jockeying currently underway would simply take longer.

He risked a quick peek at his watch. It had been twenty minutes since he'd left Judge Cook's courtroom to check in with Tactical Operations. Before he'd reached the office, Gregor's cell phone had rung. He'd answered, not quite sure how he was going to play it, but it had turned out to not matter. Irwin had just barked out an address and told "Gregor" to meet him there with the files before hanging up.

Ever since, Leo'd been cooling his heels

while the Special Agent in Charge of the Federal Air Marshals Pittsburgh Field Office and the Chief Deputy U.S. Marshal for the Western District of Pennsylvania worked out who was going to get the credit for collaring Irwin. The Supervisory Deputy United States Marshal had been coming back and forth between his own office and the chief's office, eyeballing Leo each time he passed through the waiting area.

While he waited, the courtroom deputy trotted in to make copies of the order granting Mickey's TRO and then trotted back out to disseminate the copies. Leo rapped his knuckles on the arm of the chair. No magazines, no art on the walls, no window. The waiting area seemed to be designed specifically to bore a person out of his skull.

Leo passed the time staring at a long, jagged crack in the plaster on the opposite wall. Finally, the door to the chief deputy's office opened and the SDUM came out. Leo stood.

The SDUM was red-faced and resigned. The machinations had not worked out the way he'd wanted.

"You can make the arrest, but our office is taking custody of Irwin after you do so. We've got two Inspectors who just came off a witness protection detail. They're going out with you."

Leo didn't react to the news. He said, "Sir, I'm going to need to borrow Irwin's vehicle."

"They don't issue you fly boys vehicles?"

Leo started to explain that he'd left his official car out at the airport but the SDUM wasn't interested in his story.

"Whatever, son. You can hitch a ride with Morgan and Pulaski."

Morgan and Pulaski were probably the inspectors.

"Sir, I need to go in alone first—in Irwin's car."

The SDUM stared at Leo with tired, milky blue eyes.

"Work it out with Morgan and Pulaski. They're next door."

He gestured toward the door and went back into the chief's office.

Leo checked his watch again. It had been twenty-seven minutes since Irwin called. He went next door to find the inspectors.

Morgan was a stocky white guy, average height, with brown eyes and brown hair, which he wore in a buzz cut in an attempt to hide the fact that he was balding. He deferred to Pulaski, who did all the talking.

Pulaski was the shorter of the two and bulkier. He had the physique of a guy who had spent years weight lifting, but his muscle was starting to grow soft with age and lack of use. He was completely bald and wore wire-rimmed glasses. Connelly thought he was probably still strong, just on the edge of out of shape. In another year to eighteen months, he would be doughy.

They both wore nondescript navy blue suits. Morgan's tie was red. Pulaski's was light blue. They were waiting for him, eager to go.

After the introductions were out of the way, Pulaski pushed back his chair and jerked a thumb toward the door.

"It's been thirty-plus minutes since your boy called and we're another twenty-five away from your rendezvous. Let's hit this."

He and Morgan holstered their guns under their jackets. Morgan opened a supply closet.

"You want a vest?" Pulaski asked, as Morgan pulled two bulletproof vests from a stack in the closet.

"I do. Thanks."

Morgan reached back into the closet, grabbed a third Kevlar vest, and tossed it to him.

"I need a car, too."

Pulaski gave him the stink eye. "Why?"

"Because he's expecting his guys to come in their car. Someone needs to drive the silver Camry, and it doesn't have a cage. I'll drive the

Camry, and you two follow me in a pool car to transport him back."

They looked at each other. Morgan shrugged. He was right and they knew it.

They headed down to the parking area; when they got off the elevator, a deputy marshal working the motor pool jogged off in search of the Camry keys. He jogged back with them and tossed them at Leo.

"Hey, Connelly," Pulaski said casually, as he and Morgan got into their car, "it was a pretty punk move to keep that cell phone when you turned the prisoner over."

That had been a bone of contention between the Special Agent in Charge and the Chief Deputy; Leo had heard raised voices discussing that point while he waited outside the office.

"What's done is done," he said.

Morgan gave him a look.

Leo shrugged.

Pulaski waved it away with his hand.

"You know where you're going? Ohio River Boulevard to the village square. Bistro's on the main drag on the left."

"Hang back once we get close. I don't want to spook him."

"We've done this before, Pilot Prettypants," Morgan said.

Leo couldn't help himself, he busted out laughing. "Pilot Prettypants?"

Pulaski chuckled and, a minute later, Morgan cracked a grin.

They had to give him a hard time, interagency penis-measuring tradition required it. The truth was, they were all prepared to work together to take down Irwin.

In fact, although Leo was convinced the federal air marshals received better training, most of them didn't have much opportunity to use it. These two inspectors were more active, protecting witnesses with mob targets on their backs. They'd have the instincts to act if Leo needed backup.

Leo and Pulaski programmed one another's cell phone numbers into their phones, all three of them strapped on the vests, and the two cars swung out of the parking lot, with the Camry in the lead, nearly forty minutes after Irwin had called.

Leo rode an urban wave of green lights down Grant Street, with Pulaski and Morgan right on his bumper. Leo checked the rearview mirror. Morgan was driving and Pulaski was either subjecting him to a running monologue or singing along to the radio.

As Leo joined the line of cars merging onto

the bridge, Gregor's cell phone rang. He palmed it and read the display. It was Irwin again.

He put the phone on speaker and answered, hoping that when he spoke, the background noise would mask the fact that he was not Gregor.

"Yes," he said in a clipped voice.

"Where the hell are you?"

"Uh, got lost." Leo laid on the horn, just for the noise cover it provided.

The curly-haired woman in the blue minivan in front of him raised her head and put her hands up, palms facing the roof of the vehicle, unsure what his problem was. There were at least three kids in the back. One of them, a freckle-faced boy about nine, twisted around in his seat and shot Leo a double bird. His siblings rocked with laughter.

Behind him, Pulaski was the woman's twin, hands in the air, miming confusion.

Irwin let out a hiss of frustration. "You two really are a pair of brain-dead twits. New location. Take Ohio River Boulevard—that's Route 65. You'll see a country inn on the right. Go through the next two lights, then hang a left, go up the hill. At the third stop sign, make a right. Two houses in from the end of the block, there's a big white house with a white fence and a bunch of pumpkins and flowers and shit on the front porch. Park on the street and come to the front door. Don't block the driveway. Got it?"

"Got it."

Irwin hung up on him.

The minivan nosed out into the travel lane and joined the flow of cars crossing the bridge. There was a break in the traffic, so Leo followed her. Morgan couldn't make it; he was left behind at the merge point.

Leo picked up his cell phone to call Pulaski and let him know about the change of location. He thought for a minute. If Irwin had changed the location because he was suspicious, Leo couldn't risk spooking him by rolling in with backup. He read the text from Sasha and pulled up her number instead. Four rings, no answer.

Leo hung up on her recorded message and punched it.

Morgan probably wouldn't work too hard to catch up with him. He knew where they were supposed to be headed, and Ohio River Boulevard was a straight shot. If he covered enough ground, he could easily lose the pair of inspectors.

Once he had Irwin in his sights, he'd call Pulaski. They could gripe at him all they wanted. They wouldn't want to let their SDUM know they lost him, so it would stay between the three of them.

43

Jerry paced around Laura's enormous gleaming kitchen, fuming. Bringing Vivian and those two idiotic goons into Laura's home would sully it. He had intended to draw a line between his old life and his new life with her and not let his business bleed into their relationship. It was not off to a good start.

He'd been about to leave to meet Gregor and Anton at the bistro when Vivian had called from the federal courthouse. He couldn't follow everything she was saying in an angry whisper, but he'd gathered they'd suffered some sort of legal setback that had pissed her off. She had insisted she had to see him right away and asked him to stay put.

The legal end of the plan was Vivian's responsibility. So any problems were her problems, not his. All the same, he didn't want there to be any hiccups when they were this close, so he'd decided to wait for her.

That left him no option but to call Gregor and tell him to bring the files to Laura's house.

As he waited for his unwelcome guests to arrive, Jerry tugged at his hair with both hands, thinking. Laura was out running errands. When she finished, they planned to have a quick lunch together at the house, then she would leave again for a meeting with her priest to go over Noah's funeral service.

He looked at the time display on the control panel of Laura's complicated espresso machine, just above the tangle of nozzles and wands that made him long for Folgers. It was 10:02.

He'd just have to get rid of everyone before Laura returned.

He heard the purr of a car engine and the crackle of crushed stones as a vehicle made its way up the driveway. He looked out the window over the kitchen door, expecting to see Gregor's Camry. Instead, Vivian pulled up in her maroon SUV. She had someone in the passenger seat.

SASHA STARED AT THE PETERSONS' gracious home, but her mind was still on the globe hanging from Vivian's key ring. Vivian was feeling around under the driver's seat for something, but Sasha paid no attention. Her instincts were screaming at her to get out of the Mercedes. Too many things were wrong with the situation.

Much later, when she replayed the events in her mind trying to rewrite the ending, she would chalk up her failure to react to two factors: One, she had been intimidated by Vivian because she was a client. Two, she was distracted by that keychain.

In the moment, all she knew was she turned back to Vivian to ask why they were at Noah's house and looked straight down the barrel of a handgun.

Reflexively, she began to calculate the steps to disarm Vivian. Almost immediately, she realized the conditions were no good. Vivian's hands were shaking badly. The safety was off. Sasha assumed the gun was loaded. And they were in very close quarters. A struggle for the gun in the front seat of the vehicle almost guaranteed someone would be shot.

It was better to bide her time and take Vivian down later. Assuming she got an opportunity.

"Out," Vivian ordered, hands still shaking.

Sasha complied with slow, deliberate movements. Vivian was tense and wound up tight. Sasha didn't want to spook her and end up dead.

Vivian shut the driver's side door and walked around the car to Sasha's side.

"Can I get my briefcase?" Sasha asked.

"No."

Vivian nudged the passenger door closed with her hip and jabbed the gun at Sasha.

"We're going in the side door. Hurry."

Sasha trotted up the path, unsteady in her heels on the crushed stones. Vivian followed behind, more slowly, the gun aimed at Sasha's back.

Sasha swept both sides of the path leading to the doorway with her eyes. No brush that would provide cover if she were to dive, just two glazed, stoneware pots—one on each side of the door—both home to fat, wine-colored chrysanthemums.

She reached the door and stopped. Vivian leaned forward, over Sasha's head, and rapped on the glass with the butt of the gun. Sasha could have grabbed it then. Wrapped her hands around the barrel and pulled it down, out of the bigger woman's hands. But Vivian was not practicing good weapon retention. By using the butt end of the gun to knock on the door, she was pointing the weapon up and at herself. Bad idea. If Sasha grabbed for gun now it would be pointing up and toward Sasha as she wrested control of it away.

Worse idea. Unless she wanted to get shot in the head.

Not the right time.

A man's face appeared in the door. He was wide-eyed with surprise and his mouth was set with anger. The two emotions battled for supremacy on his face.

He pulled the door open and stepped back. Vivian used the gun to push Sasha inside. She followed and pushed the door shut behind her. As soon as she stepped inside, Sasha felt Noah's death hanging over the house like a cloud.

"What the hell, Vivian?" The man's voice was tight and fast. He looked from the gun to Sasha to Vivian then repeated the circuit.

Sasha wondered if he was a relative of Laura's. She saw no resemblance. He was in his late fifties. He was bald on top, with wispy brown hair that hung in a fringe from right above his ears down to his collar. He was perfectly average in height and weight. Not tall, not short. Not fat, not thin. He wore a turtleneck and jeans. Socks, no shoes.

"Jerry Irwin, meet Sasha McCandless." Vivian said.

The man—Irwin—reared his head back, disbelief painted across his face. "Her?!" He blinked behind his glasses.

Sasha felt like telling him the feeling was

mutual. This mundane–looking man was the psychotic genius?

His eyes shifted to the cream-colored, tumbled limestone floor. Sasha and Vivian followed his gaze. Their heels had tracked in mud from the wet ground.

"Take off your shoes, please." He said it in that same strangled voice.

Sasha kicked hers off fast and lined them up beside the door.

Vivian huffed. "Is Laura home?"

"No, she went out. Take off the shoes, Vivian!" Irwin's face flashed deep red as he screamed.

Vivian muttered under her breath but propped her back against the door and lifted her right foot. She kept the gun in her right hand and used her left to pull off her right shoe. She let it fall to the floor. Mud flew off the stacked heel when it hit the ground.

Irwin frowned at the mess then stalked off toward the mud room to the right of the door.

Sasha waited, off to Vivian's left.

Vivian raised her left foot and kept her gun hand up against the door while she fumbled with the left shoe with her left hand. She was off balance and struggling with the strap.

It was time.

Redirect. Sasha wheeled across Vivian's torso and used her left hand to pin Vivian's right wrist against the door. The gun was pointed up—less than ideal—but away from everyone in the house.

Control. She stretched on her toes and pressed her elbow deep into the hollow under Vivian's ribcage. Vivian gasped. She drove it deeper and held it there.

Attack. At the same time, Sasha grabbed Vivian by the throat with her left hand. Vivian dropped her shoe and clawed at Sasha's wrist.

Sasha aimed two quick straight punches at the hollow of Vivian's throat. Followed them with a palm strike to the chin. Vivian's mouth snapped shut and the back of her head slammed into the door.

Take. She bent Vivian's right wrist back and pried the gun from her hand.

She stood, feet apart, and aimed at Vivian, who slid down the door to a seated position. Sasha followed her movement with the gun.

Irwin appeared in the mud room doorway holding a cordless hand vacuum, ready to clean up the dirt. He raised his eyebrows when he saw Vivian slumped against the door, holding her throat.

He nodded to the bright red splotches of blood that dripped from Vivian's mouth and dotted the tile.

"You'd better hope that comes up, Vivian."

Sasha considered shooting him just for being stupid.

"Put the vacuum down and help her into a chair," she ordered.

He hesitated, like he might argue with her, then cut his eyes toward the gun. He sighed, but dropped the hand vac and hoisted Vivian up, wrapping his arms under her armpits. He dragged her over to a wrought iron chair and propped her up in it.

"Sit down next to her," Sasha told him, pointing at the empty chair beside Vivian.

They sat there, side by side, like kids called to the principal's office and looked up at her, defiant and scared. Vivian was still breathing heavily, but aside from some minor damage to her throat and a bloody mouth, she'd be fine.

Sasha stood there with the gun and just looked at them for a long moment.

"Start at the beginning," she said.

She barely got the words out before the sound of a doorbell chime floated into the kitchen from the front hallway.

"You expecting company?" she asked Irwin.

His pale face lit up. "Yes, I am. Oh, am I."

Vivian looked over at him.

"My guys," he told her. "They're here with the files." He was buzzing with excitement.

"Your guys? Gregor and Anton?" Sasha asked.

"That's right," he told her. "I'm surprised you survived your encounter with them. Did you enjoy it?"

Idiot, Sasha thought.

The doorbell chimed again, followed by hard knocking on the door.

"Well, go let them in before they break Laura's door," Sasha told him.

He jumped up from the chair, then froze, wondering what the catch was.

"Irwin, for Chrissake, don't . . ." Vivian started.

"Quiet," Sasha told her, waving the gun for emphasis.

The evil genius stood for a minute, trying to decide, then raced off down the hall, slipping and sliding in his socks.

Vivian just shook her head.

Sasha smiled. "No common sense, huh? I mean, it's too good to be true, right? I'm just going to let him open the door for his reinforcements?"

"Too good to be true," Vivian repeated, dull eyed and quiet.

Irwin reappeared a moment later, looking deflated. Followed closely by Connelly with the Sig Sauer in hand.

Connelly looked at Vivian, hunched over in

the chair, blood staining her silk blouse. He nodded a greeting to Sasha.

"Didn't I tell you to go straight back to your office?"

Sasha ignored it. "Do you know whose house this is?"

"No."

"Noah Peterson's."

"That Mrs. Peterson?" he inclined his head toward Vivian, keeping the gun on Irwin.

"No. Vivian Coulter."

Connelly raised an eyebrow. "Nice client relations your firm has. She need medical treatment?"

"No," Sasha said at the same time Vivian mewed, "Yes."

Connelly rolled his eyes but stepped closer to inspect Vivian's injuries.

"You'll live," he told her.

Irwin stood slack-jawed and silent.

"Sit back down," Sasha told him.

Connelly handed her his gun and reached for his phone.

She stood, feet planted, and pointed Vivian's gun at Vivian and Connelly's gun at Irwin.

"Hurry up," she told him. She felt ridiculous.

Connelly ignored her and made his call. Spoke loudly over Pulaski's complaining and gave the U.S. Marshals the address. Then, he slid the phone back in his pocket and looked at Vivian and Irwin.

"We've got about ten minutes. Somebody start talking."

Sasha handed him his gun.

Vivian kept her mouth firmly shut, but Irwin began to prattle right away.

"After the RAGS links were installed on Hemisphere Air's planes, we planned to ride it out. Vivian thought after the administration changed in D.C. we'd be better positioned to revive the pilot program with the Air Marshals Service," he explained.

Vivian muttered, "Shut up, Jerry," but it was futile.

"But then," he continued, "Patriotech was approached by certain...private organizations that had an interest in acquiring the technology. But, each party only wanted it if I could guarantee exclusivity."

"Exclusivity?" Connelly arched a brow.

Irwin said, "Nobody wanted it if everybody else had it, too, understand? So, I organized an auction for interested bidders. They wanted to see a demonstration or two before bidding."

"Wait." Sasha was confused. "Isn't this a limited use application? Once you run out of planes that have RAGS links installed, then the winning bidder would just have a useless technology, right?"

"Yes and no," Irwin said. "I had a plan. I wasn't going to implement it, but I would license it to the winning bidder."

"License what?

Vivian tried again. "Jerry, stop talking."

He plowed ahead. "A second-generation RAGS. No link needed. No need to be on the plane. With the new version, you can crash a plane from the terminal."

"What do you need to make it work?"

"Someone on the inside."

"Inside what, the cockpit—a pilot?"

Irwin shook his head, "Pilot, flight attendant, air marshal, cleaning crew, baggage crew. Whoever. You just need someone to read you the model number on the transponder in the cabin so you know what frequency to set the RAGS to."

Sasha flicked her eyes to Connelly and saw his grip on the gun tighten.

"Did you line up anyone on the inside?" Connelly asked, his voice careful.

"No, that's on the buyer," Irwin said.

"Then why even use the RAGS-linked planes for your demonstrations?"

"Because I wanted to be certain the demonstrations were repeatable. The new system *should* work. I *know* the old one works."

"So, it's fraud. The technology you're selling isn't the one you're demonstrating," Sasha said.

Irwin shrugged. "Caveat emptor, baby."

Vivian shifted in her seat. "I think you bruised my larynx," she said to Sasha.

"Who lined up Calvaruso and Jones?" Sasha asked, ignoring Vivian's complaint.

"Who's Jones?" Connelly asked.

"Harold Jones. Martyr Number 2."

"You found something in Warner's papers?"

She nodded. "Yeah, Jones is booked on Bob Metz's flight back from Seattle tomorrow night, carrying a Patriotech-issued smartphone."

Vivian glared at Irwin. "Good job getting the files back, Jerry," she said through clenched teeth.

"Actually, Sasha figured out which planes were modified before we ever got Warner's files." Connelly told her. "Using your files."

Sasha repeated her question, waving the gun for emphasis. "Who lined up Calvaruso and Jones?"

"I did," Irwin said. "Vivian used her connection with Laura . . ."

"Laura Peterson?"

"Yes, she's on the board of the cancer center. Vivian told Laura I was a philanthropist, looking to start a fund for terminal cancer patients. Laura set up interviews with several gentlemen, and I picked the two who seemed most desperate. They both agreed to carry a phone on a plane, knowing it was dangerous and they could die. In exchange, I paid them each twelve thousand, five hundred dollars and purchased life insurance policies for them."

"Did they know they were going to take down planes full of innocent people?"

Irwin made a motion with his hands, as if to say *who knows?*

"Jones didn't ask a lot of questions. Calvaruso did. He might have known. Probably he did."

"Jesus," Connelly breathed.

"I have a question. Where are Gregor and Anton? Why do you have their car? And who the hell *are* you?" Irwin fired his questions at Connelly.

"That's three questions," Connelly informed him. "Gregor is in the custody of the United States Marshals Service. Anton is at UPMC having reconstructive surgery courtesy of Ms. McCandless. And I am Special Agent Leo Connelly. I'm a federal air marshal."

Irwin hung his head.

"Where are your boys?" Sasha asked Connelly.

"They're still a couple minutes away," Connelly said, checking the clock over the double wall oven. He seemed to take in his surroundings for the first time. "Why are we here anyway?"

"I'm not sure," Sasha said, "but Vivian has Noah's . . ." Sasha stopped as Laura appeared on the doorstep outside the kitchen door, a Whole Foods Market bag and a bouquet of cut flowers in her arms. She turned the doorknob and filled the doorway.

"Jerry?" she called, as she walked in, "is Vivian here?" She looked back at the SUV in her driveway then stepped into the foyer. She stopped.

Her pale blue eyes searched the four faces in her kitchen and her knees buckled under her. "Jerry? What's going on?" The groceries tumbled to the floor, followed by flowers. Connelly hurried over to catch her.

"Ma'am," he said, steadying her on her feet, "I'm Special Agent Leo Connelly, we have a situation here."

"Situation? Sasha? What are you doing?" She eyed the gun in Sasha's hand.

Sasha half-turned to Laura, keeping one eye on Vivian and Irwin.

"Laura, I'm so sorry. Agent Connelly will explain everything later, but you need to turn around and leave right now." She worked to keep her voice calm.

"Leave? I'm not leaving Jerry here. Honey,

what's going on?" Laura was wild-eyed and getting loud.

Honey? Sasha saw the question mark in Connelly's eyes and shrugged.

Vivian saw it, too. She barked out a laugh. "The Widow Peterson didn't waste any time taking a lover. Although, I do have to question her taste."

"Vivian!" Irwin warned her.

Vivian laughed her ugly laugh again.

Irwin saw his chance and lunged from the chair for the block of knives on Laura's counter. He scrabbled with the block, tipping it over, and pulled out an eight-inch chef's knife.

"Jerry!" Laura screamed, hands flying up to her face.

Sasha dropped Vivian's gun to the floor and kicked it toward Connelly. She wasn't going to fire it and it was just going to be a hindrance. She'd need two hands to deal with Irwin.

Connelly held Laura tight around the waist and brought her close, so he could cover Vivian with his gun.

"Do not move," he told her. Vivian nodded and pressed herself as far back as possible in the chair.

Irwin's eyes darted from side to side. Sasha flashed on the story Mickey had told, of Irwin slashing him wildly with a broken bottle. She prepared for an erratic, disorganized attack.

Instead, Irwin charged straight at her.

Active defense. She leapt to the right and he stabbed at the air where she'd been.

He came again. This time Sasha charged forward, toward Irwin and the knife in his right hand. He blinked, surprised that she was moving toward him, and tried to back away. He slid across the floor in his socks.

Sasha moved closer, swung her left arm in, and caught his right hand at the wrist.

Control. She bent his arm back at the elbow and leaned forward. She felt his hot breath, as he panted from exertion and fear. She kept pushing him back, and he started to lose his balance.

Attack. Irwin leaned forward—the natural reaction to stop himself from falling backward. She was waiting for it and brought her right elbow up in a roundhouse and smashed it into his jaw, with her full weight behind it.

Take. Still twisting, she turned so that now she was standing directly in front of Irwin, who was howling and keening, rocking with the pain. She kept her left hand tight on his right wrist. Brought her right knee up and struck his wrist bone quick and hard. The knife popped out of Irwin's hand and clattered to the floor.

Sasha stepped on the knife and then forced

his wrist back until his bones splintered and cracked and his eyes rolled back from the pain.

Laura was screaming and crying now, big heaving sobs.

"Calm down, Mrs. Peterson, please." Connelly maneuvered her into the chair next to Vivian.

Sasha caught her breath and dragged Irwin over to the wall.

"Does she know?" Sasha asked Vivian, nodding to Laura. She picked up the knife and put it on the kitchen island behind her.

"Know what? That Jerry's a homicidal maniac who caused a plane full of people to crash so he could fund their new island home?"

Laura looked up in horror. "Is that true?" she cried, asking everyone and no one in particular.

"Yes," Sasha said, "your boyfriend is a mass murderer."

"I'm sorry," Irwin said from the floor, "I know you're disappointed, Laura."

"But that's not what I meant, Vivian," Sasha said. "Does Laura know you killed her husband?"

Vivian was completely still and quiet.

Laura whipped her head around to Sasha, mascara staining her cheeks. "She killed Noah?"

"When the police gave you Noah's belongings was anything missing?" Sasha said.

Laura looked at her blankly.

Sasha reached into Vivian's purse and held the keys up for Laura to see: the globe and its bright red plane dangled from the Mercedes key ring.

Laura turned to Vivian. "You killed him?"

Vivian shrugged. Her face revealed nothing. She hadn't spent her entire adult life as a lawyer without learning to lawyer up.

"You *killed* him?" Laura repeated.

"Oh, Laura, what do you care if I did? You're moving on, remember." Vivian's voice was cold and her face was a frozen mask of disdain.

Connelly was busy examining Irwin's injuries. Sasha was busy staring at Vivian.

Neither of them saw Laura launch herself forward and grab the chef's knife. She was on top of Vivian in a flash, plunging the knife into her chest.

Sasha pulled Laura off her, but she could tell it was too late. Bloody froth bubbled out of Vivian's parted lips.

Laura let the knife slip to the floor and collapsed onto Sasha, shaking and crying. "He was still my husband," she said.

Irwin called to her from the floor, telling her he loved her. She didn't seem to hear him.

Connelly left Irwin there, shouting, and checked Vivian's vital signs.

He looked up at Sasha and shook his head.

"Her pulse is really thready. I think she has at least one punctured lung."

Connelly called for an ambulance, then he took Laura from Sasha's arms and sent Sasha out to the porch to wait for it.

Sasha sat on Noah and Laura's hanging porch bed and just swung, curled up among the richly patterned pillows, until Pulaski and Morgan careened to a stop at the curb below.

They pounded up the stairs and ran past her, as Connelly yelled out to them from inside the house, "We've got one down!"

His voice carried down to the quiet street, lined with old maple trees, their leaves just starting to turn red and gold.

44

After Irwin was taken into custody and Vivian was zipped into a body bag, it seemed to Sasha that time somehow both sped up and slowed down. In the immediate aftermath of flashing red lights and local reporters thrusting microphones at her, she remembered only Connelly, shouldering through the crowd in front of her and handing her off to Naya, who'd somehow gotten word to come out to Sewickley.

Naya and loyal Carl drove her home. Naya tried to stay, but Sasha just wanted to sleep.

Once Sasha convinced Naya to leave, she changed into warm pajamas and collapsed into a pile on her bed. It was three thirty in the afternoon. She slept until morning but did not dream.

Connelly let himself in with her spare key

and found her still curled up under the covers on Friday morning. He had an Einstein Brothers' bag with bagels and cream cheese in one hand and a takeout coffee in the other. He looked well rested.

Sasha fought through the syrup covering her brain and struggled to a seated position. She stared at him blankly.

"Hi," he said, handing her the coffee. "Do you need to call your office?"

Sasha looked at the clock. Eight thirty. In nearly eight years at Prescott & Talbott she'd never arrived after eight. Not once.

"I guess." Her voice came out in a croak. She pushed the hair out of her eyes and picked up the phone. She didn't know what she'd say. Everyone would say they didn't expect her to come in, that she should take some time.

That's what they always said—after a trial or when a lawyer had a family emergency. After all, the firm's lawyers were entitled to five weeks of vacation and unlimited sick and personal days. But, the reality was, at least for the trial attorneys, machismo demanded no rest. No one used their vacation days. It was a badge of...something.

Sasha knew male attorneys who hadn't taken the day off to be present when their children were born. The female attorneys had to be present for their children's births, but they made up for it by spending their labors sending e-mails from their Blackberries and calling in to participate in unimportant conference calls during their transition to active labor.

The associate in the office next to hers had convinced his siblings to put their mother in cold storage when she had the bad timing to die while he was in the middle of a trial. They buried her afterward, when it was more convenient for him.

An income partner whom Sasha liked a great deal had come to work every day during her chemotherapy treatment. Never mind that she'd spent most of each day vomiting and shaking—she came to work.

Sasha put the phone down. "No."

She wasn't going to call because she wasn't going in.

She sipped the coffee and studied Connelly. "Are you on the clock?"

He nodded. "I'm wrapping this up today and then I'm taking the rest of the month off."

He stood awkwardly at the foot of her bed.

"They grabbed up Harold Jones and talked to Bob Metz out in Seattle. Jones is cooperating, but he doesn't know anything. Irwin is, too. He's hoping it will impress Laura somehow. His story is they hadn't planned to kill Noah. Vivian was supposed to tell Metz about the RAGS link with the hope he'd confide in Noah."

"And he did," Sasha said.

"Yeah, but it was just to establish Metz had knowledge. Somehow, Vivian thought she'd be able to pin everything on Metz after he died in the second crash. But, Noah pressured Metz to go to the government, and Vivian had to stop him. The coroner is reviewing Noah's autopsy to determine how she killed him."

Sasha looked up at him. "I was driving that train. I pushed Noah to push Metz. Are you saying I got Noah killed, too?"

Connelly sat on the edge of her bed. "Look at me. You saved several hundred people, Sasha. You stopped them."

She shook her head. Warner. Noah. Their blood was on her hands.

"Did Irwin say why she did it?"

"Vivian?"

Sasha nodded.

"Money. She was going to invest in a startup that would compete with Hemisphere Air on its northeast routes. She figured the crashes would hurt Hemisphere Air's business and drive customers to the new airline. Her cut of Irwin's auction was just gravy. For her, it was plain old vanilla greed."

"You think it was something else for Irwin?" Sasha asked.

"I think it started out as greed. And ego. Then

he fell in love with Laura. He's deluded, no doubt, but he really thought they would move out of the country and live off the money and she would never know."

Sasha suddenly felt strangely sorry for Jerry Irwin. And tired again.

"Thanks for the coffee, Connelly. I think I'm going to take a nap. Let yourself out?"

He frowned down at her. She put the cup on her bedside table, rolled over, and pulled a pillow over her head.

IT WAS dark when she woke, sweaty and hungry. She squinted at the glowing display on her alarm clock. It was almost seven p.m. She sat up and switched on the lamp.

Connelly was sitting at the foot of her bed. He'd dragged her reading chair in from the living room. The one she'd tied Gregor to the night before.

"Have you been here all day?"

"No. I came about a half an hour ago. It's time to get up. Take a shower. We're going to get some food."

"I don't want to go out," Sasha told him.

"Take a shower. Go." His voice was firm.

She stood up. Her brain was fuzzy. She went

into the bathroom and ran the water. While the shower got hot, she stared at herself in the mirror. Her skin was stark white. Her purple bruises were dark against it. Black smudges creased her eyes from exhaustion. She turned away from the mirror.

When she emerged from the bathroom with wet hair and wearing clean pajamas, she felt more human.

Connelly looked up as she walked into her kitchen for the first time in a day and a half.

"I ordered a pizza from the place around the corner."

"Village Pizza?"

"That's the one. You want to come with me to pick it up?"

She shook her head. Not yet.

But she called after him as he let himself out, "Pick up a six of beer, too."

SHE HOLED UP ALL WEEKEND, dodging her parents and brothers. She talked briefly to Naya, who told her Laura had made it through Noah's funeral ceremony. Afterward, she had been voluntarily admitted to Western Psych for psychiatric evaluation. Prescott & Talbott's backroom deal makers were working overtime to make sure she wasn't prosecuted.

On Sunday, Daniel called to report that, after he taught his last Krav Maga class on Friday, he'd returned to her building around noon and positioned himself in her bushes. About twenty minutes later, he'd seen a skinny, long-haired white male lurking around the playground across the street. Daniel had called 911 and then watched the guy until the police arrived. The guy gave up Vivian without a second thought. She'd paid him two hundred dollars to jump Sasha and get some files.

Sasha relayed this information to Connelly for the federal investigation. He passed it along to Pulaski, because, as he reminded her, he was on vacation.

Connelly stopped by each day to make sure she was eating. He didn't stay long.

On Monday, she woke up early, before six, and felt like going for a run. So she ran. She ran farther than she'd intended because the cold air filling her lungs felt like a promise. But after the run, she returned to her condo and ignored the calls that came from the office.

On Tuesday morning, she ran again. She found herself standing outside the Krav Maga studio. After sparring with Daniel, she showered and went to a matinee that was playing at the

Squirrel Hill Theater. She didn't pay much attention to the romantic comedy, but she enjoyed sitting in a dark, quiet public space alone without fear.

Finally, on Wednesday, after her run and her class, she was ready. She walked through Prescott & Talbott's main lobby with her shoulders back and her eyes forward. She didn't stop until she reached Lettie's desk.

Lettie hurried around to the front of her work station and hugged Sasha tight, like a mother would. Then her gray eyes grew serious.

"They said if you came in at any point to send you up to see Mr. Prescott right away."

"Okay," Sasha said. What else was there to say?

She took the stairs to Cinco's office. Caroline was waiting for her when she arrived.

"Ms. McCandless, would you like a cup of coffee? Mr. Prescott will be ready for you in one minute."

"Coffee would be great," Sasha said. She wasn't nervous or excited. She wasn't anything. She sat on Caroline's striped silk couch and drank coffee from a gilt-edged porcelain teacup. She listened to the quiet classical music that played as Caroline worked.

"Is this Vivaldi?" she asked.

"It is." Caroline looked at Sasha closely. Sasha tried to smile. She didn't know if she succeeded.

Cinco's door opened and he stood in the doorway. "I'm sorry to have kept you waiting, Sasha. Come in."

She put down the teacup, shook his outstretched hand, and followed him into his orange office. He tried to usher her toward the white captain chairs, but she wanted to sit where her feet could reach the ground. She ignored him and sat on the low white couch under his naked woman painting.

He raised his eyebrows but joined her on the couch.

To his credit, Cinco skipped the small talk and got right to business. The firm appreciated what Sasha had done, of course. They were willing to overlook some small lapses in judgment and breaches of protocol and procedure that may have occurred along the way. Hemisphere Air was very pleased, certainly. As a result, the firm had decided to take the unprecedented step of moving her partnership vote up from April. In fact, they had voted on Monday, but no one had been able to reach her.

Cinco stood up and walked over to the door. Caroline appeared with two champagne flutes on a silver tray.

Cinco came back and held out one of the

flutes to Sasha. "Welcome to the partnership, Ms. McCandless."

She stared at the bubbles fizzing up in the glass for what seemed like a long time. She thought about how long and hard she'd worked. She thought about Noah and Laura. She thought about Connelly, taking a vacation. She thought about Mickey Collins, following his conscience without having to worry what a committee or subcommittee thought. She thought about stopping by the Animal Rescue League and getting a puppy. Or maybe she would start small and get a houseplant.

Finally, she looked up at Cinco. "I'm so sorry, but, no thank you. I'm not interested."

She left him standing there with a glass of champagne in each hand.

The next day, she went back to the office to clean out her desk. Lettie knocked softly on her door and then came in with a package addressed to Sasha. It had no return address.

Inside was a light pink linen card with a note written in careful, elegant handwriting:

Sasha,

I think Noah would have liked for you to have this. I am going to spend a year in France. I think he would have liked that, too.

Laura

SASHA TURNED the small package over and held out her palm. A crystal globe with a ruby airplane hovering over North America dropped into her hand.

It was almost five o'clock before she had packed up the last box. The Committee on Departures had provided her with an exit memorandum that detailed which work-related materials she could retain for her personal files. She made a few copies, mainly briefs that reminded her of good courtroom fights she'd won or deposition transcripts that included on-the-record exchanges that had become legend over the years. Like the one where Kevin Marcus said "let the record reflect that the middle digit of plaintiff's counsel's right hand is extended stiffly in the air in a widely understood gesture." She couldn't just relegate a gem like that to off-site storage.

In addition to the files, she'd accumulated more personal belongings in eight years than she'd thought. She wasn't sure how she was going to get her clothes, diplomas, framed pictures, and assorted office clutter to her car.

Naya appeared in the doorway.

"What are you going to do, Mac?"

"I'm not sure. Maybe make two trips?" Sasha said, surveying the pile of boxes.

"For work, Sasha. What are you going to do for a job?"

"Oh, yeah, I don't know that either."

"Are you going to stay in touch?" Naya gave her a fierce look.

Sasha came around the desk. "You're one of the only people here I consider a real friend, Naya. You're not going to shake me that easily. You'll be calling me Carl, Jr."

Naya laughed and leaned in for a hug. She squeezed Sasha tight.

"Speaking of Carl, I thought you might need a hand getting your crap out to your car."

She leaned out into the hallway and shouted, "Carl!"

And sure enough, Carl strolled into sight, pushing a hand cart from the mailroom.

"Hi ya, Sasha," he said, as he helped her and Naya pile the cart high with bankers' boxes.

He asked her for her car keys and wheeled the boxes out to the garage. Sasha and Naya sat on a stone bench in front of the building and waited for him to bring the car down.

"He's a good man," Sasha told Naya.

"I know he is," Naya said.

"Are you ever going to give in and fall in love with him?"

"Probably someday," Naya admitted. Then she threw her head back and laughed.

She stopped mid-laugh. "Uh-oh."

Sasha followed her gaze.

The Honorable Cliff Cook was headed their way. The judge took long, purposeful strides.

"Okay, well, you take care now, Mac." Naya stood to make her escape.

Sasha reached for Naya's elbow and tried to pull her back down to the bench, but Naya shook her off and scurried away.

Like the proverbial rat, Sasha thought. She guessed that made her the sinking ship.

"Ms. McCandless," Judge Cook said as he stopped right in front of her, "I am told by the Prescott & Talbott receptionist that as of today you have left the firm's employ."

Sasha popped to her feet.

"Yes, Your Honor."

"And what greener pasture are you off to? In-house counsel at Hemisphere Air?"

Sasha stared at the judge. Metz, who had taken over Vivian's position had called and offered her his old job, not once but twice. She thanked him gently and sincerely, but told him she wasn't interested.

Metz had understood.

But, it appeared Pittsburgh's legal gossip mill hadn't gotten the memo.

"Actually, no, Your Honor."

"Oh? Then where are you going?"

Sasha opened her mouth to say, "I'm not sure. I'm going to take some time." Instead, the words "I'm opening my own office" came, unbidden, out of her mouth.

Judge Cook cocked his head. "Is that so? Well, good for you. I'm sure you'll do quite well for yourself. You're a very persuasive legal writer."

Sasha wrinkled her brow. "I don't believe I've filed any papers with you, Your Honor."

The judge looked at her. "Ms. McCandless, do you have any idea how many pleadings and briefs written by Prescott & Talbott attorneys I've read during my years on the bench?"

Sasha threw out a guess, "Dozens? Maybe hundreds?"

"Hundreds—perhaps thousands, given your former firm's penchant for motions practice. And each lawyer has his or her own style, to be sure. But, I can tell within the first paragraph when I am reading papers that were written by a Prescott-trained lawyer. The firm's DNA, if you will, is distinctive."

"Really?" Sasha managed.

"Really." Judge Cook leaned in close. "And Mickey Collins, for all his talents, does not have Prescott & Talbott DNA."

He looked at Sasha for a minute. She thought he might smile, but he didn't.

"Good luck to you in your future endeavors, Ms. McCandless."

Judge Cook nodded a goodbye, then he turned and walked back the way he'd come.

WHEN SASHA PULLED into her parking lot it was already dark, so she left the boxes in her car and hurried inside.

When she reached the door to her condo, she heard music coming from inside.

With her heart in her throat, she silently turned the knob. The door was unlocked. She took a deep breath, and then she exploded through the doorway, ready to react if someone was waiting on the other side of the door to attack her.

There was no attacker on the other side.

But Connelly was in her kitchen. Boxes, jars, and bags littered her recycled glass countertops. Pots bubbled on her gleaming cooktop. Wine was breathing. Connelly was stirring something and singing along to music. Classic rock, from before she was born.

He looked up and smiled a lopsided smile.

"I thought you were on vacation," Sasha said,

her heart returning to normal as the adrenaline drained from her body.

"I am," he told her.

That night, he slept in her bed for the second time. He did not curl up on the bottom like a dog.

ALSO BY MELISSA F. MILLER

Want to know when I release a new book?

Go to www.melissafmiller.com to sign up for my email newsletter.

Prefer text alerts? Text BOOKS to 636-303-1088 to receive new release alerts and updates.

The Sasha McCandless Legal Thriller Series

Irreparable Harm

Inadvertent Disclosure

Irretrievably Broken

Indispensable Party

Lovers and Madmen (Novella)

Improper Influence

A Marriage of True Minds (Novella)

Irrevocable Trust

Irrefutable Evidence

A Mingled Yarn (Novella)

Informed Consent

International Incident

Imminent Peril

The Humble Salve (Novella)

Intentional Acts

In Absentia

Inevitable Discovery

Full Fathom Five (Novella)

The Aroostine Higgins Novels

Critical Vulnerability

Chilling Effect

Calculated Risk

Called Home

Crossfire Creek

Clingmans Dome

The Bodhi King Novels

Dark Path

Lonely Path

Hidden Path

Twisted Path

Cold Path

The We Sisters Three Romantic Comedic Mysteries

Rosemary's Gravy

Sage of Innocence

Thyme to Live

Lost and Gowned

Wedding Bells & Hoodoo Spells

Wanted Wed or Alive

ABOUT THE AUTHOR

USA Today bestselling author Melissa F. Miller was born in Pittsburgh, Pennsylvania. Although life and love led her to Philadelphia, Baltimore, Washington, D.C., and, ultimately, South Central Pennsylvania, she secretly still considers Pittsburgh home.

In college, she majored in English literature with concentrations in creative writing poetry and medieval literature and was stunned, upon graduation, to learn that there's not exactly a job market for such a degree. After working as an editor for several years, she returned to school to earn a law degree. She was that annoying girl who loved class and always raised her hand. She practiced law for fifteen years, including a stint as a clerk for a federal judge, nearly a decade as an attorney at major international law firms, and several years running a two-person law firm with her lawyer husband.

Now, powered by coffee, she writes legal thrillers and homeschools her three children. When she's not writing, and sometimes when she is, Melissa travels around the country in an RV with her husband, her kids, and her cat.

Connect with me:

www.melissafmiller.com

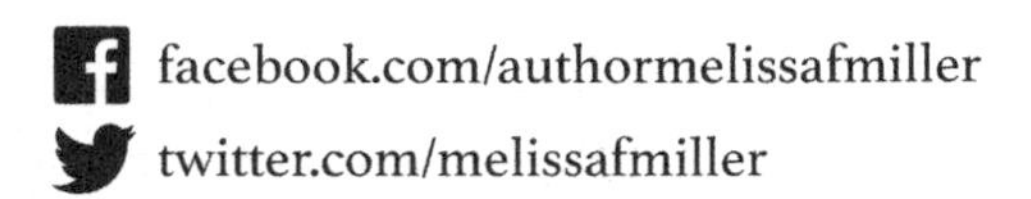